RELMS

TALES OF VISHNU & THE DREYGON

L. CENTAURI

RELATIVE
ENERGY
LIGHT
MASS
SPACE

RELATIVE IS THAT WHICH IS
UNDERSTANDABLE BY YOU

ENERGY IS WHAT OUR EXISTENCE IS IN ITS
MANIFESTATION

LIGHT IS THE LAST THING YOU ARE AND YOUR
MEANS OF TRAVEL

MASS IS YOUR FIRST QUALITY AS STAR DUST

SPACE IS YOUR LOCATION, YOUR REALITY
AND ALL YOU WILL KNOW

THE RELMS are Tales of spirituality and imagination. Infinite possibility is an attribute of the Relms. These are stories of the *inner map* as a tool to experience the frontier that has no end as do the vastness of the universe and the mind of a god as infinite possibility.

We are made of stardust. And for us it begins here. Creation is the intent of the dust of stars, and so we too are creative within the possibility of what is infinite. The mind of the universe is in a constant state of creation of that which could be known.

Welcome to the Relms. You are everything you will need.

Dedication

This book is dedicated to my son, who is always my heart and inspiration.

To my good friend Ray Holbert for always being his authentic self.

And to my good friend Shirley Nelson, thank you with all my heart.

To all the Humans on the planet, may you always be in a state of loving.

Thank you to a beautiful universe that whispers stories to me.

To my Dad who always thought I should be a journalist.

Thank you my friend Valerie Tookes for being the first to read The Relms.

CONTENTS
OF THE RELMS

Chapters

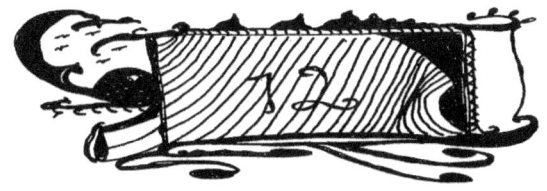

DREYGON

I have something incredible to tell you.
Before all this happened, I had spent most of my
childhood not quite fitting in.
I knew there was something different about me as a
kid.
I remember my mother telling me this story; that she
had a dream about me before I was born.
She said she was a young woman, and that she had
gone to France on a business trip.
    She was staying at the Victor Hugo Hotel in
Paris. This hotel was hundreds of years old and care
worn.
    It was run by an old French family and had
been in their possession for generations.
Her stay at the little hotel was short, but while she
was there she had a dream.
    In this dream she was standing in a forest full
of trees so large they blocked out the sun.
My mother said she looked up and could see
sunlight filtering through the tops of the trees down
to the forest floor.

She said she then looked into the forest and saw a woman approaching. The woman was small in stature with brown skin and long black hair. She had a very exotic face and wore an emerald green sarong.

The woman was carrying a baby in her arms. My mother said the woman walked toward her and spoke to her. The woman said, "This is your baby", handed her this child and that it had my face.

I'm not sure I believed my mother's tale. I think as a kid it might have just added to me feeling outside the box. I had some really good friends, but I always needed time alone. I had a vivid imagination.

I remember having dreams as a teenager of numeric equations and seeing galaxies not yet mapped by Astronomers. Most of what I seriously thought about, I told her. I remember the shocked look on my Dad's face when he found an essay I had written regarding an outer journey I had taken in my imagination. He asked me if I was on drugs. Funny thing, I had no idea what he was talking about. I laugh now at that thought. A lot has happened since then.

I am called Vishnu. I'm tall and what most women would consider very good-looking. I have my own style of dress. I guess you would call it kind of euro-American. I like to look professional at work, but I rarely wear a suit.

When I'm hanging out with my crew, I dress casual but hip. I am of mixed blood, taking my good looks from my mother who is of Native American and African descent. I have a great smile and curly hair that I have a tendency to wear long. This sometimes gives the impression of being the "party type", but in fact, I'm just the opposite.

I grew up in a town where a cultural revolution had taken place. My parents were part of this change.

Since then, the problems of Humanity have been addressed on a global scale. But it had its real beginnings here in the town I grew up in before I was born. It has had an effect on how I see the world.

I am a scientist by profession. My world consists of cold hard facts. I graduated from an Ivy League University on the east coast. I wasn't wealthy, just very intelligent. When I graduated, I immediately got a position in my field of interest.

This was definitely beginner's luck. I'm presently working with a group of extremely bright people who have some amazing ideas in innovative technology design.

We do our brainstorming in the Wheel Room. It's got its name from all the brilliant minds that have sat inside this place. You can feel the energy when you walk in. Every once in a while an idea is doable.

I had the idea for a Hieroglyphic chip for the space probe. Sometimes I feel like we make toys that really work. But there is seriousness in this creative environment and a lot of responsibility. I'm game and we all work to perfection.

I spend a lot of time with numerical configurations and the design of the Hieroglyph. I like what I do, but it can be very tedious. It takes years to complete projects like this, and because I am a young man I have mentally resigned myself to this fact.

I'm glad this is a project I really like because it could take up a portion of my lifetime to complete. Already I had developed a routine, but unknown to me, this was about to change forever.

It was Wednesday, midweek and I was feeling good. I arrived at my office; I did my "A" game. There is a lot of planning that has to be done regarding the programing of the Hieroglyph.

We are in meetings all day and the planning and design are very detailed. I'm tired at the end of each day and look forward to going home to chill and listen to some music.

Life is good. I am living in a really nice neighborhood, at the edge of the city. I bought a Victorian five years ago when there was a drop in the real estate market. The owners were in a hurry to sell. I never could understand why they wanted to leave. They took the first offer I made and the deal was done in forty-five days. I was ecstatic, but I still had my suspicions.

This house has an upstairs with three bedrooms, two full bathrooms, and a fireplace in the living room, a dining room, and a full deck off a kitchen with glass doors. There is a downstairs that is like a rec room with a patio that opens to a fairly large garden. This garden ends just at the edge of a grove of giant Sequoia trees. I always thought this was odd.

The trees are huge. It took seven or eight people to put arms around one tree. These trees had survived the great cutting and are at least a thousand years old. They are very special.

The tops of the trees can be seen from my bedroom windows on the second floor.
I have spent hours staring in amazement, and feeling really lucky to have such a great view and a house this size.
I could never have imagined that on this Wednesday evening, everything would change forever.

It was late, 11:00 o'clock. I was upstairs in my bedroom on the second floor. I had spent the whole day working with just the configurations for the Hieroglyph. I was still deciding the kind of information that would be programmed to represent Humans as an intelligent and peaceful organism from planet Earth. I was tired and found myself sitting quietly on the edge of my bed, lights off.

On this night the moon was full and it shown silver light through my windows. The moonlight was intense and reminded me of a spot light. It made the rest of the room so dark; I almost forgot where I was. This was the first time I had ever really sat in moonlight. I was bathed in silver and I was really digging it. The wind began to pick up outside and I thought I heard a sound, like a hum and then a rustling.
I thought it must be just the tops of the trees, so I gazed up to see.
At first I thought it was a really large shadow in the top of the giant Sequoia trees beyond my garden.
 But the moon was full, and I could see what my mind was not ready to tell me.
I had no name to call this Being upon our first meeting. He is called The Dreygon. (dray-gon)

In fact, I stared for a long time because I just did not believe it. What was even more amazing is that I had no fear of this vision. It was quite beautiful. I sat still, staring and did not move. It was as though I was waiting in anticipation of something.

The moonlight seemed to increase, and I could feel an eerie stillness in my bedroom. The wind picked up outside and this Being that I could see through my windows began to change color. Sometimes it could not be seen. I dare not take my eyes off him, for fear of missing something. My heart was pounding in my chest.

This Being, The Dreygon, seemed to be waiting in the giant Sequoia trees for something.
He suddenly turned his enormous head to look in my direction. I stopped breathing for a moment.

He had the head of a dragon. Three horns adorned his enormous head like a crown. There were three bone-like whiskers that grew at the bottom of each cheek. When he moved his head, I saw small bat-like wings hiding ears of an unusual shape.

His large yellow eyes gazed at me with unworldliness. His body was iridescent and bore the color of violet and emerald green. He had two enormous wings and four feet supported his long glistening body.

His face looked as though it had been in the wind. Then I noticed a very green mane that grew from the top of his head, down his back and ended at the tip of a long intimidating tail of great thickness. I watched as he began to flick his tail in the moonlight and his green mane moved in the night wind.

He was incredible to behold and I saw all this by the light of the moon. I felt as though I was in the beginning of an incredible dream that might turn out to be a nightmare. I stared, and he stared. My heart began to race. It was not fear that drove my heart, but the visual and the disbelief I felt.

He began to speak to me, but I saw no mouth move. I could hear a strange crackling voice in my head.

The Being said, *"I am Dreygon.*
Know where I fly, the center of the eye,
The knowing of a sky."
I thought, "Man you're a scientist. This is not possible!"

I stayed calm and decided to focus on this vision in the giant Sequoias trees beyond my garden. I was trying to respond like I knew a scientist would.

It was obvious Dreygon was not from my world. His size made me question what kind of being could inhabit such a form. I saw no mouth move: yet I heard him continue to speak to me.

Dreygon said, "I have twelve spirit beings that dwell within. You have only one. This is not a disadvantage for you Human, but a curiosity for me.

I behold you, Human, with the eyes of many. Yet we are all the same possibility. We all have the *inner map* that tells us how to travel from one Relms to another."

At this point, I hadn't moved at all. I sat frozen and at the same time gathering my wits.

I was about to have a conversation with this Being. I told myself again that I was a scientist and I could handle this. I regrouped and I decide to take what was happening seriously.

I had never heard of his concept before and I definitely could not imagine a Being made of twelve spirits, all of whom at this moment were looking at me. So I said, "What do you mean traveling from one Relms to another"?

Dreygon opened his enormous wings from where he was sitting in the tops of the giant Sequoias and replied, "You must be aware of the inner map when you travel, if you are to remember. At night the skies light up with the souls of many Humans.
Some Humans travel to other Relms in the twinkling of an eye.
And do not remember.
There are others who do remember their travel, but as a disturbing dream. This is the awareness of most Humans who dwell on the *Big Ground* you call Earth.
I carry twelve aspects of the Divine One that makes two. The One having eyes to see in all directions knows who the One seeing all directions is."

My mind reacted to his words, and I felt my body shiver.
I was not sure I understood anything Dreygon had just said. I kept my composure and he continued to speak inside my head.

"Enough of that, Human. You would like to know my origins, and I would imagine to what purpose my existence? Dare I ask you, Human, the same questions? You would probably tell me you were here to witness existence.

As for me, existence is my witness."

The Dreygon began to smile now and it was shocking to see a face like his smile. I saw no teeth but the light forming a smile in the shape of his incredible head. I tried hard not to become afraid. His voice continued in my head and I had to really focus to hear him.

Dreygon said, "I am invisible to most, and sometimes I travel at night. I've sat on buildings and gone unnoticed to Humans."

Then Dreygon began to flick his intimidating tail. His face became lucid, and he rose smooth and beautifully soundless from the tops of the giant Sequoias.

His wings were enormous and his bright green mane moved in the night wind. His iridescent skin made him almost invisible in a full moon sky. Dreygon's unworldly yellow eyes stared at me and I felt them to my soul.

"Would you like to come with me?" he bade. His claws were huge. Sometimes when I stared they became the hands of a Human. The visual was over whelming.

What my mind imagined was only part of the truth. I heard my heart beating louder than I could ever remember.

I watched, as Dreygon seemed to move into the moonlight.

I sat motionless on the edge of my bed. I was having trouble deciding if this was real. Maybe it was the kid in me that decided this could really be cool.

Maybe I thought I was just having a really amazing dream. I am a scientist, so there must be a logical explanation for all this. I had none for the moment, but I could use observation as a tool.
I was sure this was going to be the adventure of a lifetime and that I would experience something unknown to me. I did not answer right away. I think I was getting up my nerve.

I came to the conclusion this was really happening. He came nearer to the windows and I realized how large he really was.
His head was the size of my whole body.
It was strange, but I felt compassion emanating from this Being for now he was in close proximity.
Perhaps this was his first signal of trust.

Once again he stared at me. I had trouble looking directly into his eyes. I have never seen eyes like his. My mind began to race and all I could think of was; he also saw me with the eyes of the Twelve. I couldn't imagine who the Twelve might be. Then the feeling came over me that maybe I never would.
I didn't even answer his request to travel the Relms.
He knew.
All of this I was experiencing from the sitting position on my bed.
I stood up now and walked over to the windows.
I opened them. The moonlight was beautiful, and I felt as though I really was dreaming.
The Dreygon came closer and passed under my windows. I could feel my heart beat pounding in my chest.

I gave it no more thought and climbed out the window and onto his huge iridescent shoulder.
I felt the moonlight's intensity bathe us both.
It seemed to contain us.
I looked down to make sure I could see my feet.
In that moment, I thought myself insane, but I had committed.
Dreygon's incredible green mane brushed my face and shoulder and I held on to part of it. My hand felt something there, but not the texture of what it was.
I closed my eyes.

I felt this strange sensation inside myself of moving inward very fast. My breath quickened and I felt as though I was falling down, from the inside.
My head began to reel, and I thought I would go insane from the inner pressure.
I heard myself yell and I felt as though the very flesh was being peeled off my body. It felt as though I would be in this state for an eternity.
I saw a very bright light and then I heard a very loud clap!
I opened my eyes and was overwhelmed by the view.
We were motionless above the planet!
I could see in all directions and the Earth was floating in a black field full of stars. I looked down passed the Earth and above her.
I was conscious of my breathing and I tried hard not to panic. I had this sinking sensation and wondered if I'd ever see home again.
At this moment I realized I was sitting on the shoulder of a huge being called Dreygon. We were suspended above the planet.

11

I was in the place of endless night. The Earth was brightly lit on one side and the other side was in total darkness. I looked in disbelief, for I have never seen Earth from this perspective.

I felt a longing. Maybe that was me hoping I would make it back. I think for the first time, I knew I really belonged to the blue ball called Earth. But I still felt the inner commitment to take the ride with Dreygon.

I was a scientist and I had to be ready. This is what I told myself. Then I heard Dreygon's voice in my head.

He said, "I will take you to the Relms of Suna".

I have never heard of the Relms of Suna and I was looking at the planet from a view only seen from the Skylab. Not only that, but Earth was really called the Big Ground, and I was communicating with this Being by means of some kind of telepathy.

Dreygon turned his enormous body around. We began to move away from the Earth.

He picked up speed and we headed into what looked like dark light.

I call it this for I have no other way of describing what I saw. The planet Earth could no longer be seen.

We were moving into deep space full of blinking stars, and an all-encompassing darkness that would chill the bones of any human. I felt my hand tighten its grip on Dreygon's mane.

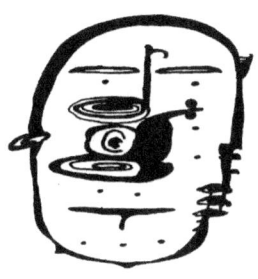

JOURNEY TO SUNA

The Dreygon glided with me on his shoulder for this is where I sat. We were on our way to the Relms of Suna. We flew through the endless night that consumed like none I'd ever known.

Night upon night and yet there was light everywhere. Then I noticed a very strange glow around us. But I couldn't see the source. I heard Dreygon say, "We carry the light with us" and he began to pick up speed.

There was no wind, but something I would call dimensional awareness. The Dreygon flew swift and silent. The further we traveled, the more colorful the vistas of gases could be seen deep within the dark light.

I had no concept of time or direction, but I became aware of something else. It was from this *awareness of something else* that I suddenly looked down at my chest.

I could see nothing, but dust. I started to panic.

13

I immediately looked down to check for my feet. This is how I know if I'm really having this experience. My feet were visible. This was all contrary to reason. But it was happening, so I looked again with the heart of an observer. I was almost transparent. Was I stardust?

We were in flight, and then the Dreygon stopped. His burning yellow eyes peered deep into the dark light in front of us. A small very bright light appeared in the distant blackness of deep space.

The light flashed and then extended itself like a long white thread against the darkness. It was amongst millions of blinking stars.
Dreygon flew in this direction at what seemed like light speed. I held on tight to Dreygon's mane. I felt a dimensional shift. It was like everything slowed down for a split second inside a wave of energy.
We passed through this flux that could not be seen and out the other side. We were closer now and approaching the rim of light.

We flew across the curve of light, which was below us and it continued to increase in size. It was huge!
Dreygon descended into the curve of light. Down we went and the light consumed us in a luminous glow.
Then we entered utter darkness and the light we passed through was above us.
I looked up as the last bit of light burned through a crack to absolute black.

We had arrived in the Relms of Suna. It was dark here, but there was light everywhere.

The environment glowed in some places. I looked down but saw nothing.

Dreygon finally came to rest on a surface so dark it could not be seen. He lowered his head for me to descend. I climbed down the shoulder of Dreygon with great unease.

The Dreygon's unworldly yellow eyes glowed with intensity in the darkness of the Relms of Suna. His iridescent body rendered him invisible here, but I could see his bright green mane. He watched me with a strange curiosity. I felt some apprehension.

It took me a moment to adjust to Suna before I could see clearly. I looked down at my feet. I was standing on burnt embers! I took a closer look and then a step. I could feel the black embers moving under my feet. I pondered the possibility of this.

I looked up and into a dark landscape that held nothing. In some places, very strange columns of light were visible. As I gazed into this semi-lit environment, I had a vague memory of something buried too deep to recall.

It made me uneasy. An even stranger feeling came over me. Something had left this place a long time ago. It was very powerful and had permeated the Relms of Suna.

I could not understand this kind of energy. But this is what I sensed. There was something about a return of the Humans

I was having thoughts about something I knew nothing about.

The thoughts just arrived and I found myself almost listening. It was as though a message was left here that I might be able to decipher.

The message was this: A massive energy field left the Relms of Suna eons ago destined for Earth. This energy field from Suna hit the planet and permeated everything. It spread across Earth in its entirety. It changed the awareness of all living things, but had its greatest effect on Humans, for which it was intended.

It was a cosmic homing device! The Humans would express it as *love*. The reason for their existence would never be known without it. Love was a direction, a cosmic homing device for the return. But I did not understand to where?

How strange were my thoughts! My head felt strange and I wondered why would I think this?

Perhaps it was Suna itself who spoke to me.

These impressions ended soon after they began.

I turned now to look behind us into the darkness beyond where we stood. I could not tell direction because of the engulfing blackness that extended to the surface of Suna.

Then in the distant darkness, I noticed a long trail of approaching lights. At first I thought they must be stars. But they were too small to be stars, and stars don't move as though they're about to lap a shore!

It had the appearance a white sea emerging out of total darkness just beyond where we stood. The lights were coming in fast like an ocean on the Big Ground. They came across the blackness moving up and up and then crested at the top in a swirl like a wave. Then it crashed down soundless and lapped an unseen shore aloft.

I watched as it receded out into the blackness and disappeared. There was no sound.
It was beautiful, and I tried hard not to become uneasy because it could be seen returning again.
I turned now to look at Dreygon.
His unworldly yellow eyes were watching my every move. In this darkness I could still see the green mane on his crown moving as though there was wind. He began to flick his long tail of great thickness.
He stared at me and then Dreygon turned his enormous head toward this White Sea.
I watched him open his huge wings, rise and dive in and completely disappear.
He could no longer be seen from where I stood. I was alone now and it was dark by my standards. I told myself again I was a scientist and that I was here to observe. So I waited.

The sea moved as though it lived. Millions of tiny lights seemed to be floating inside an invisible substance. It continued to roll in and crest, then crash down in silence. And after a while I saw him emerge out of the rising crest of the White Sea just before it lapped an unseen shore.
Dreygon was luminous and seemed refreshed as he spread his enormous wings and came to rest by my side. I realized how large he was compared to me and how unbelievable he really is.
I dare not ask him where he had gone. I wasn't ready to know. I was still dealing with his size and us being here in the Relms of Suna.
"Is there anyone living on Suna?" I asked.

Dreygon did not look at me but sat gazing at the White Sea. But I heard him answer.

"Here, Beings simply "be" in the Relms of Suna. There are no cities here, as you know on the Big Ground. This is not imagined here. Building shelter is not known on Suna because the concept of permanence and protection is not a reality.

On Suna, elements change and are not as you know them. Everything here is light energy. There is no concept of time, as you know it. You will not be able to see what is here. This is your first journey to what is Relms, Vishnu."

I heard Dreygon say my name for the first time and I was startled, because I hadn't told him. I said nothing else and continued to stare into this environment. I thought I saw something moving in the distance near the strange columns of diffused light. I felt the presence of many and I saw no one. The horizon bore only columns of a light unfamiliar to me.
Suna had no structures.

My observation did not allow total comprehension. I had to be satisfied with what I sensed.

"No nightclubs?" I asked. I'm not sure why this thought entered my head. I think I was trying to imagine something that would reflect a culture I could understand. I couldn't see anything living.

Dreygon's turned his huge head toward me. His unworldly yellow eyes pierced the darkness of Suna. He moved down to look at me. I was shaken to my core. I stood fast and kept my composure.

"Come, I will take you to the music sphere" he said.

Dreygon lowered his huge head so that I could climb onto his shoulder. We began to glide across the blackened embers toward the unfamiliar columns of light in the distance.

Did he say music sphere? He did! We were on our way.

The eerie columns of light were further away than I anticipated. I looked to my left and then to my right as we moved across Suna. Nothing but blackness could be seen. In some places light seemed to be emanating in columns from somewhere below the burnt ember surface. This was not a planet, or at least this is not what came to mind. This was the Relms and I have no other term to use, which would explain my observations. I could feel the strange nature of this environment and the darkness that surrounded Dreygon and me. It wasn't hostile. It was almost like a womb. We were nearing the columns now and Dreygon stopped and waited. I stared at the eerie columns of diffused white light. We were close enough now for me to see the source of the light forming one of the columns. The light was soft and seemed to rise from a very large circular hole deep below the surface. The column of light ended in the blackness above us. I tried to see inside the hole, but the diffused light blocked my vision. We were moving again, and Dreygon entered the eerie column of diffused light. I admit, I was scared and everything happened very quickly.

As soon as we entered the column, the diffused light engulfed us. We were moving up very fast. I looked above me to see where we were headed. I saw nothing except us riding in a column of light. The light seemed to extend itself to a place above us.

Dreygon and I arrived there, and the column of light disappeared.
We were in the middle of hundreds, maybe thousands of long gaseous columns, floating in a black open environment!
The gaseous columns were colored and hung suspended in all directions. The visual was immediately intimidating and the sound was so loud, I couldn't understand what I was hearing.
The sounds seem to clash with each other and for a moment I felt what it must be like to go insane.
I could hear Dreygon's voice below the clamor.

He said, "Human, this is the Relms of all music known to you".

After he said this, the sounds seem to slow down. It was as though understanding hearing came out of nowhere, and this was music.
I stared in awe. I could hear music coming from every column and I gasped at the enormity of this place.
The gaseous columns were diffused orange and a very light red. The music seemed to weave across its vastness.
Dreygon lowered his huge head so that I could descend his shoulder. I did this without looking down, having already seen the darkness of the

surface. I think I was really unnerved here. My senses were responding out of control. I stood by him. I needed time to prepare myself for what I was seeing and hearing. I took a deep breath.

I could hear very faintly the sound of some music that was familiar. It floated across the blackness that was filled with colored columns. It was music I knew. It seemed to travel to where I stood with Dreygon.

I could not control my reaction as the music became louder upon reaching our location. I was overpowered by its sensations. It was all consuming and I began to remember. This was an experience unknown to me. The music reminded me of feelings that were no longer mine. Sometimes I felt me, but I wasn't sure who I was. I could hear music and almost see when I heard this music, but I couldn't remember where.

Those mental pictures did not present themselves clearly because then was also now. I was in every song written throughout the history of the Humans.

Somehow I couldn't question this experience, just be in it. Dreygon was silent and assumed a resting position that was odd to see.
We were both floating motionless in a darkness filled with colored columns of music. I was experiencing the laws of physical physics in the Relms.

In my head I continued to hear Dreygon's voice. He suddenly said, "I will wait here for you". Without any effort on my part I began to float away from him toward the colored columns. I could feel the darkness begin to surround me.

The colored columns were not close to each other or me. I tried to remain calm as I floated across a bottomless black chasm before reaching the first column.

I could hear melodies barely audible dancing across the blackness.

I watched the diffused light of the columns extending into the darkness below.

I saw no end to the columns and when I looked at my feet they seemed to be riding on nothing. I felt fear and panic.

I turned around to make sure Dreygon was still there. I could see his huge yellow eyes amongst the colored columns watching me. I felt some reassurance.

I was now close to one of the long colored columns. It was gaseous and a diffused orange color. There was a large oval sphere suspended inside the column.

I could hear music emanating from inside, but it wasn't quite audible.

At first I couldn't quite make out what was inside the sphere. The orange gas diffused a clear view.

I moved close enough to touch the gaseous column. Then, I saw the unimaginable. There was someone inside the sphere! It was floating in a semi reclined position. The Being had a long body and looked almost Human. But we were not of the same essence. I could feel the music pulse inside the sphere.

I immediately looked for a face.

It was the Being's eyes I noticed first. These eyes were large and unnatural.

There was no pigment and they seem to open and close randomly.
When the eyes closed, the Being became visible. I could see features that would be human. When the eyes opened the Being would almost disappear.
I stared in confusion.

A clear view was hidden by the color of the column. I know the Being could see me because of where I stood. But I wondered if I could be seen?
I hesitantly reached out to touch the gaseous column. I was surprised to see my hand go through and touch the sphere inside. The volume of the music inside increased. I was alarmed and immediately removed my hand from the sphere.
I took a deep breath to regain my composure. I did not ask myself for the logic of this.
More than anything else, I wanted to know what music this Being heard.
I readied myself and again I put my hand through the gaseous column to touch the sphere inside.
The volume increased immediately.

This was music unknown to me. I heard what sounded like a deep rumbling, except it never stopped. It began so deep, that I could physically feel it. The rumbling sound increased its intensity and became the sound of thunder. I felt this thunder in my heart and heard it in my head. Slowly, very slowly I could hear other sounds arriving like the wind and the long low notes of a violin. I knew my mind was translating the sound into what I could understand. It was penetrating and with great movement.

The sounds seemed to dance and were arriving in streams. I heard them separately, then as they moved together. All the sounds in their separateness wove together, and then could be heard as one sound. That sound became this music. I was sure I was hearing something long forgotten, but it seemed to be mixed with everything I had ever known. The volume increased and the music evolved into something more complex. Then the color inside the column began to change, and now there was a pulse.

I kept my hand steady touching the sphere. Each sound became a vivid color and I was shocked to see the Being inside change color with each pulse of music. The opaque eyes opened and the being would almost disappear. The eyes closed and the Being became visible. I saw no facial expression but I could feel and hear everything.

The music kept changing as though it was revealing its history. But there was no break in the sound. On and on it played without ceasing. I could not tell where I was in this music.

I heard the music arriving from somewhere far and I was riding the stream from beginning to end. I couldn't distinguish its arrival. It would play in my head and move on and the next movement would arrive without a space in between the two. The colors continued to change as I stared at the Being floating in sound. It stared with eyes that had no pigment. Maybe it could see something I couldn't and its physical appearance was the effect of being inside the music sphere.

The music increased its volume and my head began to ring. I snatched my hand off the sphere inside the column. The sound inside immediately became muffled.

I turned now to look for Dreygon. I could see his burning yellow eyes in the darkness among the long colored columns. He was not near. I returned my gaze to the Being in front of me. I could still hear the muffled music playing inside the sphere, but the pulse was no longer present. I stared as the Being continued appearing and disappearing as its eyes opened and then closed.

I wondered if the Being knew of my presence. I could still feel the thunder of the music inside me. I looked in all directions and all that could be seen were the eerie gaseous columns. There were too many to count.

I realized that you could get lost here and never find your way out. There were no visible markers in this darkness. Dreygon was the only marker I could see. Without him I would be doomed to wander here for eternity, is how I felt.

I immediately began to move as soon as I had the thought. I was not headed toward Dreygon, but continued to float further into the blackness of this color filled place

I was approaching a reddish column. I could see there was a sphere with something inside. It had large eyes without pigment that began to close and the Being became completely visible!

Its face was different than the other, but they were the same essence. Its features, never the less, were still vague and without real distinction. I heard music emanating from inside. I didn't try to touch this one.

The eyes began to opened and the Being slowly disappeared, but not completely. I looked at the other floating columns. I could see Beings floating inside all of them!

Then the music coming from the spheres inside the columns of color began to increase in volume. This music seemed to move out of the spheres in streams, weaving itself around the music of the others. It seemed to change direction and began to fill the blackness of where I was. I became nervous because the sound of the music continued to increase.

I began to feel its maddening effects. This was intensified by what I could see. I turned now to find Dreygon.

He was already moving towards me and his incredible wings were open. The music was getting louder and the weaving more complex.

"Human, it is time for our departure", I heard Dreygon say. He lowered his huge wing so that I could climb onto his shoulder. I looked at his body as I climbed and I thought I saw eyes move across his flanks. I was shocked and I tried to keep my fear under control.

Shall we?" said Dreygon.

And he began to rise. I tighten my grip on his green mane and decided to forget about the eyes I saw moving across his flanks. We began our ascent into the darkness above us and could now see a view of the columns below.

I was now looking down on thousands of columns of colored gas!

I could still see the spheres inside the columns. And not only that, but the faces of the Beings inside! I watched as they randomly opened and closed their eyes appearing and disappearing.
It was like nothing I could have ever imagined. The music became louder and now the Beings began to open and shut their eyes in unison.

Dreygon and I were motionless above the columns. I looked to my right and I could see a wave of some kind of luminous cloud approaching. It was enormous and it moved toward the columns below us. The music was now deafening. It had reached the fevered pitch of what it was when we first arrived. I could no longer understand the sounds and the music clashed.

My head reeled, and once again I thought myself insane. The luminous cloud began to cover the gaseous columns of color. Lightening began to flash in its midst as it moved like a wave. Each column it covered became silent. It was almost over as quickly as it began. The colored columns were disappearing under the luminous cloud.

The music came to a crescendo and then a whisper. I looked down to see miles of luminous cloud cover. Flashes of lightening continued in the distance. The columns could no longer be seen. Dreygon turn his enormous body around and we headed in the direction behind us. He picked up speed and I held on tight to his green mane.

We ascended into the darkness above us and out through a thin crack of light. I turned to look behind us and could see the rim of light of the closing Relms. I saw a white flash. I felt a shift and

we entered deep space. It seemed to open up before us. I was again looking into the blackness that was filled with millions of blinking stars.
I was riding on the shoulder of the Dreygon.

"Human, you have begun the journey of what you do not know. All that you experience is what you are ready to understand." I was listening to Dreygon from the inside of my head. I was trying to understand his message to me. My head was full and I thought I might be falling asleep. How was that possible?

I don't remember what I saw on the way home or how much time had passed. The sensation of incredible speed was hard to take.
Sometimes it was so fast I only saw small black and white specks. This was scary. I closed my eyes and just fell asleep. I was having a dream and I woke up! I sat up startled in my bed.
The room was dark and moonlight filtered in threw the windows.
I immediately looked up into the branches of the giant Sequoia trees beyond my garden. I could see something resting high in the trees, glistening and iridescent. The branches shifted with the weight of this incredible creature.
His large yellow eyes held mine in an unworldly gaze. My heart began to pound in my chest. I could see him there. This was no dream! I remembered his name, Dreygon.
I laid down in the moonlight and closed my eyes. I fell into a deep sleep. When I awoke, the sun was

shining on my face. At first I had no memory of what had happened. Then it all came rushing in.

I am a scientist. There must be an explanation. I told myself this as I brushed my teeth. I would deal with this later. Now I was headed for my office and life on the Big Ground. I laughed to myself at this thought. I did not allow myself to ever think about this experience again.

A lot of time passed before I saw Dreygon again. And I was glad...then it was time.

A TRIP HOME

I had dinner plans with some friends at our "hang" called the Daygone. I arrived and everyone was already at our table that was nestled underneath a huge green plant by some windows in the rear of the restaurant.
There's about eight of us, and we do things together. We've all known each other for years. Most of us grew up together. We are a diverse group of friends. I must say they're all very interesting and intelligent. It's always a cool hang.
"Hey, Vishnu"! This is how they always greet me.

It's always a cool set. I sat down with my friends who were already having very profound conversations.
Someone pour me a glass of wine. I was silent. I listened intently to adventures, ideas, politics, and visions. I listened to numerous stories, both written and idealized and ways to keep the economy stable.
I was silent. I smiled a lot. A friend commented that I was looking wise.

I wasn't sure if that was a compliment.
Perhaps I had just dreamed the whole experience of meeting Dreygon. If I told anyone, it was bound to dream format. I was silent.
I didn't sense any changes in myself. Maybe my eyes looked different.
I excused myself and went into the restroom. I stood staring at myself in the mirror and thought I saw a light in my eyes I hadn't noticed before.
I blinked in disbelief. There was a flash, and for a moment I wasn't sure where I was.
Plenty, I thought. I've seen plenty!
I washed my hands and threw some cold water on my face.
I rejoined my friends and hoped they didn't notice. They didn't. We had a really good dinner and laughed a lot.
Someone commented on me doing a disappearing act, and for a moment I thought they all saw me disappear. The look on my face must have been priceless, because they all rolled with laughter.
I laughed myself, but out of relief.

We meet often at the Daygone. It used to be an old warehouse of unusual artifacts. The building is medium in size and completely made of redwood and polished old oak floors. It has high-beamed ceilings and there are lots of windows.
Hanging from the high ceiling is a colorful fake trapeze artist and her partners sitting in red swings. There are several very large green plants placed strategically in each corner of the restaurant.
In the middle of the restaurant is a medium size tree accompanied by a red bench. This is the spot that

31

everyone gathers before sitting down. It's amazing to see a tree thriving in this environment. The tables are in between the plant life and are made of old antique doors. The seating is very comfortable. I think the owner has a really unusual sense of décor, but it is a very beautiful place to be in. It overlooks the ocean. The music and atmosphere, food and drinks are great here.

We are never the only ones laughing loud. The Daygone is always full of people. Seems everyone is here for the same reason. The most interesting people I have ever met, I met in the Daygone. It has the vibe that attracts the unusual personage. I've never been in a place filled with so many happy people.

The evening went quickly. That old saying about time flying because of fun is true. I said goodbye to everyone and I was out.

I arrived home by taxi. I was feeling good but really tired. I turned on the lights and sat down in the living room to relax. I played some music. I decided to keep my thoughts about meeting Dreygon to a minimum; this was avoidance. I knew that.

My work kept me occupied with what I knew as reality. My responsibilities were major at the moment. Besides, the Hieroglyphic chip was cutting edge and I had to use my imagination to visualize its format. This required a lot of concentration and searching through the known. This was plenty, in regards to my intellectual workout.

I decided to watch the magic box, but with dulled sensitivity. I tired quickly and thought it best to crawl into bed. I slowly climbed the stairs and I could hear the wind blowing through the Sequoias. I stood staring out the windows from the top of the stairs.

I can't remember how long I stood there or why. It was like being on pause. Then I decided I should just get ready for bed. Sleep arrived this time. I don't know how long I slept before I heard this high pitch ringing. I sat up and looked around the room still half asleep.

The moon was full again and it played shadows of the tree branches on the walls of my bedroom. I took a deep breath and lay back down. I'm not easily spooked.

I closed my eyes and fell sleep. I was dreaming. I could see a small circle of light and it seemed to be in the back of my head. I heard a voice say, "Human".

I sat up in my bed like the house was on fire with my eyes wide open. I am a scientist and I moved to this mind set immediately.

I got out of my bed and walked over to the windows. I was still in my bedroom trying to decide what kind of dream I was having. But this was no dream!

I looked up into the giant Sequoia trees beyond my garden. There was Dreygon, who seemed to appear on some kind of wind. I'm sure of this because I felt it blow pass me in my room and he was outside my window.

I still felt the same rush upon seeing his size and those unworldly yellow eyes. He was looking directly at me. I stood perfectly still because I found all this hard to believe.

I told myself I was a scientist and immediately checked to see if I could see my feet. I always do this now, for this is how I know if I'm really having the experience. There my feet were as plain as day. I was astonished.

I'm not sure I'll ever become accustomed to this. I must be the only human on the Big Ground having these experiences.

I continued looking at Dreygon, my heart pounding in my chest. I decide to ask him a question. So I began with the greatest of reverence. I know that I have to think the questions, for with Dreygon there are no words.

So I thought, "I beseech you Dreygon to tell me of your existence, and of the Twelve that lie within?"

I thought I heard laughter emanating from the body of Dreygon. Must be the wind.

Dreygon moved his enormous iridescent body into the moonlight. His mane was bright green and he flicked his enormous tail. His unworldly yellow eyes burned through moonlit night. Then without warning, the eyes of the Twelve moved across his flanks. They were silvery in color and they seemed to be peering out. I was unnerved! The moonlight was soft on this night and seemed to comfort me as I stood staring trying not to panic.

I heard Dreygon's voice in my head. "Human, do not be afraid of what you see. The Twelve within make up my one consciousness. There is no real separation. They are of the same essence. Each comes from a different part of the galaxy, with all the knowledge and vision of what each calls home. Home is really the same place with variations of the same possibility of awareness. Perhaps I can make this simpler for you to understand.

I set perimeters or measure distance as I enter the time-reality of Humans, by using feelings, as you call them. I use this measurement only on the Big Ground, Earth. In this place the dimensions are within, but only manifest as being. This is how you know you're really here. For the Twelve within, the inner and outer awareness is the same. They know the *inner map* that points to all the Relms of possibility. This is discovery at its best, and the road to destination without end.

This may seem overwhelming to you, Human. No entity will ever see the end of the Universe, nay the end of consciousness. At that point, you would not know experience, so this is not the answer."

Was this a parable? I thought I heard laughter. Was this coming from the Twelve within Dreygon?
The laughter continued as though the conversation was absurd. I did not respond because I did not believe I was really hearing laughter. But somewhere inside of me, I knew exactly what he meant.
So I asked, "Dreygon, are these real places that each of the Twelve call home?"
I could not leave this conversation yet because this was a map unknown by any Human.
The moonlight seemed to flicker and Dreygon turned his head and looked in the direction of the moon.
His mane looked like green silver and it began to wave in the moonlight.
I stared and did not move. He then turned to look at me with his intense yellow eyes that seemed to burn through the moonlit night.

Now the Dreygon answered, "Yes, just as you are at home on the Big Ground. I am a different reality, and all who dwell as the Dreygon know the reason for existence. I am without discord. This "cord" is like the chord of a music note in harmony. The "dis-" means to be without, or unable to hear the note. On the Big Ground, few can hear the note and most are unaware of its existence. Physical existence has its challenges and suffering is the note heard by most. The discord is lack of awareness of the note, and not hearing the note of the Big Ground."

This conversation with Dreygon had taken a sudden turn. I knew I had to stay focused so that what I heard in my head, I could understand. I didn't understand the concept of the "note".

I knew music, lots of music: but the note? So I asked Dreygon," How do you hear this note? Have I heard this note?"

I knew I was being literal.

He suddenly began a smile that was light and took the shape of his face. I felt myself tremble, but I wasn't afraid.

Then he said, "When was the last time you had your head and ear to the Big Ground?"

Somehow I knew this part of our conversation was over. It was difficult to not sound insecure as an observer. I was still dealing with the concept of there being a real note to hear and I sensed he wouldn't offer a further explanation on this.

I said nothing. I was expecting something more complicated, but this was simple. The Dreygon continued to tell me things I have never considered. He said, "You cannot use desire to travel with me.

It is your own evolving awareness that will
bring you to where one of the Twelve calls home.
On this journey, desire nothing and look within for
where to find the *inner map*."

Once again Dreygon spoke of this *inner map*.
I didn't quite understand the concept. I had spent
most of my time in my head. As a scientist I used
numbers and calculations to determine location.
This is what I learned being human.
Now I was being told of a map without numbers or
location. How is this possible? Not only that, it was
most likely more advanced than anything on the Big
Ground. Maybe it was even connected to the *note*.
I stood in revelation, looking at Dreygon. This was
still overwhelming to me and I had to remember to
breath. So I took a deep breath. The conversation
ended and I felt relieved.

I was anticipating my next move. I came closer
to the windows to open them. It was time to go.
Dreygon's huge iridescent shoulders passed below
the windows. They gleamed in the moonlight. I
glanced back into my bedroom as though I would
never see it again. I felt strange but confident.

I needed to go with him, be the scientist that I
am and observe the Relms of Dreygon. I climbed out
the window and on to his shoulder. Dreygon's bright
green mane brushed my face. I grabbed on to it.

The moonlight was still soft and we were
inside of it. I automatically closed my eyes. I had the
very same sensation as I did on our first encounter
of moving inward very fast. My breath quickened
and I felt like I was falling down from the inside.
I felt myself reel and then a pressure inside my
head. This time I knew for sure I would go insane.

I heard myself yell from the inside as I felt layers being peeled off me. It seemed to take an eternity. I saw a very bright light and heard a loud clap!

I opened my eyes and Dreygon and I were once again motionless above the planet! I was breathing heavy on our arrival. It seemed more intense this time. Maybe it's just been a while and I had forgotten the incredible physical changes that I go through to travel with Dreygon. He is not having this experience, just me.

Dreygon and I remained suspended gazing at this view as we did before.

I tried to see his eyes from where I sat. I think I was wondering if he gazed at the Big Ground seeing its beauty. I know as I stared, I was definitely filled with the awesomeness of it from this view. I was observing a wonder. There was life down there on the Big Ground. It seemed so unlikely from here, and for a moment I couldn't understand what I was suddenly feeling. This experience was way beyond anything known in my world. I took another deep breath.

Dreygon turned now and flew out into the dark light behind us. The planet was no longer visible. I was surrounded by the blackness of this endless night, but there were millions of blinking stars everywhere. We were moving smooth and swift and I could not calculate the speed or the distance we had traveled. There are no physical markers in deep space.

I felt us fly through an unseen wave of energy. It passed over me like a ripple of time in the vast blackness of the dark light.

I heard Dreygon asking me, "Tell me Human of your origins?"

But before I could answer, we had entered a strange empty space, and in the distance I could see a house that looked vaguely familiar. It was sitting in semi darkness in the middle of nothing. I didn't understand how or why this would be here. Dreygon made no mention of the Relms, and somehow I felt this was about me. As Dreygon made his approach I realized it was the house I grew up in.

This house was a little different version of the one I knew so well.

It was as though the house had a soul and I was looking at it. It sat on the same perfect lawn in a twilight setting. The pink stucco was gone, and it was sleek white with a green trim.

Dreygon stopped directly in front of the house. He then took a resting position and lowered his shoulder so that I could descend. I remained by his side. I looked down to see what he was resting upon and where I was standing. I saw nothing but grey empty space below us. I looked away because I could feel uncertainty and fright moving into my head. I wasn't sure what was happening or the reason we were here.

It was strange to see this house that had been torn down years ago.
I regrouped my thoughts and took the demeanor of observer. I decided I could walk up to the front door, but changed my mind and walked around to the rear of the house. I became anxious about going in. Dreygon was not with me.

The stairs leading up to the back door were in front of me and appeared to be made of wood.

I took the stairs that somehow seemed longer than what I remembered. The old door at the top of the stairs was dark green and the doorknob red. I hesitantly touch the nob.

The door opened and I cautiously looked inside. I saw two people sitting in a golden light at a table. So I went in.

This was not the kitchen I grew up in. The table in front of the old couple was filled with all kinds of objects. They both eyed me and the woman spoke first.

She said: "You used to live here." As she spoke to me I looked at her face.

Her face was old, but I saw no wrinkles. Her eyes were very blue and mysterious. I stared. She knew me, but I could not remember her face. I glanced around this room and it was filled with nothing but tables.

The old man immediately caught my attention, gazing at me steadily.

He was lucid and dream like. His face was gentle, and it was obvious they were here together. They wore clothes from a time period long passed. Now the old man spoke:

"We are Guardians. We have been at this table, in this house for thousands of Earth years, he said. "Here, time is irrelevant. Deed is the governor. Only Humans are concerned with how long it takes."

The old woman held me in her gaze as the old man spoke and then she said, "This place is the continuation of what was not done in deed, come to completion."

I looked closer at what was on the tables in front of them. At first I thought I was imagining this.

It was not possible for these things to exist here in these numbers.

There were all kinds of gadgets on the table in front of them! Some I recognized and others I could not even imagine their use. I was astonished!

I began to walk around in this room that wasn't large and had a very odd shape. On every table there were: drawings and grafts, formulas on pieces of paper, clocks, and plane parts, wheels, springs, and every kind of tool imaginable. On top of the tables I saw paintings so incredible that their beauty touched me.

On other tables there were small human statues made of what appeared to be wood. There were gold and silver statues bearing the faces of humans.

I saw tiny machines made of pure gold. I wanted to touch them, but decided it wasn't a good idea.

Where am I? I thought to myself. How could all the inventions of the humans be in one place? It was even more amazing to discover that everything was in one room.

I tried to look on every table and remember what I saw. As I looked at each item, I could not remember seeing the previous item. I couldn't even remember looking at it. I have an incredible memory, so it was hard for me to fathom this possibility.

I turned to look back at the old couple, the Guardians of this place.

They were seated in the same place and both turned to look at me.

It was at this moment I noticed the old man's eyes. They twinkled blackness. I was so shocked I reacted with alarm. I looked at the old woman. Her very blue

eyes did not react to my apprehension, but held me in her steady gaze. I felt their eyes to my core.
I wasn't sure what I should do, so I just stood there staring back at them.
Then the old man spoke, "Humans who visit here sometimes remember what they've seen.
The Humans awake from a deep slumber with a brilliant idea."

The old woman's eyes seemed to fill the room as she spoke to me next.
She said, "Everything here is present and cannot be held in memory. This is not about possession. This is infinite possibility on the Big Ground."
I was intrigued.

The door I entered opened. This was my cue to go. I saw nothing outside the door but a light grey atmosphere. I took my last look around this room and everything on the tables. I then held a gaze with the old couple. They had continued to look at me as though I was kin. Their eyes still in character, I was afraid to smile.

I walked toward the door and the steps appeared. I descended the wooden stairs and I heard the door shut. I couldn't see Dreygon. I wasn't afraid, just confused.

I finally reached the bottom of the wooden stairs. I was in the back lawn of the house that felt like mine. I looked around for Dreygon and his unworldly yellow eyes appeared out of the greyness of this place. I was shaken. Dreygon was directly in front of me and his huge wings were open. He looked directly at me and I thought I saw the eyes of the Twelve move across his flanks. It was scary.

I must be insane to be here. I told myself again I was a scientist and I was here to observe. The experiences were becoming more than I anticipated. I had to get use to his appearance.

Dreygon's huge head moved toward me and he lowered his wings so that I could climb onto his shoulder. His bright green mane brushed my face and I grabbed onto it. I watched as the house that felt like mine began to fade away from the back lawn and disappear. Dreygon and I were once again suspended in deep space.

The Dreygon said to me: "Ah Human, you are beginning to not understand". I heard this in my head and I thought he must have been joking. But he was not.

We began to fly and I watched Dreygon's huge iridescent wings from where I sat. They were the most incredible wings I had ever seen. I held on tighter to his mane for sometimes they were unnerving in the dark light. The blackness is penetrating. The millions of lights hold their place and when I look around there is nothing except where we are. I cannot determine distance or how far away anything is.

Dreygon moves here with knowledge unknown to any human. We are not in a ship.

A small blue light appeared in the far distance in front of us. I watched as it flashed opened. It looked like a giant blue crack in the cosmic. Dreygon immediately arched his flight in that direction.

I wasn't sure why Dreygon was traveling through the dark light with me. Each time I go to what I now know as the Relms, I am sure the field of my mind's imagination changes.

Is it important to use these experiences as a starting point for this new reality? Perhaps it was. I was certain that now I was becoming more of what is infinite possibility. This has to be the answer.

The Dreygon and I continued to fly through the deep space of the dark light toward the crack of blue, which looked like a horizon.

"How far can we go?" I asked with utter excitement, and some disillusionment.

Dreygon told me, "This cannot be known with an answer that is irrelevant in the Relms. This is truly without end, and so it should be, as you, when you validate your existence by saying it is so."

His response made me think about atoms and quantum physics. The awareness of "I am and some kind of divine intelligence that even now is able to see itself through me. Dreygon turned as we moved and I tightened my grip on his bright green mane.

"The Universe was here without me", I said.

"Yes, but you were always here, just different," was what I heard Dreygon reply.

This "just different" was a vast over simplification. I had no memory of this, and even then I must have desired physical existence.

Feeling is the reality of humans on the Big Ground. Matter is the means of existence and expression, matter that has consciousness. We had become evolved cell beings of the Big Ground.

These thoughts were beginning to change how I perceived everything. Perhaps I was now looking at all my scientific concepts with a greater understanding of origin and purpose. Dreygon heard my thoughts, and said, "You're beginning to see the *inner map*".

The map? What map? Was Dreygon telling me about the map again?

I thought I saw eyes move across Dreygon's flanks and I was sitting on his shoulder. I heard myself say, "Oh shit!"

Dreygon did not respond. I'm sure he knew this was human expression.

Then I heard him say: "The more you remember, the more vivid the *inner map*. Yes, it is the map of possibilities."

So I asked, "What should I remember and how can there be a map of possibilities, and where is the treasure?"

Dreygon began to smile and I watched the light move to the side of his face from where I sat on his shoulder. It was the strangest thing I have ever seen.

Then he said, "You are imagining a map to a place, some place, any place, and singular destination. You see, the map I speak of leads to all destinations, all possible destinations. Inner distance is the reality of possible distance, distance becomes possible."

Dreygon spoke these words to me and for a moment I thought I had a glimpse of the infinite. I felt myself move in and then return to where I was, but where was I?

Dreygon heard my thoughts and answered: "Why Human, you are in the Relms!"

I was on a roll now, so I asked,

"Can you tell me of the living beings that give me physical form on the Big Ground?"
The light of the Dreygon smile was still present. He answered, "It was I who asked you to tell me of your origins. Now you ask me who you are?"

I knew I was asking an unanswerable question. The Dreygon continued to speak, and I was sure I would hear what I did not expect. "Well, I will answer you in a way you can understand. I will tell you a story.
You are the Seer of the Big Ground called Earth. It is you who looks in all directions and marvels at the beauty. You are called by the name Human. It is an expression of two words: "Hu" and "mum". "Hu" is the spirit energy and "mum" means the Doer, which is the collective consciousness of your cells. Your cells are all the small life forms that give you physical existence. The Seer and the Doer together makes a third, which is divine expression. This is your Trinity. This physical form has expression and music. The small life forms or cells vibrate a note that attracts and also stimulates their rebirth. It is also tuned to the harmony of the Big Ground.
Whether or not you can hear the note so that you may know the *inner map* is up to you. In the Human Relms this is called awareness and conscious choice."
I was now remembering him telling me earlier about hearing a note. This was getting interesting and I was sure I would get a full explanation. It was time, and I was trying to understand what Dreygon meant.

"So are you telling me, my molecules are singing?" I asked.

Dreygon answered, "More like a hum. Your planet rings, hums. Yes, everyone you see on the street is a walking orchestra. For some, the music is sad, and notes are missing. Others are looking to take the notes from someone else because they can no longer hear their own. This is another awareness without awareness.

Still there are those who now are beginning to hear and remember their note on the Big Ground. Their song is almost complete. You are here until your last note is played. It's very loud, I should tell you. No one leaves in a whisper. In the Human Relms, Gaia, the spirit of the Big Ground, gave the songs. This was the first physical map for as you know in the beginning all the chords where of the same physical place. The Seers were inspired by beauty. Each song was a reflection of the physical place on the Big Ground, so that Seers would remember where they had been as they began their great walk across the planet.

There was no discord."

Dreygon continued, "Things changed because Seers are a wandering spirit, and as time passed could no longer remember. They were soon to meet others with a different song, given by Gaia. Instead of realizing this was the other part of the map, the Seers chose discord. They choose to not hear the song of the others. Some thought all Seers should be controlled and have the same song.

In doing so, these Seers forgot their own song for the map, and as time passed were unable to hear or remember their own note."

I was listening to him telling me all this and it sounded like a great whisper in my head.

Dreygon continued the story.

"Some of the Seers now calling themselves Human, wanted control of all the chords, desiring all to be the same. They claimed the music of all the Doers. The Seers without the awareness of the Doers purpose, no longer heard their own note. I am speaking of the physical self of the humans; each existed on the Big Ground with one note. Without the knowledge of the note, the harmony of the trinity was broken.

Seers lost their awareness and ability to be in harmony with the Big Ground. A great separation took place in the Human Relms. This meant the inability to understand existence. The Big Ground became a place of struggle.

Seers no longer remembered they were here for creative expression through matter.

At times some Seers remembered their note, but were forbidden to sing. This was the beginning of the great discord. This absence of the chords became the reality of the Humans. Gaia became just the Big Ground called Earth.

The Seer-Doer in harmony is divine expression. Divine expression is the third of your trinity.

The Trinity of the Humans is a simple one made complicated over time with legends of conquest. This discord has become what you call the norm or shall we say music of the Big Ground, but not the song of Gaia.

This is the reason we have met. I have said this in this way.

I am sure it can be understood."

This parable was nothing I would consider as a scientist. In fact in my circles of thought, this idea would be nothing more than a fairytale. I had asked the question and I was getting the answer from the Dreygon who was of the Relms. It couldn't get any stranger than this.

I was trying. I had to contemplate the idea of being a walking orchestra. Yes, this could be true to some degree. I realized this was just the beginning of some very unusual conversations I was going to have with Dreygon. I had to prepare myself for what most humans would call the absurd.

Dreygon continued speaking. I'm sure he heard my thoughts.

"It's not the nature of the Doer, the Human form, to destroy itself. It has oneness with the planet because it is of the planet. You must remember the Seer is the one present and residing within the form. This Seer is the directive of the Doer that is the carrier of the note and knows the nature of the Big Ground. The note can no longer be heard."

This was Dreygon's second parable to me that I might begin to understand the nature of the Humans. Dreygon finished the incredible tale:

"This is your discord. This is seed.
All that you would ever imagine could happen did happen. Even on the Big Ground there are infinite possibilities of discord. The laws are the same."

This was getting a little deep for me. I wanted to remember to check myself when I got to the Relms of the Big Ground. I hardly finished this thought when Dreygon flew through the crack of blue.

I saw a flash in the blackness of the dark light. We had reached our destination.

We were once again above the Big Ground! I was still holding on to Dreygon's bright green mane in utter shock. I felt light headed and slightly disoriented and I prepared myself for reentry into my reality. I closed my eyes and I could feel the strong pull.

It is like nothing I would have ever imagined as possible or true. I have trouble describing this. But I will say I felt like everything was returning to me physically at an incredible speed. I felt myself fall fast from the inside. This time I could feel outer pressure and I heard unrecognizable noise. The pressure continued to increase with the return of my own weight along with whatever else that makes up me on the Big Ground.

It happened in seconds along with me yelling and then hearing a loud clap! When I opened my eyes, I was in my bed!
I could hear the birds chirping. I don't remember ever hearing them in the giant Sequoias behind my house. They were chirping loud, louder than I could recall. It was 4 a.m.

The changes were not subtle. My life would never be the same again. Sleep came easily.

TRAVELING THE RELMS

The most obvious thing was that my scientific life was being influenced by my encounters with Dreygon. My day-to-day reality was colored with these past events. In fact, I began to look forward to the journeys into the Relms. I found myself thinking about them during the day at work.

I began looking at some things as Relms dimensional. Maybe this new information could be helpful in imagining how the Hieroglyphic chip would work. It was too soon to tell. The changes of elements in the Relms did not fit the reality of the Big Ground and what I knew as a scientist.

The Relms was new to me. I found myself trying to balance all the information, but found it impossible to do. I asked myself if my appearance would change from traveling the Relms with Dreygon. I could not bring myself to the possibility of that reality, so I just left the idea for the moment.

There was a lot to be done on my project and I needed to stay focused.

I could not help thinking about the Dreygon's words to me. How he explained the word Trinity. I kept in mind Dreygon was not of my reality. I was a Trinity occupying the same space. I am the Seer, the Doer, and Divine expression. Most religions on the Big Ground would consider this religious blasphemy. The idea of a trinity was given only to the gods. Now here Dreygon was telling me that the Trinity was a human aspect. It became obvious that there was a lot to this unraveling and more.

I realized the belief of a Satan has nothing to do with Divine expression. I was still a scientist. Perhaps this concept of "Satan" is a manifestation of the discord.

It was hard to believe I was spending so much time thinking about this. I have never cared about any of it because of the bloody history of most religions on the Big Ground. I surmised that being in touch with spirituality has nothing to do with religion.

The idea of a Seer being responsible for the hearing of some chords was unfathomable. This means me. I thought about it again and came to this conclusion:

The hearing of the note of the self is Divine expression. The Trinity is the Seer spirit and the Doer coming together to make up the physical body. It is these two together that make up the third which is Divine expression. This is the Trinity of humans. I was sounding like Dreygon.

I'm not sure I fully understood this, but I knew it to be infinitely possible.

One morning, I was on the street headed to my office while some of these thoughts ran through my mind. I took this opportunity to check everyone I passed on the street. I imagined living cells moving, pulsating all over each person who passed.
Some Humans looked uncomfortable in their bodies, even though evolution had made them upright.
I wanted to laugh. It was funny.

As a scientist I know everything is attached to the ground or kind of integrated by means of the force of gravity.
I could now imagine beyond that concept. It was more like the finer energy fields of humans blended with what was coming from the Big Ground in the form of energy.
It had a different feel to it because I was now aware of something more. I thought about all the things Humans have done on the Big Ground.

A week went by.
I knew I was resisting and processing all that had been shown and told to me by journeys to the Relms with Dreygon.
Relms travel requires a certain amount of bravery.
I had to trust the journey and the Dreygon, and be the observer. Somehow the universe chose me.
I was being shown a reality that existed along with mine. I knew this to be true because here I am.
I arrive here without a plan.
It's almost like some inner self knows the map.
I asked myself how could I do this and still feel at times this deep trepidation?

Somehow there was nothing else to know but this: as a sentient being I had experienced life as most know and now I had traveled the Relms.

So far, I had never seen Dreygon arrive on a new moon. It has been a full moon and I wondered did this have anything to do with the law of physics. I thought about the gravitational pull of the full moon on the oceans and on the human psych and that everything living on the Big Ground responds to this planetary cycle.
I found myself thinking how glad I was that there was only one full moon a month, but I know the moon has nothing to do with the Relms.
Dreygon's arrival was not governed by a full moon. I think I needed time to digest all of this. Suppose my life was like this forever?
I really had to get a scientific grip on my reality. This would be ok until Dreygon's next arrival on a full moon.
I never pay much attention to the moon or when it's full. I'm a scientist and my colleagues and I have deadlines on our projects. I have been working for weeks on the design of the Hieroglyph that the chip will fit inside. I have an idea of what kind of communication to imprint on the chip and how it would represent the Humans as living. I think my colleagues will find this concept could also be useful in more immediate areas of earth life.
I had some ideas around the *note*. The note for me was sound. Each note was unique to each human who made it. The sound could be read as human vibrations that could also determine a person's

physical health. The sound would be programed into the computer to make a picture that would show the health of a human on the energetic level based on these vibrations. Using a color spectrum to represent the note, disease would appear as darkened shades in areas of illness.

I thought about the Relms and its relationship to my idea. The Relms were a different dimension. I had to change my normal physical self to travel. I laugh knowing that I have to drop this synopsis as useful information my colleagues could understand. I was on the Big Ground and I would never tell them about the Relms.

It was Friday and we were all at the office until 7pm working on the physics of the chip. We always order Indian food on the days we stay late. It's kind of a tradition and we all really enjoy the food.
The week had been long and my head was tired from thinking. I told my colleagues this, and we all had a raucous laugh. I think we just need to laugh to remove the stress of the week.
Sometimes I'm funny.
I was ready to be at home and in the chill mode.
I left as fast as I could after dinner and the early evening air was refreshing.
I didn't see a moon. I think the buildings blocked the rise from the horizon. I walked for a while and then flagged down a cab.

My house was a welcome site. I went in; turned on the lights, threw down my briefcase and headed straight for the kitchen. I needed a good strong drink.

I made myself a martini, which is something I never do.

I actually enjoyed the process. I think I was decompressing from my week at work.

The deck-looked great through the glass doors so I went out and sat down at my old bamboo table to relax and have my martini. It was at this moment that I could see the beginning of the moon's rise through the giant Sequoias beyond my garden. It was a yellow moon. I took a sip of my drink and I thought how beautiful.

My thoughts were my own and I closed my eyes for a moment and took in a deep breath. There was no wind and the air was dead still. I opened my eyes to the stillness of a navy blue night sky and a yellow moon that was slowly rising through the giant Sequoias. I must have dozed off because when I opened my eyes again, I was under a full yellow moon.

The moon was just above the tops of the giant Sequoias and seemed to be sitting right in the middle of the grove. I was fixated. I stood up took a sip of my drink and walked over to the edge of the deck. I leaned on the wood railing that overlooks the garden. Everything had a yellow hue and the plants looked like dark shadows of themselves.

The stillness was eerie and the view like nothing I can remember. I didn't want to over think this or even imagine it was unusual.

I looked up at the full yellow harvest moon so big I was in awe. I turned around and gazed up at my bedroom windows on the second floor of the house. My bedroom looked darker than usual. No moonlight seems to enter.

This was unusual, but fascinating and a little spooky on a full moon. My mind was racing. I turned and peered back into the giant Sequoia trees.
Only the yellow moonlight was present.
I slowly gazed up.
There seemed to be a shadow just to the left of the moon. It looked far away, but seemed to be headed in my direction and fast. At first I thought why would an eagle fly at night? Then I got this very strange feeling. I knew it was Dreygon!
His wings were open full. His body just a dark shadow and his eyes penetrated past the yellow moon.
My heart started to pound in my chest as he approached.
I don't think I'll ever get use to his sudden appearance. The vision of him was still overwhelming to my senses and I always have the sensation of dreaming while awake. Dreygon was close now.
        It was at this moment that I really noticed his eyes. I was afraid.
I thought I heard him laughing as he got closer. Couldn't be! I told myself I am a scientist, but my fear increased for I have never had a sensory experience that was so physical.
I felt every molecule go into alarm. The experience became overwhelming.
I had to use all that I am, just to begin to remember that this was Dreygon.
His unworldly yellow eyes penetrated the very air. He was in front of the moon now and he was motionless. I couldn't move and then it began: the pictures in his eyes.

I could see space in his eyes that was moving inward very fast. I saw a distance that was more than I would ever see as a human or could imagine.

There were landscapes of very strange colors and places so bizarre that it was startling. Everything I saw was beyond the elements of the Big Ground. Of this I was sure.

In Dreygon's eyes I saw a room that had no evident end. I had the sensation that there were several rooms. Their size so large I could not understand. I saw stairs of what looked like some kind of luminous marble and they were several stories high. Who lived there?

I saw colors I had never seen before as I looked in and what felt like out the other side of Dreygon's eyes.

His eyes burned into the back of my head and I could not understand some of what he had seen. My mind had no reference to explain the experience. I was looking, and trying to remember what I saw.

My breath came quickly, and I felt I was at the edge of the mind of God.

Dreygon slowly closed his eyes and the pictures stopped.

I had seen a view beyond the concept of question into experience of being. I said this to myself once and did not try to explain it any further, for as the observer I must not forget. My mind did not have all of the explanations of the experience, but me as the observer did.

I felt like my very existence was being stretched into some unknown dimension that ended at a point in all directions.

I had no questions because this experience was already beyond what I could imagine for myself. I could no longer see Dreygon. I could only see the yellow harvest moon above the giant Sequoia trees. His shadow was no longer visible against the backdrop of the moon. Then I heard a voice in my heard.

"Tell me, Human, what I shall call you?" I answered automatically, "I am called Vishnu". I was surprised Dreygon asked because I was sure he knew my name.

I heard nothing more and I continued to stare at the garden and then the tops of the trees. Nothing unusual and it was as though nothing had occurred. The moon was still yellow and silently beautiful. I suddenly felt very tired. I had more than I could deal with at the moment. I headed for the inside of my house and up to my bedroom on the second floor. I took a long shower and got ready for bed.

The harvest moon was moving across the night sky and had changed positions by the time I retired. My head hit the pillow and I was asleep in seconds. It felt good. I slept for what felt like hours.

I began to dream. In this dream I was standing at the edge of an ocean. I could see something in the sky headed in my direction. It appeared small and black at first because it was so far away. As it approached it became larger and larger. It had huge wings and intense yellow eyes. From the shoreline I was staring and yelling, "What is that! What is that"?

It was very close to me now and it was enormous. It would appear and disappear and was an iridescent color of emerald green and violet.

I saw a bright green mane on its head. I thought, "Where did it come from?" In this dream I did not recognize Dreygon. My heart started to pound in my chest as I slept and I continued to yell. Then slowly ever so slowly I began to remember. This was Dreygon! In my dream I was actually glad to see him.

I felt relief that it was he and not a nightmare. If this was a dream, then I was sure at some point this was going to get real. I suddenly woke up!

The room was dark except for the yellow moonlight on the far wall. It was strangely quiet and I took a moment to gather my thoughts. Then I got out of my bed and walked over to the windows. I hesitated before looking up at the giant Sequoias beyond my garden. I wasn't sure what I would see. I had to become the scientist, and remember that I was here to observe. I looked down at my feet as though I hoped they were there. The light of the harvest moon lighted them and I didn't recognize them as my own. This was a very weird feeling.

I looked up now to see if Dreygon was present. He wasn't there! Then I felt the air moving pass me where I stood in my room. I knew he was coming.

I reached out and opened the windows slowly. Dreygon's iridescent shoulder appeared out of nowhere. I was startled, but I knew this. I seem to always have the same thought of; I must be insane to do this. This was how I checked in with myself before each journey with Dreygon.

I was ready, so I climbed out the window and on to Dreygon's shoulder. His green mane brushed my face and I grabbed onto it.

I closed my eyes. I felt the same sensation of moving inward very fast. I started to breath heavily and feel as though I was falling down from the inside.

My head felt strange and then there was the intense inner pressure.

My head began to reel and I thought, "I'm insane". I heard myself yell without a voice and felt the peeling of layers off me. It seemed an eternity. I saw a very bright light and heard a loud clap!

I opened my eyes and once again we were above the planet. I was again breathing heavy upon our arrival. It took me a moment as always, to gather myself from this experience.

I looked in disbelief! There was the blue planet Earth, now known as the Big Ground. It was beautiful.

"Shall we?" In my head I heard Dreygon asking if I was ready.

"Yes, we shall", I answered.

Dreygon turned around and headed in the direction behind us, his enormous wings spread. Into the dark light we flew. I looked out into the blackness of deep space.

Light is always present. The flickering lights known by the Humans, as stars seemed very close. But their distance never changed. It was a constant of this I was sure. The appearance of the stars was different from how I remember them on the Big Ground. The light from the stars was intense and I started to imagine the incredible amount of energy. Some stars no longer existed but their light continued and finally arrived at my location. This was fantastic to consider.

The stars had the appearance of sitting inside of something dark and too vast to imagine. The perception of view changed dramatically from this far out in the dark light of deep space. I looked in wonder and asked myself how is this possible? We were moving fast and I had all the sensations that come with speed. My perceptions were definitely increasing.

Each journey into the Relms introduced another possibility. It was only here in the Relms with Dreygon that this was knowable. I wanted to ask why me? But I already knew this question was irrelevant in the Relms.

THE WALL OF SOULS

In deep space the dark light is so present; it's always hard for me to know direction. When I look around everything looks the same no matter where I place my vision. I am out of my element. I feel surrounded by something. Dreygon is a master here.

I watched the side of his incredible face from where I sat adjust to the speed we traveled. The bright green mane on his enormous head trailed as though there was wind. So far, I felt none. I had only experienced dimensional shifts.

In the distance I could see a very small violet light. It seemed to flash open. Dreygon arched his flight in that direction. I tightened my grip on his green mane for fear of being swept off his huge shoulder. As we got closer the violet light flashed open like a giant crack across the blackness of deep space. It did not extend far, but seem to be resting in the middle of this dark vastness. I tried not to panic for it was both beautiful and scary to see. We entered the crack that was a horizon.

We entered another world that was violet in color. This was the Relms and the violet open space had no end. Nothing could be seen. Dreygon said nothing about the Relms we were in.

He banked to what felt like the left and we passed over a clear space. This was not so, but how my mind rendered the visual. It was luminous. Dreygon stopped and we remained suspended. I was waiting for an explanation, but he gave none. This time we floated down. It was amazing. I felt like a kid at the amusement park. Down and down we floated. The thought left quickly as we entered a place that held nothing.

This Relms was as clear as a blank piece of white paper.

We stopped moving and Dreygon lowered his enormous shoulder for me to climb down. He was silent. I didn't quite understand why he did this, for I could see nothing on which to stand. I descended his shoulder, but stayed close to his side. I was suspended in midair. Dreygon assumed a resting position and seemed quite comfortable here. Still he offered no explanation that I could hear.

He turned to look at me. His unworldly eyes burned like two small suns, and he began to flick his intimidating tail. I watched the eyes of the Twelve move across his flanks. I kept my composure.

His iridescent color was incredible to see in this place and his bright green mane gave him the appearance of a creature of magic. He was the only thing visible. I was slowly becoming used to his appearance, but I will forever be shaken.

There seem to be nothing here. I looked around and just waited. By now, I had become accustomed to the unimaginable. I dare not leave Dreygon's side. I needed time to gather my thoughts. Then I heard a voice in my head. It was Dreygon. He said", Human, you can walk here. Look for the stone stairway".

So I began to walk out into the blank whiteness of where I was. I was cautious somehow and I thought if I walked in a straight line I could always find my way back.

But of course there was Dreygon big and sitting in the middle of this blank space, how could I get lost? So I took a walk out into white nothingness. This was the Relms of White.

I categorized it in my head. I kept walking and I was hoping I would see the stone stairway very soon. I was nervous. I took a few more steps and noticed the top of what looked like some old stone stairs. The stairs led in one direction-- down.

I could see the stairs were lit but I could not determine how. I hesitated but remembered Dreygon's instructions to find the stone stairs.

I looked at the stairs and descended wondering if I would find my way back. The stairs seemed familiar. It was as though I had been here before, but in very different circumstances that I couldn't remember. These were strange thoughts for me. Remembering details about something is what I do.

Here in the Relms I am an observer. I have new experiences to which my mind has to relate. I am definitely becoming surer of myself here. I know there will always be another experience in the Relms of infinite possibility.

The stairs descended for a long time and then took a sudden left and merged onto a path. I was in semi darkness here. Directly in front of me was a wall that was lit and seemed to go on forever.

The path continued alongside the wall. I looked up to what looked like an overcast sky. There are no skies in the Relms, as I know them.

I took the path and there was a very strange light emanating from the wall. I touched it. The wall seemed to darken under my touch and I quickly took my hand away. I looked behind me and the stone stairs were gone. There was nothing but the wall in its place.

Dreygon was nowhere to be found. I was alone. The only thing visible was the wall. The wall had a golden hue with darker shades of brown. It seemed to be moving. There was something inside the wall, but I couldn't quite make out what it was. The wall was definitely not solid. I looked closely at the wall as I was passing. I realized the darker shades of brown began to look like the shape of humans! They looked as though they were immersed in the golden hue that made up the wall!

I kept pace for I wasn't sure what would happen next. The Human shapes inside the wall became more visible and appeared to be in between places. I saw only arms and legs.

I couldn't imagine where the place could be. The wall suddenly changed direction and merged into an immense room and disappeared.

This was a room filled with rooms! I stopped and stared at what was in front of me. I have never seen a room filled with so many rooms. It was unsettling.

I decided to enter the room to my right. I immediately saw someone inside. I had no explanation for his presence. This Being looked Human, but grey in color. This humanoid had small eyes with prominent features, and the skin on the face had the appearance of small grey moving molecules. I was astonished!

The Being was squatting over some things I could barely see. It seemed to obsess on these objects that glowed and were sometimes undistinguishable. I saw objects of all manner and some were gold coins and jewels. What I did not recognize the Being seemed to obsess with even more.

It did not look at me. Around and around its eyes passed over each object. I could feel the pull of the Being's desire for each object upon which it gazed. What was most bizarre was that all the objects were beheld only with the eyes.

I had the feeling it was not the objects that were important. It was the endless desire. Nothing was ever touched! The Being only looked at the objects it obsessed on.

I think touch was not imagined. I thought this and I'm not sure where it was coming from.

This was hard for me to understand and I stared in disbelief. These were new perceptions for me and I wondered how I knew.

The other rooms had a dream like quality, and they were empty!

The Being was the only one here. It was visually strange to see just him and all these empty rooms.

I was ready to leave this place. I backed out of the room and the path appeared to my left so I just got on it. I could see the Humanoid suddenly turned to watch me as I left.

I quickened my pace and the wall reappeared. It was eerie.

I realized there was nothing linear here. Everything seemed to merge in and out of everything else. It was like watching realities metamorphous into other realities.

What seemed like a wall to me, in truth was not. As I walked along the path the wall continued to change shape as though it was some gateway in between Relms. Where the wall began and how it ended could not be known.

I looked up again to what looked like an overcast sky on the Big Ground. But it wasn't. I felt the whole place rotate. It was the strangest sensation I have ever had. But I had to stay focused. I could not see the size of this place because in the Relms everything seems infinite.

I walked in what I thought was the direction to leave. The path took a sudden right along with the wall. Directly in front of me I could see an old woman sitting in a small room. She bore the same essence as the Humanoid I had just encountered, except I could see her eyes. They seemed unnatural against her grey skin that seemed to be moving. I was nervous.

I continued my approach. I could see the old woman was squatting over a pot of something. The old woman seated herself with the pot in front of her.

She beckoned me to come closer. She eyed me as I approached. At first, I stood still watching, using my intuition to render me the truth. As I came near,

I could see that her face was stranger than I imagined. The old woman's eyes were transparent. I ventured closer.

The skin was moving on her strange grey hand as it extended me an invitation to sit down. I sat down directly in front of her. The old woman began to stir the pot, the contents of which I could not see. I took this opportunity to look into her eyes for I thought their transparency was my imagination. Now I saw stars and a galaxy of planets pass in her eyes as though she was a window.

Somehow I was sure she knew I didn't quite believe it. I watched the old woman now as she continued to stir the pot, the contents of which could not be seen by me. She never took her eyes off me.

The top of the old woman's head began to emit a light. The light was a soft white and it began to glow.

The light increased in intensity, and then opens like a fan. Before I knew what happened I was being pulled in the old woman's direction. I saw a flash and I was standing on the other side of the old woman's eyes. To my left, stars for as far as my eyes could see inside utter blackness. To my right colored gasses swirled and moved in such darkness I thought I could touch it. I put my hands out to steady myself. There seemed to be something in front of me, but I could not see it, I sensed it. I tried not to panic.

I looked directly in front of me at a smooth black surface that seemed to extend to a dark horizon. The smooth black surface moved out and around and did not change the presence of the stars on my left or the swirling gasses to my right. I looked down and I could see my feet. I dared to move forward.

I extended my arms and took a step. The black horizon immediately came to meet me.
I stopped, sensory overload!
My scientific mind told me each step took me to the edge of where I was and the beginning of the next place.

I took another step and again the dark horizon arrives at light speed. I thought to myself that maybe I was taking giant steps across the cosmic. So I took another step, and another. Then I started to run.
I ran fast!

I was not aware of how long I ran. I didn't know why I was running. I didn't think of where I was running to or what I might be running from.

I ran because I could and I ran with abandonment.

As I ran, I thought I heard a whooshing sound pass my ears; maybe it was the black horizon that arrived so quickly I could no longer see it. The blackness was like nothing I had ever experienced. I ran even faster and my mind began to leave me. And then I just leaped up into the blackness with my arms out stretched and felt myself moving out into the unknown.

I suddenly realized I might not find my way back! I gazed out, but the blackness rushed in or was it myself I sensed rushing in?
I turned to look back! What I saw was unexpected.

I could see the old woman's hands stirring the pot in front of her, the contents of which I still did not know. I had never left! I was still standing in the same place. All my realities arrived at the same moment.

I was still looking from the inside of the old woman's head. The old woman was still stirring something in the pot as though she was not aware of my presence. I tried to understand how. Looking through the old woman's eyes was like looking through windows. I came closer to see. I extended my hand to touch this place I was in and in a flash I was pulled through the old woman's eyes and once again I found myself sitting in front of her.

I saw her smile. Her eyes were once again transparent. I kept my composure.

My eyes fell once again on to what the old woman was stirring in the pot, the contents of which I could not see. The old woman looked at me with transparent eyes and then into the pot.

I knew I would never see its contents.

"Knowledge cannot be seen," I heard her say. "Knowledge is a manifestation of experiences understood."

She spoke to me with lips that did not move. The old woman's transparent eyes locked with mine and I shuddered.

Then she began to tell me secrets. I knew she was telling me secrets because upon hearing these secrets I had trouble understanding it all.

Her thoughts were advanced and moved into me with eloquence. There was an absence of opinion and she spoke as though this was for me to know. She told me of infinite possibility as though it were an energy grid. She spoke of a place unfamiliar to me but said we had the sameness of energy. It was not the Big Ground.

She planted something in my consciousness that would change my life forever. I could feel the sensations moving and then become hidden.

The old woman, who stirred the pot, the contents of which I could not see now pointed toward the path and the wall behind me. It was time for me to leave. I bowed my head to her in acknowledgment.

I stood up and turned to go.

The path and the wall were visible. I got back on the path and followed the wall. I was shaken by this experience.

I continued to walk in what I thought was the same direction, the direction to leave!

This time I took note of the wall that seemed to be a place in between places. I kept walking but I slowed down enough to really see the wall.

I looked with a scientific eye and I thought I saw a head. Not possible! I thought. But now I saw an arm, then a leg. Not only that, they seem to be many. They were intertwined with each other and attached with the golden light. I was unnerved. The wall was moving now as though they were all expressing something with each movement.

I quicken my pace for as I looked ahead I saw no end to the wall.

I began to see faces. As I stared it was as though the heat of my stare made individuals turn to look upon me with expressions of which I have never seen.

The golden light hid their eyes.

I saw faces that contorted to express something, which was absorbed by the light of the wall.

Did I see anguish and then emergence? There were voices now, many voices speaking, and then thousands of voices whispering.

Then I heard them all whisper the same thing, "Continuum!"

What did this mean?

The wall pulsed with the spirit forms. I had this feeling there really was no end. It was like a Wall of Souls. I wanted to run, but there was only the path in front of me. I knew fear was knocking on reason.

The Wall of Souls was changing again and arms began to emerge. I was close enough for one of the arms to reach out and grab me. I felt pressure from a very strange hand on my wrist. I tried to pull away but could not. I was being pulled inside! I felt myself hit the wall and begin to merge through.

I saw golden light and a glimpse of a long line of souls that were caught in between. They seemed to be flailing. I heard myself yell because it was frightening. I was now completely immersed inside the Wall of Souls. I felt myself still moving. I began to reemerge out of the other side of the wall and I watched as part me was still entrapped and the rest of me free. I was not in control and wall just spit me out. I was on a ledge.

I gazed down to find myself at the edge of a precipice. Light extended down and disappeared. The light was almost blinding. I leaned over the precipice and then the unimaginable happened. I fell!

Over the edge I fell. I fell down toward the light below. There was nothing to grab onto. This was a free fall. I tried to see this place of light, but the speed at which I passed things made it impossible. It felt like a long fall and I hoped I would not hit bottom.

I was relieved when I finally stopped moving. I was right side up and in a great stillness. The light was in sheets and seemed to form walls. But there were no walls here.

Suddenly someone came out of the sheets of light. The figure was elongated and the light seemed to shuffle for me to vaguely see. The figure wore no attire. She said her name was Sotsah, but I never heard a word.

The stillness seemed to increase with the arrival of this Being. It was now absolute silence and I could feel it. What does silence feel like? It was so intense it felt like pressure.

I thought I was going to blackout. Resistance was impossible. I could see a hand extended out of the shuffles of white light. The silence increased and became penetrating silence. I could not see where I was, and I couldn't hear anything. So I extended my hand to meet the one coming through.

I couldn't hear my heart beat or any sound of breathing. Then I felt the touch of the hand that came through the shuffling light in this place to which I fell. The touch was light, and if I thought it was quiet before, the silence increased even more. It was now deafeningly silent. I felt silence to my very core.

Now this being of the Great Silence came very close to me. Does absolute silence have a face? I saw the face of silence, which bears the name Sotsah. She conveyed this to me, and I still cannot remember how.

Perhaps the silence told me. The light shuffled and I saw her face. The face was elongated and could be seen only with the shuffling of the light.

She was unusual and looked almost human. Her face was strange, but beautiful and seemed to be the same white color as the light. Her eyes were completely closed when she looked at me. I didn't understand.

When she opened them, they were the reverse of those of humans. She only saw in. I'm sure she told me this for how could I possibly have known?

She held on to my hand and we were on the move. I called this place the Relms of Silence.

We penetrated the Relms of Silence that was made of more shades of white than I could imagine. I was moving with Sotsah, the Face of Silence, through a Relms of every shade of white possible. The white light shuffled and moved in long sheets that blended into each other. There was no obvious separation. I could see she held my hand as we moved, but I could not see her clearly. Sotsah became visible only as the light shuffled. She told me she was here to absorb whatever sound could be heard.

The sounds of which, for the moment, I could not hear. Sotsah never spoke to me directly and I heard her thoughts as an afterthought. This took some getting used to. I felt a sudden sensation on the hand she was holding.

Once again the unexpected occurred. We were already in absolute silence when out of this Relms of Silence; a wall of sound began to approach us.

I could actually hear the sounds approaching us. I have never heard these sounds before. These sounds were much more energetic than what I was used to hearing on the Big Ground. It was like hearing sonic hums that were distant. I realized I could not determine if I liked or disliked the sounds. I was silent to my core. This was not logical but is all I have in explanation.

Sotsah became very attentive as though she was ready to absorb the approaching sound. The light continued to shuffle in front of us and I could hear sound approaching like a wave. I heard it moving through the shuffles of light as though it had form. Then it stopped!
The great silence and the wall of sound were both present. The wall of sound was inside the Relms of Silence.

The face of Sotsah began to move and contort. I tried not to become overwhelmed by this sudden visual change of her. Sotsah's face took on the character of all the whites of the Relms of Silence and we were still moving. Our speed quickened.

The Relms of Silence began to vibrate. I didn't understand. Sotsah's face was changing at an incredible speed to absorb all sounds present in the Relms of Silence. Her face shuffled like the light and became even more elongated. I felt the energy change in my hand she was holding and now I could hear the sound just as it hit the face of Sotsah. I was trying to understand the possibility of this. These were sounds unfamiliar. I heard sonic hums; and then very low rumblings began. I almost became afraid.

We continued moving through the shuffles of light. The light began to change and the silence grew

76

more intense. We arrived at a place where the light was diffused and stopped. Out of the shuffles of light emerged a high-pitched sound. I felt it move toward us as though we would be over taken by it.

Sotsah's expressions quickened. The inverted eyes seemed to darken to an unusual shade of white. I didn't understand for she told me she only saw in. Her face became undistinguishable in the shuffles of light. The facial contortions increased in speed until it became a face of its own! I dare not think of the face of sound. I dismissed this thought, as an explanation of what I was experiencing.

Faster and faster Sotsah's facial contortions continued. I stared in disbelief at the appearance of this new face. I felt like I was looking from somewhere else, but I was here and finally everything stopped!

Then there were no other sounds heard by me. The final quiet was deafening. I heard it from inside myself.

Sotsah, the Being of the Great Silence turned and looked directly at my face. The light moved so that I could see her. I stared. I saw no garments. Her face and body were elongated and the light continued to shuffle. Sotsah's hands and body blended together in the shuffling light. I could feel myself being drawn into the silence of Sotsah's face. This was all so unknown to me.

I told her my name is Vishnu, but I never said a word. I asked her if she was here alone. I saw her point through the shuffles of light behind her.

Were there others? I could tell Sotsah did not understand "others". Perhaps she knew no separation. Others had no meaning to her.

She lifted her arm and still holding my hand; we began to travel up from where we were. I could see the precipice. It was far.

The silence continued and wrapped us in a blanket. Up and up we traveled. I looked down and I could see the light extending down in soft columns. I could feel the deep silence below. I heard a moan leave my body. Man, what was that? And the silence increased.

The silence was intense, and I turned to look into the face of Sotsah and then I was again at the Wall of Souls.

I looked behind me and the light was still emanating from far below. Sotsah was still difficult to see because she seemed to be made of the same emanating light from below. It shuffles so that her face could be seen.

Sotsah pointed to the Wall of Souls and let go of my hand. I knew this was how I had to go back.

I did not see her leave.

I merged through as the Wall of Souls was disappearing. This was so strange.

I immediately took pace and felt the second rotation. I looked up.

You must never judge anything by appearance. Appearance is only an assessment relative to oneself. I was rationalizing my experience. I had to settle into what I could understand so that I could continue. The color above me was now a soft grey and a path in front of me became very visible even though the wall of souls was slowly disappearing.

I forgot about Dreygon. Somehow I could not imagine him here. Perhaps this part of the journey I had to take alone. I continued on this path that somehow seemed lit. The Wall of Souls continued to disappear and I stayed on the path along the fading wall. I noticed the colors of the wall were changing. Red and very dark green colors emerged and dripped a luminous essence through the gold and brown hue of the wall.

I sensed these were memories and feelings lodged inside the Wall. Perhaps filled with the passions of existence and transcendence. They were now oozing out of the Wall of Souls as perhaps the final end of their existence.

My sense of reality changes in the Relms. These reflections occur only here. As a scientist, I was becoming very aware of this change and the need to remember.

Even now as I glanced back, I could no longer see the place of the old woman. She remained and I had moved on.

The path was still lit and it wound around and up a small hill. As I reached the top I could see up ahead something that looked like a forest. I stopped, looked and my head flooded with thoughts. I was still reeling from the silence and the meeting of Sotsah. I told myself she was beautiful, in a very strange way. Could I fall in love with silence?

Of course, and I started to laugh to myself.

This was not the moment to take myself too seriously.

I hardly knew her. It must have been the light. I laughed again. I had just gotten the silent treatment. I found these thoughts humorous but I knew I was freaked. Not only that, there may have been others! This was pure speculation and once again very human. I was looking for a way to deal with what had just happened. My logical mind found repose in my sense of humor.

I cleared my head and decided to keep moving. It seemed to take a long time to reach the forest, but I finally did. It's hard to determine what's really happening in the Relms. I looked in front of me and there was no horizon. Is that possible? This was not basic quantum physics, I thought. Does this mean this goes on forever?
I was entering the Relms of trees without leaves.

There must be thousands of trees here, all in a state of winter. This is what I surmised. They all seemed to be frozen in a pose that told a story. I wondered what had happened here. I saw no two alike.

These trees were very tall and their leafless limbs spread cross to form a canopy. As I passed under the leafless tress I got this very strange vibe. I really didn't want to touch them. I think I was a little unnerved because I felt like they knew I was here.

This is not how I see the world; I'm a scientist. But the trees were talking to me, and I could not escape this. I had to let myself have this experience. I kept on the path that was lit and headed directly into the interior of the leafless forest. I turned to look back to see how far I had come. The lit path behind was not visible and in its place was nothing but the leafless forest. I was completely surrounded! I kept my composure. The possibility of all of this was zero, but here I was.

The only thing visible now was the path in front of me. This was getting really eerie. I picked up my pace hoping to see the end, but there was none insight. The longer I walked the deeper into the forest without leaves I became. The Relms had begun to change color now, as I looked out in front of me. I looked up at what was a sky in the Relms and observed the change to a deep olive hue. I could see no reason for this shift. It changed without warning.

The silhouettes of the trees were a soft black against this new background. I felt as though I was entering a very strange painting.

THE MAN WITH THE CRYSTAL EYES

I was walking fast now and I continued in the same direction, straight ahead. It seemed as though I had been on a visible path through the Relms of leafless trees for a long time.

Up ahead, I could see something that did not fit the outline of the leafless forest. It looked as though someone was attending to something, as one would do on the Big Ground. I stopped dead in my tracks. I stood staring for a long time. Perhaps he is tending the leafless trees, but this was not the case. He seemed close, but I realized he was even further into the Relms.

I could see him clearly, as if he was next to me. I have never seen anyone with his features. This was mind baffling. I decided to keep going and as I came closer; I could see he was squatting in front of a very large chest. The chest seemed to be made of gnarled wood. This was only in appearance for it was not solid. It was luminous and seemed to vibrate.

The man squatting in front of the great gnarled chest eyed me as I approached. It was not until I was directly in front of him that I could see the true nature of his features.

His eyes were crystals! His face was angular and a dark burgundy color. I tried to understand the texture of his skin. It looked like a woven cloth. I saw no hair on his head. He wore a fitted brown garment that was made of a material I have never seen. His hands were the same texture and burgundy color as his face. He then sat down in front of the great gnarled chest and crossed his legs.

The Man with the Crystal Eyes slowly opened the chest. A soft glow came from inside. He put his hands in and they moved rapidly as if to confuse anyone who was the watcher. Over and over again his hands passed over something inside the great chest and it was not an object.

I was trying to see what it was. It was obvious that to him, it was of great value. He bade me sit next to him that I may see the world from his perspective. This is what I heard him say inside my head.

I hesitantly walked over and sat down next to the man with the crystal eyes and crossed my legs. I looked at him and I was shaken by his appearance.

His crystal eyes were even more frightening against his angular face and dark burgundy skin. I turned away quickly and looked at his hands and then into the great gnarled luminous chest. His woven dark burgundy hands gleamed and I watched as they shape and reshape something that was inside the chest.

His hands began to move like flashes of light. The man with the crystal eyes said nothing but somehow I knew his intent. Then, inside the great gnarled chest, I watched him reveal possessions created by Humans on the Big Ground. It was hard to believe what I observed. All were made of the same essence. I didn't understand, and then I remembered what I knew about the composition of the universe. The Man with the Crystal Eyes began to mold and reshape this essence. It looked like colored light.

It was beautiful to see and I felt this incredible pull of desire attached to each vision he shaped. I was trying hard to control myself. The intensity of desire was greater than any I had ever known. In his hands he possessed all that could be acquired on the Big Ground. This is what I heard him tell me, and he spoke no words.

The Man with the Crystal Eyes had the ability to use this colored essence to manifest what we both knew Humans desired most. I wondered how he knew this and why would he show me? Until now, there had been no real communication between us, but maybe that's exactly what this was. The man with the crystal eyes turned and looked at me. He could hear my thoughts. His eyes were gleaming like diamonds and I heard him say; "Even though I have the eyes to see essence, and the hands to create, this is only a small part of what is infinitely possible."

I was impressed and overwhelmed by him. His crystal eyes gleamed colors I have never seen. He held me fast in his gaze. His dark burgundy woven face was frightening. I quickly look back into the great gnarled chest for I could not gaze into his eyes for long. He was still moving his hands. I saw objects I recognize. I also saw things I could not understand as to what was their purpose?

Maybe I was seeing symbols that took the shape of things. Perhaps these things would exist on the Big Ground in the future. But for the moment those concepts were truly otherworldly.

Then the unthinkable happened. Our minds began to merge. My vision changed in a flash of light.

I saw the essence in the great gnarled chest as energy and then color.

I had to relax because for a moment I could not tell him from me. I could understand everything he did. We were still looking inside the great gnarled chest when I felt us begin to travel with great speed from where we sat, into the chest. We entered the great gnarled chest, and inside was a white space of nothingness. We began to move and I could feel the pressure of moving through the nothingness of this white space.

We stopped. In the distance I could see two colored objects approaching us. As the objects neared I could see their composition. I saw a small cube made up of smaller cubes, and a cubed circular object. They both rotated and with each rotation a change of color combinations. These were colors unknown to me. I could only comprehend them with the mind of the man with the crystal eyes. These objects were moving toward us fast. The colored cubed cube was closest and arrived first. These colors were fantastic! They glowed and vibrated and seemed to change quality as we watched. My mind could not calculate the use of the cube, but with him I would understand.

The imagination has such great potential. I attribute this experience to just that. Here in this place, what were infinite had already become objects of possibility. And there was more.

It was here that I realized as a scientist that a great attraction was always in play. Even when the results of this attraction became visible, there would always be things still unseen by me. To gaze upon the colored cube was indeed to open a door of what was possible with only this essence. This I heard from the mind of the Man with the Crystal Eyes.

I felt him smile because our minds were still joined. I watched as he extended his arms and his hands began to change. Hands that had appeared human melted flesh, to bone, to dust, to light. I kept thinking, I've just seen the last bit of what holds dust together, and it left as light energy.

His transformed hands of light energy merged with the colored cubed cube from the tips of his fingers.

He immediately began shaping the cubed cube and I could hear his thoughts on creation. The objects he fashioned were fantastic.

His thoughts became even more intense and his hands began to rotate the colored cube.

We began to move again, our minds still merged. We increased our speed through the white space.

We neared the rotating cubed ball of color that was now approaching. We anticipated this together. I watched as the luminous hands of the man with the crystal eyes took the cubed ball of color from midair. He then added the cubed ball of color to the cubed cube. Together we viewed an object, which was a cubed cube on one side and cubed ball on the other.

Before I could respond to what I was seeing, the Man with the Crystal Eyes began to rotate the objects. His hands combined the two objects. The colors changed as the man with the crystal eyes moved the objects with increasing speed and the two became one new object.

Our minds stopped moving in the white space. The Man with the Crystal Eyes tossed this new colored object into the white space in front of us. It bounced out to a distance that only became evident with the arrival of the colored object.

Then it began to open from an unmarked horizon in this place we were only in with our minds. It unfolded toward us and took form as it approached where I thought we might be. It looked like the beginning of a place. I could see it was made of the same essence as the cubes, but only one color. It looked orange, but it wasn't. Buildings appeared and a street in front of us. All was outlined in this very strange orange color and made of something that looked like membranes to me.

It continued to unfold and take shape. The final shape was that of a city! This city was made of the essence of the cubes. It extended out in front of us and we could see it in its entirety. I was mesmerized. I felt myself breathing quickly again for I was in shock. I could not use my sense of things to tell me anything about this. My mind was joined with the man with the crystal eyes and I sensed I was only stardust.

I thought I felt the Man with the Crystal Eyes hit me in the back of the head. But how could he? I could see his hands. Suddenly, I detected the feel of the city. There were no doors. The feeling of safety and separation was absent in this place.

It was hard to tell where we ended and the city began.

We move in and through the city with our minds. This time I felt us separate enough so that I could see my companion again.

He looked so strange with his burgundy skin and unusual attire. His eyes were alien. I had to gather my courage even though we were sharing minds. I could see him in his entirety. I sensed his calm, and I wondered how one being could create an entire city. The Man with the Crystal Eyes was smiling. His eyes became more lucid; the colors transparent and in them he held the doors to the city.

I thought I heard him tell me; these were not doors, as I knew them, but markers of infinite possibility.

I'm not sure what he meant by this statement even as I still shared part of his mind.

Where were the inhabitants?

It was obvious I responded like any Human would, look for like kind.

No Beings live here. The power of the Man with the Crystal Eyes was essence and illusion.

Now I remembered he was sitting alone. I still asked for the others. I heard him tell me that he wasn't sure how he got here and that he was following a great desire but had no image of it. The man with the crystal eyes said, "I am not aware of what you call alone for I am in the journey of infinite possibility."

This was the only explanation given for suddenly I could see someone standing at the very edge of the city.

The Being's form was hidden behind a blue light. I knew my companion could see who or what it was. My vision was blocked. Maybe this was done for my protection. Perhaps the form of the Being was unusual or maybe too high a vibration for me to comprehend even though; I shared his mind and I was traveling in this lighter form. I held steady and relaxed into what I could see.

I knew they would be communicating with each other. I was most curious about the language they would use. I know that language can be a reflection of evolution. Perhaps their language would sound like cosmic music. The Man with the Crystal Eyes and the Being inside the blue light began to speak to each other. Now I could hear something. The words shook my frame, but were not hostile. I had the sensation I was really hearing something unusual and in a very unusual way. The blue light became much denser.

The conversation flowed smoothly and the blue light flickered as though it was breathing. I could not understand what was being said, but I had the emotional response as if I had.

The conversation was about the Relms. The Man with the Crystal Eyes had entered his own creation with me. The Being inside the blue light arrived at the edge of our reality. The Man with Crystal Eyes had the ability to look beyond the blue visitor into the Relms still unseen. But the Being inside the blue light was the marker for where we were. This information arrived quickly. I had a difficult time understanding the physics. The man with the crystal eyes wasted no time and together we began to move again with our minds and we looked passed the blue visitor. I felt everything move to extend itself into a state of comprehension.

The visual on the way was incredible. How could I see in a curve all things above and all things below? I saw a great blackness that was filled with small lights. We were moving fast, and we passed places that were floating in this blackness as though they were dreams. We seemed to be headed for a point that I anticipated with the mind of the man with the crystal eyes. It was almost like seeing a dot on a page except I never really saw the dot. It was like looking at a point of convergence, but I didn't know of what. We arrived and moved pass this pinpoint.

Still, the crystal eyes searched and looked for that which had not been seen.

I felt myself breathing very quickly.

The vast magnitude of his vision was overwhelming. We increased our mental speed and went through what felt like a thin skin of ethereal essence.

Another horizon made itself known to us, as a pinpoint where silver and pink gasses reveal a city. It seemed to be resting in the middle of this blackness from which we looked. We stopped moving with our minds.

The man with the crystal eyes was gazing upon his next great desire. His mind had reached its destination, but this time there would be others. I surmised they were in the city behind the pink gas we saw together.

Then as in slow motion: we did a rewind, and there was a sound. I'm sure it was present the whole time, but there was only so much I could comprehend at once.

Perhaps it was more audible because in rewind, our minds had slowed down considerably. It was a beautiful sound and I felt I was hearing it with another part of myself. We were moving backwards. I watched as everything we saw on the way, I now saw in reverse. It was almost like falling from some place you have been and passing everything on the way back.

The city behind the pink gas had appeared as a pinpoint and then it disappeared. The sound I heard continued like some violin music played backwards. Together our minds melted back through the membrane. The first pinpoint we saw reappeared. It was so close I thought I could touch it. We were moving away from it and even though we were moving slow, the pinpoint was gone before I could fully register its existence. Now the Being inside the blue light could be seen and we stopped just pass the place of its location.

I understood now that the man with the crystal eyes had sent out a signal. The Being inside the blue light had received it and arrived. It was at this moment that I heard the man with the crystal eyes tell me who he was. He said, "I am a Navigator of the Relms".

I heard nothing more about who he was even as I was one mind with him. I could see the Being's blue light was dense. Our minds were still merged and we were now just outside the city. Then as if in a revelation, I finally understood the purpose of the city.

This city was really a beacon! Impossible!
I thought this with the part of my mind that was still mine. The man with the crystal eyes had forged a city made of essence unknown to me with his hands. But it was really a beacon, a signal that could be seen the distance of stars!

I was trying to imagine the size of this beacon, and that was my only frame of reference.

The city made of cubed cubes and cubed circles seemed endless.

The appearance of this Being at the edge of the city meant this Navigator's signal had been received. This Being inside the blue light arrived to mark the edge of the beacon. This was where we were outside the mind of the man with the crystal eyes, whom I now knew as Navigator.

Even with this, "where" would never be sure. The Relms were always shifting, the horizons disappearing. Reality as I knew it had become one with infinite possibility. Right now, the Relms was the extension of reality. The Being inside of the blue light began to speak to the Man with the Crystal Eyes. Their language was like some kind of music. I just knew this was how they would communicate, and now I listened. This was language in its highest form.

I cannot say any of this was familiar. This was a form of communication I would never have imagined. I had to listen in a stream to understand the experience I was having.

It flowed from us to the Being inside the blue light. This being spoke with sounds not audible on the Big Ground, and as a scientist, of this I was sure.

I could only understand in this way. Imagine the happiest music you ever heard along with the saddest music you ever heard not separate but played at once. What was sad wrapped around what was happy and vice versa to make a perfect equation of balance. In this music were all the mathematical equations Humans used on the Big Ground. Here that knowledge was a language of sounds. Sometimes it felt like a Morse code.

This would be the closest to what a Human could understand as a tool.
It made sense to me now. If this was their language, of course one person could create something the size of a city. I wondered was there a metaphor.

Navigator, stuck with me, or maybe I was receiving the answer to my question. I was asking. who would navigate the Relms?
The Man with the Crystal Eyes was on his way somewhere, and he looked before he left. This was incredible navigation. His mind maps or was he following the *inner map*? Who was the Being inside the blue light?

I wondered: how did the Being inside the blue light know how to locate the beacon? It must be huge here!

I had to stop thinking. It was hard to ask myself all this and still have part of my mind merged with the man with the crystal eyes. The sound of their language continued and then came to an end.

I watched the Being inside the blue light leave its location in a flash of blue and disappear into the blackness of where we were. Our minds still merged we continued our retreat from the city. The sound of the backward violin music returned.

We were leaving the city in rewind and I watched us retreating in perspective. The city changed as we retreated and it began to completely undo itself beginning at the horizon.

The city seemed to be moving toward us and undoing itself on its approach. The Man with the Crystal Eyes held his hands steady as the city continued to rewind. The orange membranes of the city began to vibrate with each movement as if the cubes were being reformed.

This city, which had really been a beacon, flashed in the darkness as it rewound to a place of stark white. I watched in awe, as it unfolded to become a small cubed object. It was now suspended in front of us in stark white. I imagined this to be the mind of the man with the crystal eyes. I had witnessed his thoughts on creation through our joining of minds.

The Man with the Crystal Eyes moved his hands, changing the colors and the shape and then there were two.

In his left hand he held the cubed ball. In his right hand he held the cubed cube.

I looked upon the cubed cube of color and the cubed ball of color as they pulsed and glowed distance in this white space. Then he began to move his hands and I saw them coming towards me.

The Man with the Crystal Eyes turned his incredible face to look at me and vanished!

There was a blue flash and I was sitting in front of the great gnarled chest alone. It was closed, and it rumbled and blue light came out of the sides. I just sat there, not knowing if I should.

I was breathing quickly now, for I had seen and experienced something that was not part of my reality. The man with the crystal eyes, that I now knew as the Navigator was gone without a trace. I had no desire to open the great gnarled chest. I really just wanted to get up and leave, so I did.

The magnitude of the beacon that was a city and the Being inside the blue light was incredible. My head felt full.

I knew this Relms journey was not over. I stood up now and the path through the forest was very visible in front of me. My mind was racing and I was trying to remain a scientist of observation.

Then I noticed that the forest of trees with no leaves began to grow in size. The soft black color of the trees became even more pronounced. I looked up and the space above me was an olive green sky. I thought I sensed a great rotation, for here all could not be seen. I still felt like I was in a very strange painting.

The dark yellow glow of the Wall of Souls re-emerged briefly. It was in the forest of trees with no leaves in the distance in front of me, further up the path I was on. It was gone before I could come near. There was no one here to ask questions. So I decide to make my own conclusions. Here there must be cosmic memories of the Big Ground. The endless forest of trees with no leaves was not a sad place.

It was incredible to see. All the branches and trunks of each tree could be seen. All were different. It was hard to comprehend the amount of diversity in each.

The branches looked like arms stretching toward each other: each holding a moment of movement in time.

I was unnerved in a good way.

I was still on the path in the leafless forest when the stairs became visible again and I stepped onto them as they curved left and up and continued through the forest. I was thinking the appearance of stairs meant I'm on my way out of this Relms.

The stairs ascended slightly before becoming the path again, and now the glow of the Walls of Souls could be seen again deep in the leafless forest ahead. Again I felt a great rotation. I stopped on the top stair to look up but could not see how this could occur. The olive green sky remained unchanged.

When I looked down again the forest was gone and only the path was present. I turned to look behind me from where I stood on the stairs. The leafless forest was still there, but I could see a human looking woman and a small child literally bleeding through the olive sky to where I was!

They were moving toward me but stopped. They seemed to occupy a Relms of their own. They were standing inside something that looked like a very large eerie colored circle. The colors were paler than any colors on the Big Ground. It encompassed them with a gaseous quality that rotated around them so slowly it was hard to detect. I was baffled! I wondered how this was possible. And were our Relms crossing paths? I stared in disbelief.

I waited on the stairs in anticipation of what would happen next. I couldn't quite see them in detail, so I decided to approach them.

I tried to retrace my steps down the stairs, but could not.

Each move I made found me in exactly the same position I was previously, at the top of the stairs! I tried again to arrive there and could not. I finally decided to remain where I was and wait. The Relms of the woman and the small child began to move again, toward me. Soon they were both in front of me.

The woman continued to console the child and turned her eyes to me. She looked surprised, and then began to speak.

"What are you doing in this place?" she said without greeting.

She seemed to be concerned about my presence. The first thing I noticed was her attire. She wore a dark colored jacket with a high collar that seemed large for her. It was held closed by a silver cord. She had curly red hair and it was pulled tight at the top of her head. Her complexion was dark brown and I couldn't see the color of her eyes.

My name is Vishnu. "Who are you?" I asked, amazed and intrigued.

She seemed so much like me in essence, but there was an unworldly aura surrounding her.

I was trying really hard to sense why she was here.

"My name is Elbah and I am Agnamani. I am the guide for children who leave the Big Ground."

Big Ground? This was getting interesting.

Once again I could not tell if I was reading her thoughts, for I never saw her lips move. The child was wearing loose clothing made of very small patchwork. He looked content and confused. It became obvious to me that the child had just left the Big Ground.

Elbah continued to speak: "Yes, the child's memory has been put to rest and does not recall what was experienced.

This small child is an ageless entity. I travel the Relms in search of those who leave the Big Ground under duress, and are too young to use their *inner map*."

Once again I was hearing about an *inner map*. How was this at all possible? My journey with Dreygon began with him telling me of an *inner map*. Here I am in the Relms, and out of nowhere this person called Elbah appears with a child and she has the same information about the map.

I didn't understand. This made no sense to me. Who were they, really?

I could ask the question and expect an answer that would have been relevant only in the Relms. Instead I said, "Elbah, tell me more of what you know about the Relms. Perhaps it is the very reason we have met."

She did not answer me right away. She looked at me for a long time before she spoke. I could see small circles of light in eyes that were too dark to see a color. Elbah the Agnamani then began to tell me things that would change my concepts forever.

Elbah said, "The *inner map* to the Relms can be known. It's better to use it before you leave the

Big Ground for good. Most children are not aware of it.

I am here to insure they know where they are 'being'."

I had not heard it put quite like this. She sounded like an Angel of mercy. But I knew Dreygon had already introduced me to this reality. It took a moment for everything to register. Then I seized the opportunity to ask Elbah the Agnamani the mundane.

Does anyone ever get lost in the Relms? I asked.

"Yes, but only if you bring the reality of the Big Ground with you.
This is the Relms, and the Big Ground is not a place on the map", Elbah replied.

Now this was a real surprise. Not on the map? How did I get there if it's not on the map?

My perception of things was changing, and I was holding on to what I thought I knew. The Big Ground was home, so how could it not be on the map? I think she heard my thoughts. I was staring at her mouth and her lips were not moving. But I heard everything she began to say.

Elbah began to explain:
"There is no time millennium in the Relms. You cannot use the concept of thousands of years to measure its existence into your reality. Its existence is before time, yet everything moves as though time was its master. The Relms vibratory rate cannot be known, and it changes to expand into existence. The Relms is moving in the present and what has been created in the past becomes a part of the future.

What I am saying is this: Where you have already been is of no consequence in the Relms. This is the first viable concept to understand its reality.

In the second concept of the Relms: awareness of being is essential for the Humans to understand the existence of the Relms. The third concept means; inside of your being ness lays your memory of what you did, but not who you are. It is under these conditions that Humans have the ability to know the Relms and the *inner map*."

I was slow to understand what she was saying. I summarized that; because I am on the Big Ground, I need the *inner map to* experience the reality of the Relms. The 'inner map" is for my journey in the Relms from my existence on the Big Ground. As a scientist I tried to rationalize this as a formula, but this was a formula I could never write down. It was something to be experienced.

It was infinitely possible that, this was the next stage of Human evolution on the Big Ground.

It is a probability that the Humans might need a map to find the map. I was chuckling to myself. I looked at her. I still had the question of Why?

I was staring at her. Elbah's deep brown face was beautiful. Her eyes were so dark I could not tell who she really was. I kept looking and once again I saw a very small circle of light in her eyes. I was silent. I could not tell her age. Sometimes she looked like a young girl, and then a mature woman. I wondered would I ever see Elbah again.

The child suddenly caught my attention. I gazed down at him. He had the same unworldliness as Elbah.

He was small in stature and I would guess in earth years he was six or seven years old. He was smiling and I could not understand why. I felt something strange coming from him, so I took a really good look at him. I thought I saw something changing in his face and then in his eyes.

In his eyes it almost looked as though there was a picture of the Big Ground. I was really curious now, but I wasn't sure how to respond to what I observed. I decided to just watch it all happen.

It was like watching a very small television screen. In the first vision of his life I was with him on his arrival to the Big Ground. I saw his birth, his guardians; where he was born on the Big Ground and a glimpse of his life. I became suddenly aware of the intent of his heart and I shuddered.

The pictures continued. I saw his understanding of who he was and his relationship to the planet. I saw why he left, but not how. I was relieved; for I was not quite ready to know this and somehow I got that it was not so important. A lot happens on the Big Ground.

His eyes blinked and I saw no more.

His whole life was in his eyes.

It was so strange to see his life played out in this way. I saw no emotional attachment. There was no sense of tragedy. Perhaps this is because sadness is not known in the Relms. Perhaps happy means to finally be near the infinite and free to travel in the Relms of infinite possibility.

Elbah never told me how she got to the Relms, and I knew they would be gone before I could ask another question. I heard a sound and so looked up.

I tried to see what it was or where it came from. I felt everything rotate.

When I looked again, Elbah and the child were moving away. The pale colored circle was in retreat and they were inside of it. It moved along the olive sky at eye level and then melted back through from whence it came.

I raised my hand to wave, but they were gone. I was alone again and ready to leave. I was still standing on the top stair, so I turned and took the path for a short distance.

The stone stairs reappeared and were headed up in a spiral. I climbed around and around the staircase and then I just stepped out and into a blank white space. I was back and I immediately turned to look for Dreygon. I could see him a distance away in a resting position, suspended. His unworldly yellow eyes were like two huge suns in the blankness of this white space.

Dreygon's iridescent body glowed emerald green and violet. His incredible green mane stood out in this whiteness. He seemed to appear and disappear like the sound of a Human heart.

I wasn't sure why I felt this. Perhaps I had finally become aware of my own heart.

I walked toward him, glad to see him.

The Dreygon began to speak as I approached: "Ah Human, this is good. Tell me of your awakening."

I found it curious that Dreygon said awakening and not journey. I began to tell the tale. I turned to point to the stairs and they disappeared, but not before I caught a glimpse of them merging with what I could not see.

I became a little confused and for a moment I couldn't remember where I was. Hearing my thoughts Dreygon answered: "We are where we began, but just a little different. The Relms have shifted and you will be traveling back with a different approach."

Dreygon lowered his enormous head that I might climb onto his shoulder. I gazed into the blank whiteness of where we were. It was the most incredible sensation I have ever had of clarity. Dreygon spread his huge wings and we began our assent. Up we floated through the great whiteness and into the blackness of deep space. The violet crack flashed closed below us. It left no trace of having ever existed.

I heard a rumbling and then a hum. Dreygon turned his enormous body around and we headed in the direction behind us. He was moving fast, so fast I closed my eyes. I knew I was going to fall asleep before we got to the Relms of the Big Ground.

And then I just woke up in my bed!

I was breathing heavy. I immediately looked around and didn't recognize anything at first!

Then, I realized I was back. I felt light-headed and disorientated, but relieved. I have never been so happy to be home.

It was difficult moving from one reality to the next. Does anyone else know about the Relms: this relative, energy, light, mass, space?

I was never in control of how things happened on return. In fact, not even how or when I would leave! I wasn't really in control of anything. This has nothing to do with me, and everything to do with me.

Ok, so maybe I was being guided and I wasn't ready for this. I wasn't sure what it all meant, if anything? I had to always be mentally prepared. My mind was flooded with too many occurrences. Traveling with Dreygon brought me realities I couldn't imagine. I knew this.
All I had to do was observe, after all, I knew the world's greatest secret.

The phone rang, startling me. Who would be calling at this hour? The clock read 4 a.m. The ringing seemed to be coming from far away.
"Hello!"
I spoke as though I might have a surprise. This time I was ready for something. There was silence on the line.
I looked out of the window. I thought I saw something glimmering in the tops of the giant Sequoia trees.
I suddenly felt uncontrollable fatigue. I fell back in my bed and was fast asleep.

ELBAH THE AGNAMANI

It was Monday. The sun was shining on my face warm and soothing. I was back all right. Daylight had arrived and my night awakenings had vanished. There was much to contemplate and my head swirled from the visuals.

I got up, took a shower, and did my normal routine of getting ready to go to my office. I made a strong cup of java and just stood in the kitchen drinking it. I didn't feel quite the same. The giant Sequoias out my window looked different.

At first I was apprehensive and then I realize I had to take this slow. So I relaxed. I went out on my deck and down into my garden. It was nice, and everything was green and the flowering plants were in full bloom. I took a deep breath. I felt good. It was simple here and a reality I knew. A light breeze passed through the trees. It smelled sweet like honey suckle and something I couldn't quite remember. I didn't go into the grove of Sequoias. I stood staring at them.

I viewed them in a way I never have. The energy from these ancient trees was intense. Perhaps my sensibilities had increased after spending so much time in the leafless forest of the Relms. Nothing felt or looked the same. I was ok with this. I understood I had become more in tune through these travels. My awareness had increased a hundred fold.

Now there was this great curiosity about everything I saw. I could see the huge roots of the trees from where I stood. I admit I felt a little intimidated.

The giant Sequoia Trees contained the energy to live for thousands of years on the Big Ground. This was amazing here and irrelevant in the Relms. This would take some getting used to. These were strange thoughts and new to me. The trees seem to have their own message for me, but nothing I could put into words.

It was time to go. I went back inside to grab my briefcase and finish the java. I was out the door in no time and on the street again, headed for my place of employment. The air was fresh and a warm breeze blew pass me. I decided to walk for a while. A time check said I should flag a cab.

I arrived at work the usual time, which was 9am. I went directly to my office. I passed several colleagues, who greeted me with surprised eyes. I began to wonder if I looked strange, so I took a detour to the men's room to have a look in the mirror. Was my head glowing?

I thought I saw some lights and then I didn't. I washed my hands and thought I saw them become the water.

That's it! I'm out! I knew I could not get too involved with what I perceived as some kind of physical change. I was probably carrying some of the Navigator's energy. I most definitely had a head full of what I had seen, and now I had to be at work.

I could do this. I was doing this. I left the men's room and slowly walked back to my office. I sat down at my computer and began to answer several emails. I told myself once again that I could handle everything, and so I began to answer everyone and send out all of the updated information requested.

After I finished answering all the questions, I headed for the *wheel room.* This is where my colleagues and I work on the hieroglyphic chip together. The space is well equipped and pleasant to be in. I smelled fresh coffee and pastries as soon as I entered the room. I headed straight for the pot and poured myself a cup inhaling the aroma. The aroma was dark roast with just a hint of black berries. This was my favorite. I took a sip and headed for my work area.

We have windows and the walls are painted a sea mist color. I often wondered who chose this color. We all admit it's very calming. This is always a plus because our work is very intense. All our equipment and the work we have completed up to now, is in the *wheel room.* I think it got its name from all the thinking that has taken place here over the years. This room has a special kind of vibe. You can feel it when you first walk in. We say it's the residue of brilliant minds.

We are now working on the final Configurations.

My idea was that we would put one note from every Human in the chip. We have the technology to gather and record this data. Pressing a combination of the hieroglyphic symbols can play all these notes.

There will be two hieroglyphics that represent the northern and southern hemisphere of the planet. One will play all the notes from the Humans living in the northern hemisphere, and the other will play the notes from the southern hemisphere's inhabitants. This recorded data is the harmonic sound of both hemispheres together and separate. I'm sure the results will be fascinating and informative.

The idea is the Human harmonic story through notes and hieroglyphics, which are the first written language of humans. You can imagine the amount of thought that will go into making the chip comprehensive. The hieroglyphic chip will contain an incredible amount of recording. I am still working on the physics. We have enough room on the chip to include the songs of birds and the calls of other animals from earth.

We are hoping the duration of the hieroglyphic chip is thousands of earth years like the information on Voyager 1.

The hieroglyphic chip will be part of a communication-exploratory probe that will be sent into space, as a record of life forms based on harmonic sound.

It's thousands of light years to the nearest solar system that could contain life. This chip can make the journey and function upon arrival. My colleagues and I are excited about working on this project every day.

On this morning, I was the first to arrive in the *wheel room*. As soon as I sat down to work, I heard someone knocking on the door.

"Come in!" I said without looking up from what I was doing. The door opened. I heard a voice before I saw the person.

"Hey, my man, got the glow going on today, hey?" It was my colleague, Sidmond. Sidmond is Chinese. I teased him relentlessly about his name. He does not look like a Sidmond. He is average height, fairly good looking, wears a goat tee, black hair, and does not wear glasses. He wears a suit to work every day and they are all a different color with the shirt and tie to match.

He dresses likes a hustler from Harlem. Sometimes I find it humorous when I see him, but he always wears a pair of really nice and very expensive black shoes. Believe it or not, he looks very cool and Sidmond has a brilliant mind. I guess that's why no one ever reproaches him in regards to his attire.

If anyone could understand me at my job it would be Sidmond. I am always happy to see him at work. We've had many very interesting conversations over the years inside the *wheel room*.

But this was the time I would have to remain secretive about any information regarding the Relms.

"Is it that obvious?" I said, like it was true.

Sidmond began to laugh. "Hey man, I stopped by to tease. You look electrified, but in a good way. Copasetic!"

This time Sidmond was looking at me with curiosity. "Vishnu, did you have some kind of experience that did this?"

109

Now I was really freaked. It could not be that obvious.

"I'll have some of that!" Sidmond was being his humorous self, and I was using him to gauge how obvious this change might really be. Sidmond continued to talk to me.

He said, "Vishnu, my man you look happy!"

I was relieved that happy was what my colleague observed. This was typical. Their sense of things spiritual was happy or as Sidmond would say "copasetic", meaning, for the moment everything is cool.

He had to know my friend Harper. I didn't ask. The door closed and Sidmond was gone. I was alone in the *wheel room* most of the day. I was so busy I took no notice of the door quietly opening and closing. We had deadlines and everyone was in full gear.

The day went by quickly. Days turned into weeks, then months. It was fine with me. Everything was going very well with our project. I needed the time to be present on the Big Ground. The Relms were changing me.

A long time passed before I saw Dreygon again. I saw no trace of him in the giant Sequoias beyond my garden. One spring evening as the sun was setting, I saw a very large flock of birds perched in the top of one of the old trees.

I thought to myself that there was this vague similarity to their perch formation and the shape of Dreygon's body. I smiled because I knew the time would arrive and I had to be mentally ready. I thought about Elbah the Agnamani.

She was a spirit guide in the Relms. How does someone become an Agnamani? Her face was so beautiful.

A few more weeks went by after seeing the flock of birds. Summer had arrived. The weather was hot and the evening breeze carried a smell of leaf and earth. The sunsets were beautiful and I stayed out on my deck with friends late into the evenings. Sometimes the smell from the grove was so strong I wondered if there was something else going on in there. I had to check my sanity. I would just close my eyes and breathe deep.

On this particular evening I arrived home late as usual.
Turning the key in the door I anticipated being inside. I was so tired. I put down my briefcase and sat down on the couch to gather my thoughts. It had been another long week, but I was feeling confident about what we had accomplished regarding the hieroglyphic chip.

I felt the pangs of hunger and went into the kitchen to make a drink and look for food. I still had some left over Italian food, so I put it in the oven to warm. I decide to have a glass of wine. The sound of the cork popping was good to the ear. I poured myself a glass, took a sip, and immediately looked out the window pass the garden, and into the grove of Sequoias. The wind picked up and I could hear it rustling through the tops of the trees. It was a familiar sound and I listened with total contentment.

I knew Dreygon would soon return. I wondered why he had been gone for so long. In truth, it was I who had been gone. I needed time to synthesize the experiences.

111

I had changed realities so many times. As a scientist I tried to analyze the Relms, but could not. I was becoming aware of a being ness. And for the first time I thought this might be a spiritual journey. My mind juggled both realties. I came to the conclusion that I had to be both mental and spiritually prepared.

It was time to eat the leftovers. I put everything on a plate and went out on the deck to eat. I wanted to take a break from all the thinking. I ate in silence. The food was good, and the wine relaxing. I sat staring out into the night sky wondering now where Dreygon might be at this very moment. I was ready to see him again.

It was getting late, so I took my plate and glass inside and put them in the sink. I was too tired to wash dishes. I just wanted to lie down, so I went upstairs. I could see the tops of the giant Sequoias as I stood in my bedroom.

The moon was full again, and gave the appearance of a small eye sitting in a very large space.

I brushed my teeth and got ready for bed.

My head hit the pillow and I was out cold. I slept deep. I began to dream. In this dream I was falling through midair. There was a hum then a flash of violet light and I landed on something that seemed to be covered by brown mist. It was hard to see. I said out loud, "Where am I? And I woke up.

I was wide-awake and I immediately looked toward the windows. I could vaguely see something resting in the top of the trees beyond my garden. My eyes slowly adjusted and sure enough I could see

Dreygon glistening against the night sky in the treetops of the giant Sequoias.

I was both surprised and elated. I spoke to him immediately. I said, "Pray tell me Dreygon of your existence?" This was our greeting.

I always notice his unworldly yellow eyes first. I'm will forever be unnerved. Dreygon iridescent skin and bright green mane was almost shocking to see again. I looked as I always do in absolute awe. Then I watched as the light that was his smile took form on his face. It was still one of the strangest things I have ever seen.

The Dreygon began to speak to me, and in my head I heard him say:

"Know where I fly
The center of the eye
The knowing of a sky"

I was hearing these words again from Dreygon. This was my invitation to travel with him again in the Relms.

I got out of my bed and walked over to the windows. I opened the windows and felt the warm breeze of the night air on my face. I looked down to check my feet. This is habit and how I gauge my reality. My feet were there as plain as day.

I am always in reflection at these moments. I find myself with the same thought that I must be insane to do this. But I felt no inner hesitation.

I watched Dreygon rise silently in the night sky. The moon remained a small eye as if it watched from afar. Dreygon spread his enormous wings as if to remind me of the power of this moment.

113

His unworldly yellow eyes stared at me, and I shook at my core. He now moved toward me and soon I could see his huge iridescent shoulder as it glided along just outside the windows and stopped. I was ready and I just climbed out the windows and got on.

His green mane brushed my face and I grabbed it to hold on. I closed my eyes and the physical sensations began immediately. I had forgotten how incredible it is. I felt myself moving in very fast. My breath quickened and I felt like I was falling down from the inside. My head began to reel and then the pressure that was so intense I thought I would go insane.

I started to yell from the inside and then peeling of layers began. It felt like an eternity. I saw a very bright light and heard a loud clap!

I opened my eyes. Dreygon and I were above the planet. I looked again as though I could not remember ever seeing it from here. We remained stationary just looking at the view.

The planet was green and the ocean very blue. It was beautiful. We could see cloud systems moving over landmasses and storms taking form over the vast oceans. I looked above the planet and the dark light was forever present. I could feel the blackness and what was the never-ending night. I was humbled, and as a scientist, absolutely intrigued.

Dreygon turned his enormous body now and we headed in the direction behind us. We were moving away from the planet and into the dark light with speed.

It was incredible and at times I thought I am dreaming. I watched Dreygon's mane flutter as if there was wind, but there was none. I thought about Elbah and the bizarre way we met. It felt like a weird dream. I needed to see her again. I had to know more about her being the Agnamani.

Who is Elbah the Agnamani on the Big Ground? A lot of time had passed since our first encounter. It was on my last journey to the Relms with Dreygon that we met for the first time. I remember now, I was just leaving the Relms of the leafless forest and it wasn't the only Relms I had been in. This was profound.

I felt Dreygon and I move down now and then to the right. We passed star systems. I have never seen stars move. They were very far away. The stars seemed to be moving in the same direction--out! I wasn't sure how I could have this sudden perception. We had the ability to calculate but no one had seen this with the naked eye.

I held on tighter to Dreygon because seeing this made me very uneasy. Dreygon slowed down and stopped. I watched him gaze into deep space, as we remained motionless. A small dark red light appeared. It suddenly flashed across the blackness of the deep space in front of us. It had the appearance of a distant horizon. Dreygon moved in an arc toward this destination just under light speed. I could feel it. Inside of me I yelled. I could see a stream of light merge in a streak. Suddenly we were directly in front of a ruby red crack that extended across the blackness of deep space. It was a very scary sight. It seemed to glow as we approached, and then we just slipped through.

We entered the ruby red atmosphere of this Relms. The color floated separate from the space, yet they seemed to be perfectly balanced. Dreygon glided through and immediately came to rest on a grey surface that didn't appear to be solid. Strangely enough, this Relms felt familiar and it was stone silent.

I sensed a fluctuation at times. It was as though something passed through where we were but it was impossible to see. Dreygon lowered his huge head for me to climb down from his shoulder.

"You are in the journey", I heard Dreygon's voice as I was climbing down. The surface of this Relms felt solid. I am always curious about composition. I had no way of telling what I was standing on. The surface looked grey and the ruby red atmosphere floated just above it. I stayed close to Dreygon and he immediately took a resting position. He turned his enormous head to look at me. The red atmosphere filtered the color of Dreygon's unworldly yellow eyes. I stared. It was like a horror movie, but I knew the Being.

I could hear Dreygon's voice, always in my head. He said "Human, do not be alarmed, I am with you. This Relms is important in your journey. Look deep into the atmosphere".

I turned to look in the other direction. The ruby red atmosphere was changing. It swirled and then it parted. Something was coming through. I was shaken to see it was Elbah merging into the Relms I was standing in!

I was flabbergasted! At first I said nothing. I watched as she melted into visibility coming from someplace else. The red atmosphere seemed to spit her out. "How did you get here? Do you live here?" I asked immediately.

She looked so real and this time there was no circle of pale color around her. And she was alone. I watched her mouth move.

Elbah began to laugh. I looked for Dreygon, who now seemed to be hidden behind a veil of ruby mist. I could still see his yellow eyes.

I heard Elbah answer, "How did you get here, and do you live here!" She was not asking as a question.

I thought to myself that she does not know questions, only what she knows and this was without question. She must be someone who has traveled the Relms for a long time. I wondered if she lived on the Big Ground.

Then I heard a beautiful voice. It was Elbah's. She said, "Vishnu, my traveler, this is not a place you live for living, as Humans know. That kind of reality does not exist here. Living is transitory and belongs to life on the Big Ground. Being is the door to the Relms.

Who am I? I am love personified on all fields of the Human understanding. It's like being all the possibilities of love all the time."

I understood Elbah's words. They describe the constant relationship she felt with existence. Agnamani was the word she had spoken that I have never heard.

She then said, "To travel as Agnamani you must be prepared or you will lose yourself in the changing of reality, which would end your journey on the Big Ground. Her face moved to a smile. You can make no mistake so do not worry, she continued to say. If you are here, you have an understanding and I am pleased to see you again."

At that moment I sensed another fluctuation in the ruby red atmosphere as something moved through, but could not be seen. Elbah's expression changed and I saw her look pass me into the red atmosphere of the Relms. She then turned her gaze to me and said, "I am the Agnamani of the young who leave the Big Ground under duress. I make sure none are lost. One has the experience of many. I'm sure there are other Agnamani; I have never met any other. I think this is how it's meant to be."

I asked Elbah if there was anything beyond the Relms as somehow I thought they might begin and end somewhere, but where? I was laughing at my small vision of possibility.

Elbah's expression did not change. I felt she spoke from those lights in her very dark eyes. "The Relms is the gateway between origin of the great light and manifestation on the Big Ground. This energy field is a continuum of thought form and some unexplainable places. You will experience what you are capable of understanding."

I turned now to see the location of Dreygon. He was watching us and I could still see his yellow eyes behind the ruby mist. The eyes of the Twelve suddenly appeared on his flanks. The ruby red atmosphere made the eyes more eerie that can be imagined. The eyes of the Twelve stopped and seemed to peer out and then continue moving. I had to keep my mind steady so that I would not react. I realized Elbah could not see Dreygon.

"Agnamani is a state of being and an entity," Elbah continued.

118

This was getting deep for me and I continued to stare at her. I didn't understand how Elbah became an Entity in the Relms. This was a stretch for my reality. I wanted to ask her if she is Human on the Big Ground. If she is, then she must have very special qualities. I'm a scientist so I could not imagine what those qualities might be.

I wondered would we ever meet, but in fact we have. Right here!

There was another fluctuation, and I felt it move through the ruby red mist unseen. Without warning Elbah said,

"I must go." Before I could respond Elbah began melting back into the mist in front of me. She was gone in the blink of an eye. I wasn't sure how to respond to all this. I just stood there looking at an empty space of ruby mist.

The veil of ruby mist that hid Dreygon faded and he became very visible. I was still trying to understand what happened? Maybe at the moment there were no answers, only observations that could be made by me.

Dreygon was no longer in a resting position so I knew it was time to leave. He stood still for a moment. I watched him spread his huge iridescent wings and flick his great tail in the ruby red atmosphere of the Relms. It was something to behold. He looked talismanic. He turned his impressive head and looked directly at me.

Dreygon's unworldly yellow eyes burn through the red atmosphere.

I was uneasy. He lowered his wings. I heard him say, "Shall we?" he began to move.

119

We were walking, I was walking for I never saw Dreygon tread or heard his footsteps. We began to move through the ruby red atmosphere. It parted as I walked and swirled around in a circle. I looked at Dreygon. His iridescent body became almost invisible in the ruby atmosphere of this Relms.

The atmosphere did not move as he glided through. I was spooked.

I wasn't sure where here was. I tried hard not to feel discomfort, but for the moment I did. I wanted to ask about Elbah, but I knew I could not. I had to stay in the present and observe these experiences in the Relms as an unfolding of a reality beyond mine.

A new set of tools was needed for this: mostly definitely a different reaction.

RAINBOW PEOPLE OF THE RELMS

The Relms with the ruby red atmosphere and grey surface continued for a while. I felt as though I was moving through red smoke. It was alien to me and I had to remember I was with the Dreygon. There was nothing in the Relms that was normal. The ruby red atmosphere came to an abrupt end and we stopped. We had arrived at a point and there was no color in front of Dreygon and me, just the absence of anything.

This was my first experience of this kind. It took a moment to register. This was another reality shift for me. I looked to my right and then to my left and the atmospheric line was there as ruby red and it held steady.

I became nervous now and I moved even closer to Dreygon. We went through. My eyes were open and we slipped from a ruby red atmosphere into a colorless world. It was brief as though we were passing from one Relms to another and in-between there was empty space. It was unbelievable. I could feel the strangeness of this brief passage. My head was the first thing to pop through to where we were going.

I was shocked to see an environment that was completely green!

It was so green I became dizzy. I had never seen this color of green. I was inside the color and green had a completely different hue. I could feel myself being consumed by the color as Dreygon and I continued moving into this world. He glided and I was even walking upon something that was green.

Thoughts of Elbah came racing back into my head. I wasn't sure why now? Meeting her again was really strange. I admit I was very happy to see her. It was a validation that she really exists. It was also kind of weird how she just appears out of nowhere. I don't have any answers about the nature of the Relms. All of this was still new to me.

I turned to look behind me and I saw nothing but the intense green environment of this Relms. Dreygon and I were inside of it, and we were on the move. He was silent and my head was filled with questions regarding the Relms. Now I was walking through the Relms of green with Dreygon.

I looked around wondering who was in charge? Only a Human would have that thought. Humans live in a world of rules and physical limitations.

Life on the Big Ground meant someone was in charge. Someone had to be in charge. If no one were in charge we would have endless possibilities. Why would we want that?

I was smiling to myself. I realized I now had both experiences. I was on a roll now, and I just had to rationalize the "why" of my reality.

Everything on the Big Ground was magnetically charged. In charge also meant that two vibrations polarized the energy. Positive and negative vibrations are needed for physical manifestation on the Big Ground. Humans can read this energy and know: and then create from this reality. Everything had a charge, and some Humans were always in charge. They had made big fires.

This was the nature of existence on the Big Ground. I'm a scientist and there is always a logical explanation for everything. I told myself this knowing I would have to change my perception by expanding my reality.

I stopped myself from all this analyzing. I was thinking too much and walking with Dreygon in the Relms of green. I was in a multi-dimensional world! I was not aware of any sides and sometimes I couldn't tell what was up and what was down.

I looked at my feet. I was surprised to see that they were green! I looked at my arms and watched as they became green. I was green! I had become what I could see. This was terrifying. I was trying to understand with my eyes and all of my will.

My rational mind was glad it was only a color! I was green for the first time in my life. Somehow that struck me as funny. I began to laugh without control. I laughed out shades of green and I scared myself! I was so shocked, I laugh again. This time Dreygon turned his incredible head toward me.

His unworldly yellow eyes were now pea green. His iridescent body was emerald colored and his bright green mane was almost undistinguished inside this green environment. I turned to look in the direction we were headed. The green atmosphere made it impossible to see any horizon. I have never been in a placed that seemed to have no end. I was at the edge of my reality. I heard Dreygon in my head again. He said, "Human, be in observation of this. Do not try to rationalize your experience, be your experience."

I looked at Dreygon for a reality check. He continued to glide next to me and he flicked his intimidating tail of great thickness. Green was an environment here, and then it was a place. I tried to understand what part of this Relms was related to me? I was again at the edge of my reality and breathing heavy.

It took a while before I became accustomed to my state of green. I tried not to laugh as I regained my composure. I felt good. I was vibrating green now and I have never felt so tranquil. My heart felt happy. I became aware of the other shades of green and they made the environment transparent. Dreygon and I stopped moving.

My eyes made the adjustment to this green world and I thought there was nothing in it. I was looking around and then I looked above me. The green above me was in the shape of a very large arch. It extended out in front of me and I could see no end! In my head I calculated it as infinite. This arch could not be measured on the Big Ground. I was dumbfounded. This infinite green archway had more to reveal.

I could just make out the outline of something moving inside the arch directly above my head. I noticed the outline of the figures first. There was more than one and they stood next to each other. They had no distinguishing facial features.

They were ethereal and looked almost human except for the shape of their heads. Their heads were elongated and round on the top. The sides of their heads sloped up to a jagged point on both sides like a pair horns.

I have never seen horns in this shape. As a scientific observer I could see they were not horns. They were translucent and blended with the green of the arch.

These entities appeared to be standing on something upon which they rode. It took them to the top of the arch and then down. There was nothing apparent that I could see. They seemed to be communicating with each other. Sometimes they were directly above my head in the arch.

They would then move down in a slope and disappear at the bottom into the Relms of green. They had energetic hands and they held them in an upright position.

Their fingers looked human even thought they were translucent. There was some kind of energy field that came to a point on each finger of their hands: they moved their fingers as they communicated. I surmised this was how they spoke with each other. I stared because I really wanted to see facial features.

They seemed to be veiled but I could still see the shape of their horned heads. They were indeed very strange entities, but I felt no hostility. Now that I had taken notice of them I began to hear voices.

Voices speaking in whispers filled the space above my head. I was listening because I wondered what they could possibly be saying to each other. I could not hear well enough to understand. Some words I recognized. I thought I heard the word "infinite" or maybe it was something that I felt from them.

They took no notice of me, so I looked at Dreygon for assurance. Dreygon seemed to take no notice of them and I wanted to ask why? But decided not to. Then I saw the eyes of the Twelve begin to move across Dreygon's flanks. The eyes looked like jewels moving in Dreygon's emerald green body. The eyes of the Twelve glistened and searched as if they were peering out to see experience.
It was shocking and my heart started to pound in my chest. The eyes of the Twelve looked as though they were crawling and then they were gone. Dreygon turned and looked directly at me. I know he could hear my thoughts. Then in my head I heard Dreygon's voice. He said,

"Human, this is just the beginning of this journey. You are in the Relms of the Rainbow People. Here you will know part of who you have been and a glimpse of Human potential. You are standing in the middle of the Rainbow Relms, and the middle is the color of green."

I looked to my left and I could see the archways of other Relms and the colors were all different. I looked to my right and the same transformation was occurring. I wasn't sure what it meant. Except now I could see all the colors of a rainbow on the Big Ground.

I felt a little overwhelmed. I looked at Dreygon. I'm sure the expression on my face revealed how I felt. His unworldly yellow eyes looked back at me; he looked surreal. For a moment I couldn't remember where I was.

It was like of wave of an unchecked reality passed into my head through the vision of my eyes. It felt like a ripple in time, but I really didn't know what that meant until now. This concept was in theory, and now it was in my Human experience. There would never be a moment when anything in the Relms, was what I call normal.

I took another look at all the archways on my left. I could see through the Relms of archways that had become: blue, blue-violet, and violet. There was something just beyond the violet archway, but it was too far away to be seen clearly.

The horned Entities with the raised hands of energy were coming from someplace, but I couldn't imagine the origin. They continued to move up the arches and down in a slope and disappearing into the Relms of the color they were in. As one group disappeared, another group would reappear slowly ascending the arches. There was no evident end to their procession. Once again, I didn't understand the reason why?

There were more archways to my right and they were becoming the other colors of a rainbow on the Big Ground.
These arches had a definite effect on me. I felt lightheaded when I looked.
The archways bore colors that blended: green to yellow and yellow to orange and orange to red and then deep red. The deep red archway was far from where I stood. I could barely see the arch in the

distance. The Relms of the colored archways melted into each other. I was in the middle of a color scape.

Then I heard in my head Dreygon's voice. He said, "Ah Human, you are having your first experience of the vibration of color. Each color is a field of knowledge and a Human energy field of possibility. You are in the heart, which vibrates a color of green. Here are known all things of the heart for Humans." Dreygon began to smile and the light that was his smile took the shape of his incredible head. It was so strange to see, but on him it seemed natural now. His penetrating yellow eyes seemed to search my very soul.

Dreygon continued, "It is the color of breath. It is also a color of life on the Big Ground. In the Relms, the reference to the Big Ground is the *mother whose heart burns with fire.* Therefore it is your heart that's most sensitive.

It is from this place of heart, that you realize your existence and your natural connection to the *mother whose heart burns with fire.* It is the only place you will know love as a Human. Your heart is your guide on the Big Ground. Since you cannot see where you are, you must be in the Relms that is most important to you. Maybe you are experiencing the color of your heart for the first time."

I had always thought the color of my heart was red. I knew this was allegoric.

I stared into the archway on my left. It was an incredible blue. I'm not sure why I was attracted to this arch. Maybe it reminded me of the color of the sky on the Big Ground. It was definitely the most beautiful blue I have ever seen.

I guess the law of attraction got the best of me. I was ready and willing to observe whatever was there. Dreygon was at my side and he glided as I walked. I heard no footfall and green was becoming blue-green. The green archway blended into the blue, and I became aware of the transition. I could feel myself begin to blue, and then there were the voices. I could hear voices as the archway blued itself. The voices became loud whispers to the point of maddening.

At first I understood nothing.

But as I blued I began to understand and the voices became small whispers. I turned my head quickly to look at Dreygon wondering if he could hear the voices. He had become an iridescent blue and he looked larger than I remembered. Dreygon slowly turned his head to look at me, and his enormous yellow eyes pierced the blue color of the archway. His bright green mane glistened and the eyes of the Twelve moved across his flanks and peered out as if floating in a blue placid lake. I was unnerved. He then flicked his intimidating tail of great thickness. I heard him say, "Human, you have the ability now to read the message in the archway of the Relms of color. As you become, therefore you are."

Dreygon and I stopped under the blue arch of the Relms. He assumed a resting position and I realized how large the space was that we were in. I looked at my arms and legs and they had completely blued. We were completely inside now. I looked up and the horned entities were moving up the archway of the blue Relms. They all held their energetic hands in an upright position.

They spoke in whispers as they communicated with each other.

I could hear them whispering things I have never imagined. Their voices seemed to move across the top if the blue archway. Many voices became one message.

I heard them say, "Blue is the place of speaking experience for the Humans. Blue is where things were said, or not said. The naming of things becomes part of your world. Truths, concepts and insights from the collective consciousness, all spoken doctrines, and high ideals of the Human evolution are here as infinite possibility."

These are the whisperings I heard under the archway in Relms of blue. Suddenly I heard a voice coming from far away. I listened as only one can in the Relms.

It increased in volume. It seemed to come from everywhere and nowhere. The sound of the voice was so familiar. It arrived to where I was under the blue archway of the Relms.
It was the sound of my own voice!
Then I heard it say in a whisper, "You dream awake!" I was spooked.

I was hearing the sound of my own voice and it was almost alien to me. There was no place for a reality check.
Dreygon did not respond to any of the voices I heard, including my own.
Perhaps the voices were just for me.
I looked into the next archway.
It seemed to be an unstable violet color.

I just stared. I thought it might just disintegrate me.
Foolish thought, I was with the Dreygon.
I was still apprehensive. I really just needed time to
adjust. I took a deep breath.

He remained in a resting position and we
began moving toward the violet arch of the Relms.
I watched my blue arms slowly dissolve into violet,
rendering me almost transparent!
My eyes did not understand this color and I became
a little disorientated. I turned to see Dreygon and he
began to appear and disappear. He turned his
enormous head to look at me.
Dreygon's yellow eyes looked like static yellow light
flashing inside the Relms of violet.
I began to feel a very strange sensation in my head. I
was looking, but I was not sure from where.

Faces began to appear near what seemed to
be the door of the violet archway. I knew these faces!
I stood still as the faces slowly passed in front of me.
The sensations in my head increased.
I felt my self-regressing to remember me, and there
had been many. All of them felt different but the
sensations in my heart were the same.
I realized the faces were my own!

The expressions on these faces were sometimes
terrifying. Sometimes they were different
nationalities.
I knew these faces, but I had no previous memory of
the life belonging to the face.
I thought, "How could that be me"?
I saw facial expressions of people who were
strangers to me now, but previously determined my
reality.

The last face that appeared looked just like me!
It moved close enough to touch.
The eyes searched mine. The expression on the face
was one of disbelief!
Then it just passed right through me. I was shocked!
I could feel myself breathing quickly.
I knew I had to remain the observer so I tried to
remain calm.

I looked above me to see if the rainbow people
of the Relms of violet were present. I could barely see
their outlines.
I could hear them whispering, "Many faces all of
whom you have been." I heard them say this. Their
energetic hands were in an upright position. I could
see the violet archway extended way beyond what
any Human could imagine. I was not ready for this.
I dare not venture forth.
I remained where I was and I looked to see what
archway was next. There was one more. I didn't
remember seeing this arch when I looked in this
direction the first time. Maybe it was too far away to
see. I found no comfort in that thought.

Dreygon and I began to move again and I
walked toward the arch of Indigo. I experienced no
physical changes as I left the archway of the violet
Relms.
I really didn't pay any attention. I think I was
completely mesmerized by the strangeness of the
Indigo arch. It was different than the other arches
we passed under. It didn't have the same quality. It
seems more like a door than an arch.
I began to feel some discomfort as though everything
was out of control. I looked for Dreygon at my side. I
watched him just disappear! I suddenly was alone

and I stopped. This was not the best moment for Dreygon to disappear!

I was under the archway of indigo. It looked unstable and seemed to fluctuate in appearance. The Indigo archway had the appearance of a very strange entrance.

I glanced at the top of the arch. I could see something moving up the arch and down the arch, but there were no riders in the Relms of Indigo.

So I walked further under the archway of Indigo toward its strange entrance. I wanted to locate the source and the nature of this movement. It appeared to be coming from an energy pool moving in a circle very slowly at the base of the archway. It was slowly spiraling up from deep below the side of the archway. As it came to the surface it formed a bridge that moved up to the top of the arch, and then down the other side and disappear into the Relms of Indigo. I followed its movement with my eyes from where I stood. It was against all laws of physics I knew, but then I was in the Relms. There were no explanations of occurrences here. The only thing possible was the observation and then the experience.

I stepped upon it. It continued to move with me on it. I went up and into the top of the archway in the Relms of Indigo.

When I reached the top of the arch, everything stopped. I looked up. Where was I? The top of the arch was almost transparent. I could see an indigo beam of light and it continued out through the top of the indigo archway. I suddenly felt a great pull of which I had no control. I went out the top of the arch headfirst.

I arrived in darkness so deep it glowed. I couldn't remember who I was. I saw a body that looked like mine stretched across the blackness. I could see my own eyes and a light that pulsed deep within.
I started to gasp for breath. I could see the entire rainbow Relms.
The seven archways extended pass what I would perceive as horizon in both directions! I was so over whelmed by what I was seeing that I started to panic. I immediately started to fall.
I fell backwards! It was like falling a hundred miles an hour.

I could not see Dreygon and for a moment I did not know him. I continued falling and trying to remember who I was as I fell. I thought I was the only person in the entire universe. I fell for what felt like an eternity backwards. I had the sensation that I fell into myself! And in a flash I was back standing inside the green archway of color! I was breathing heavy on arrival.

The green Relms was soothing and I soon regained my composure. I put both my hands on my heart.

All of my memories came flooding back to me. I knew where I was and how I got here.

I looked to my right and there was Dreygon. He wasn't looking at me, but was in a resting position staring out beyond the endless archway of the green Relms in front of us. Just seeing Him this way was something I will never forget. It was moving and I felt it in my heart. I was surprised by my response, but I owned it.

Dreygon turned his enormous head and looked at me.

I know he could hear my thoughts. I would be insane to think otherwise. I looked up and I could still see the Rainbow People moving with their energetic hands toward the top of the arch. I gazed to my right beyond the Relms of green. I could see the beginning of the Relms of yellow.

I felt apprehension. I didn't know what to expect. So far it had been a lot for me to understand and synthesize as a scientist and a Human being. I looked at my arms, they were now green, and so were my feet. I had the sense of wellbeing, but I also felt at the edge of what I knew as reality. I heard Dreygon's voice in my head and he never looked in my direction. He said "Human, your journey of color continues so that you will experience all aspects of yourself inside the colors of infinite possibility."

I was resolved upon hearing Dreygon's voice, but baffled by his words. Perhaps I was just destined to have this experience. This is how I began to feel. I made myself get ready to move in the direction of the yellow archway.

Dreygon stood up and spread his enormous iridescent emerald colored wings. His bright green mane moved as though there was wind. I watched as he flicked his intimidating tail of great thickness. He looked at me with his now pea green eyes and said nothing more. Dreygon lowered his wings and began to glide toward the Relms of yellow.

I followed him. I watched the change in me, a change I also could feel. The color green peeled as though it were a skin that was blending with yellow. It was eerie and I had to really focus so I would not start to scream. There was no reason for me to over react. The change felt quite natural. I was becoming yellow and I extended my arm. It became so bright; I thought this must be the divine part of me. I could feel me glowing yellow from the inside out.

I was not accustomed to this kind of intensity, and then I looked at my feet. They were amazing. I stared at my feet for a long time. I had this sudden awareness that this was the color of travel. I was reading the Relms of yellow.

My feet began to glow a dark yellow color. I tried to see me, but only my feet were visible. Inside this dark yellow glow, my feet began to change. I watched my toes and the feet that were mine became unrecognizable.

I saw feet that ran and feet that walked very slowly. My feet were sometimes small and young, and then old and large. I saw feet that were brown in color, and sometimes having no color. Sometimes my feet wore sandals and then boots that I have never seen. All the shoes I wore were different!

Feet inside of shoes that were new, and feet inside of shoes that were so worn, there was hardly any shoe left. I saw my feet bare and dark with thick soles for walking the Big Ground barefoot and feet inside shoes with gold trim. So many places my feet had been.

The visions were rapid, and I was so surprised I began to panic.

Not a good sign. I looked up to find Dreygon. He was still in front of me. His bright green mane stood out under the yellow archway and it began to move like there was wind. Dreygon's body was now an iridescent yellow, and he flicked his intimidating tail from a resting position. He was not looking at me, but was gazing out beyond the bright yellow archway in front of us. It seemed infinite.

Dreygon's eyes were almost the same color as the archway. Then I saw the eyes of the Twelve move across his flanks. They were almost invisible inside the yellow iridescent color of Dreygon's body. I put my hands on my head overwhelmed and looked once again at my yellow feet. I could feel all the places my feet had been but I had no visual.

I could hear Dreygon's voice.

He said, "Human do not become confused by all you have seen of your infinite self". As soon as he finished speaking to me I was merging into orange without my will. I was being pulled and the yellow and orange archways began to blend. I watched my arms peel back yellow to reveal orange.

I was aghast! I looked at my chest and I saw half of me yellow and the other half orange as I passed from one archway to the next. I didn't think of Dreygon or even look to see if he had made the transition with me. I was focused on my physical changes. I looked up and I was under the archway in the Relms of orange.

I felt myself vibrating and there was a sound. It reminded me of a note.

The note grew louder. I heard Dreygon's voice before I could see him. I heard him say.

"Ah Human, This is the sound of your own life".

I listened intently. I have never heard this note before. If each life were one note, what would it be?

It wasn't a note that I decided was mine. I could hear this note at my core and then it passed right through me. I felt it and I heard it at the same time. I had no idea a sound could be so beautiful.

It was definitely singular and as I listened it became the only thing in my existence.

The note suddenly stopped. I felt as though I had left the Relms and gone somewhere else and now I was back. I felt different but I had no logical explanations for what that meant. I immediately looked for Dreygon. I could see his yellow eyes burning through the red Relms of the next archway. He was still in a resting position and he was looking in my direction. He flicked his long tail. I stared at him.

Dreygon was bright red and his iridescent body seemed to pulse. The three horns that crowned his head and the whisker like horns on each side of his face were very pronounced. I was amazed. I could see his bright green mane moving, but there was no wind.

I could barely see the eyes of the Twelve as they moved across his flanks. The eyes seem to be lit and they sparkled like dark diamonds. My head reeled. It was hard to believe what I was seeing and what I had just heard. I didn't move at first. I needed to take a few deep breaths.

I had to gather my thoughts for the red archway. I couldn't allow my imagination to run rampant. It would have been easy given the visual of Dreygon. I knew I had to just make the move toward the archway in the Relms of red. I gave no thought to the Rainbow people, but I noticed I could not see them.

I began to walk toward the red archway and I did not look to see myself change. But I could feel it happening.

I felt red slowly consume me and I became confused. I felt red as a world and it seemed to be moving. I felt the intensity of the color red move inward. Then I felt it leave but still be there, red. I felt red on my face and on my chest. I finally looked at my arms and red had penetrated the orange. I was consumed!

I could see Dreygon watching me and I was still moving toward him.

My imagination got the best of me and I became a little scared, as I looked at him in this red environment. Any Human from the Big Ground would swear Dreygon looked like their devil. But looks are deceiving, and this was something I was experiencing as a truth.

His appearance was other world. But his knowledge was based on infinite possibility. This was what I understood as a scientist, but I was also a sentient being. Dreygon continued to look at me even as I now stood at his side. I heard Dreygon say, "Red is the Big Ground".

I was surprised by this information. This was going to be another unwavering experience. I had to prepare myself mentally. Dreygon was still looking at me as he lowered his shoulder for me to climb. It is always an intense experience when I am this close to him. I have never seen eyes like his and I never look directly into them. I climbed onto the shoulder of the Dreygon. He stood up and spread his huge wings.

Dreygon's bright green mane brushed my face and I grabbed on to it. He turned and glided out under the infinite red archway in the Relms of color. We were moving fast. I wondered how Dreygon could see in so much red. Then I noticed two yellow lights burning through the atmosphere in Relms of red in front of us. It was the light from Dreygon's incredible yellow eyes.

I had an unusual sensation with the intensity of this red environment. I kept looking at my chest to see if I could see red passing through me. Maybe I'm really just dreaming.
I looked back over my shoulder, and now I could see the Rainbow People moving up the archway in the Relms of red. I couldn't see them before. Perhaps I could only see them as the past.

I knew Dreygon could hear my confusion. In my head his voice answered, "Experiencing is the only road to remember knowing."
I had to really contemplate things he said to me.

I looked above me as we flew through this archway of red. We were flying fast underneath this red canopy. It reminded me of nothing I have ever seen. It was both scary and beautiful at the same time. The bright red archway continued out in front of us. I saw no end. I kept wondering how it was possible.

I looked below us. It was here that I detected a color changed. Dreygon slowly descended in this direction.

We were moving away from the bright red archway above us. It looked as though it continued out into infinity, but we were taking another route.

The red darken in the Relms below us and became more of an earthier color. Down we went further and further into the ever-deepening red color of the Relms. Dreygon leveled off in his flight and now I had the shock of my life as I looked below us.

I saw Humans! They were hidden by the color of the Relms. I saw only dark red shadows of their physical existence. Some seemed to be disappearing down through the darker red below us.
I saw others coming up through the deep red, and just disappear!
It was impossible to imagine their destination in either direction.

The figures of Humans soon dissipated as we continued our journey. The view below began to change and some very strange objects appeared, the shapes of which at first, I couldn't quite understand.

Then like a revelation, I saw this as a wasteland in red. Here were the objects of the Human imagination. I saw bicycles, umbrellas, cell phones, toys, cars, and houses with parts missing. Discarded clothing, everything you could imagine a Human might want in possessions lay here as waste. Discarded feelings, thoughts, and not the good ones could be heard as faint echoes.

The echoes didn't rise very high, but seemed to float across the deep red Relms below us.

Dreygon said, "You look worried, my companion. It's just an illusion. Thought matter that was dark matter and has been discarded. It will blow away on the Stellar Winds."
He began to fly in a spiral. Down and down we spiraled through the deep red Relms below us.

We came out through the red cloud cover and into the dark light of deep space. We increased our speed. Dreygon was on the move. The darkness had returned and the million blinking stars was a welcomed sight. I looked back for any view of the Rainbow Relms. There was none to be found. It was as though it never existed.

Dreygon was silent as we continued moving through the dark light at an incredible speed. I was holding on to his bright green mane and the ride was awesome. Dreygon accelerated his speed again and I thought I would lose all my stardust. I could see a bright blue light in the distance. I knew it was the Big Ground. We were headed in that direction. I just closed my eyes. I think I passed out, because I remember nothing after that!

I awoke in my bed, tingling.
I sat up and watched my hands become solid. I could still hear a note or maybe that was a ringing in my head. I decided I better remember it as a note.

The wind was blowing hard and it startled me. I looked out the window at the giant Sequoias. They stood still against the wind. I checked the time.
It was the usual time, 4 a.m.
It seemed like a lifetime in the Relms. No awareness of time, but the body knows when it's time to return.

I did not expect to see Dreygon resting in the Giant Sequoias as I checked the tops of the trees.
He had a way of arriving on a wind that only brought Dreygon and he left on the same one. Must be really cool, I thought.
I should sleep, and I did.

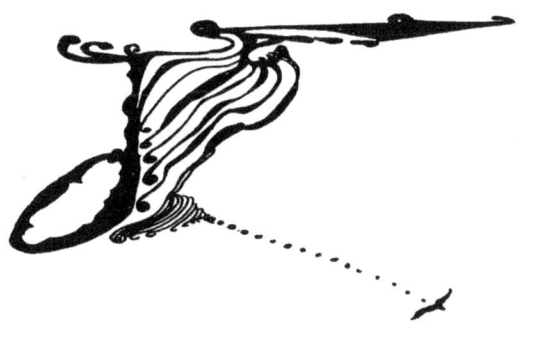

THE NOTE

The sun was on my face again. Morning arrived in all its glory; I wasn't sure where I was for a moment. I sat up and looked around as though I had never seen this room before. What a rush! It was weird. I know myself very well. I also thought the dimensional changes might have an effect after entry from the Relms. Actually, I sometimes thought it was cool, but not always.

I laughed to myself. The sun was warming my face and I could feel myself here on the Big Ground. It was Saturday and I was feeling good.

I was beginning to really appreciate being alive. This is a beautiful planet. I had no theory on how these worlds were touching each other. I was having an experience unknown. I felt closer to the Big Ground than ever.

In fact, I appreciated this place even more now, after having been to the Relms. This was a different kind of awareness for me.

I showered and dressed in no time.

143

Time to take a walk outside. The day felt wonderful.

I was beaming and I was attracting attention. Everyone was looking at me, or so I thought.

My thoughts turned to Elbah and how cool it would be to meet her here on the street.

Yeah, I was being esoteric. The point was: Is she in my town? This is the real deal, I told myself.

I realized this was already an incredible life. I said life because I knew the changes. The evolution of Humans was forever and we were never going backwards. The whole universe laid before us in its infinite possibility.

I was sure the Relms was a place of destination. Had I told anyone of my new discovery?

No one would believe there is a place called the Relms.

We have no working theory that explains this.

I could probably talk about the Relms as a mathematical equation. I was smiling all the way down the block. This was fun, with a long n.

I turned the corner. I was in my neighborhood and headed for Zenobias Cafe. This café is known for its atmosphere. It has the smell of espresso and fresh pastry like a French café in Paris.

There are lots of small tables and customers can stand at the bar and drink java, wine, or beer from the tap. It has a very old beamed ceiling made of oak. The floor is red Italian tile, unusual and very well preserved.

There is always music playing, mostly classical and jazz. The java is strong and the pastry great. It was 10:00 AM, and for the moment

144

Zenobias was the place. I needed time to digest all that had happened. I needed to just chill.

Someone suddenly brushed passed me. She was humming something. And then I heard the last note as it floated on the wind. I was unnerved.

I stopped in the middle of the sidewalk turned around and stared at her back as she disappeared down the street.

It was the note! I had heard this note before. I really needed this java now. Instead of finding out who she was, I made my way into Zenobias as quickly as I could. I ordered, sat down to drink my java, and realized that she might have been Elbah.

I wasn't ready! This is what I told myself. This could not be real! I fought my way out of non-belief. I knew this path already, so I just stopped thinking. I smiled to myself and remembered this was my awakening, and I was on a journey. Watch it unfold.

Was that Elbah? No, couldn't be.

I took another sip of java. I decided to read a magazine that someone had left. It read, "Sounds of the Universe". This was getting to the point of weird.

I remembered hearing someone say something once about road signs from the cosmic. At that time I just laughed. That kind of thinking was not in my scientific journal. Needless to say, I have had a very rude awakening since then that was not rude at all. It was incredible.

Ok, I thought. Maybe I should just really chill with this and enjoy. I read the magazine and drank the java slowly. I finished it and ordered another cup.

Now I was thinking maybe she recognized me and wanted to let me know. This did not make sense. I was digging really deep now. This was my imagination. Elbah would have spoken. She did not see me, and somehow the Relms had given me a note to remember. I wasn't even sure that was Elbah. Whoever she was, she sang the note.

I needed to be very practical about all this, or so I thought. Logic, logic, yes, logic, I kept saying to myself. There wasn't any, so I just put it to rest. I was now out of my comfort zone, but with revelations.

The java was better than ever and I savored each sip. I was on a roll.

What about the Navigator, the Man with the Crystals Eyes? Would he have met Elbah in the Relms?

This was getting exciting and I was trying hard not to over- think the possibilities of unlimited possibilities, if that's possible.

What about Sotsah in the Relms of Silence? No, this had nothing to do with Elbah. All of this has to do with me. I was at the center. Perhaps that was exactly the point. Centered.

The note returned to my head and I tried to hum it. Maybe it was part of what the Dreygon had told me regarding the Human song, and what happened in discord.

But this was different. I heard the note in the Relms and I heard Elbah, or the woman that I thought might be her, sing it on the wind. The note was like the end of some crazy jazz-rock indie concert. I'm not sure it was the same note that I heard in the

Relms as my note. It was close enough for me to remember that I had heard it. I truly had forgotten about it.

It was time to go. I would be working at home today. I didn't mind that it was a Saturday. I tell myself I have a career because I really like what I do. It's not exactly how I imagined it, but nothing in life ever is.

It's either a bigger version of what was hoped for or one so small it goes unnoticed. The one that goes unnoticed is usually the reason why each of us is here.

THE RETURN

The rainy season was upon us. It was dark early on the Big Ground. I had gotten used to that name for Earth along with the name Gaia. Perhaps the Humans were trying to reunite with something lost. Maybe it is a kinship and belonging that had been erased.

No one would know the name the Big Ground. Gaia could be known. Big Ground was a concept from the Relms, and only known with the *inner map*.

Most Humans were not ready. I was ready--of this I was sure. The Relms was a new frontier. Because its reality was all unseen from the Big Ground, it could be easily dismissed. I knew something more now.

It's hard to visualize nuclear fission if you're not a scientist, until you get the Big Bang!

By then it's too late. I was smiling to myself.

It had been three years since the meeting of Dreygon. I could never calculate my journeys out. They seemed to be out of my control and Dreygon had a way of arriving unannounced.

So it was one evening after the rains had stopped. I came home early, changed into my sweats, and decided to continue working on my project at home. The work on the Hieroglyphic chip was tedious and time consuming. After a few hours, I fell asleep on the couch.

A loud clap awakened me! I was startled at first and quickly sat up. My head ached for a moment. Now a wind blew and ruffled the collar on my shirt.

The lights were still on and the glass doors were closed in the kitchen. I was unnerved for a moment and then I realized it must be the arrival of Dreygon. I got up and turned off the lights and climb the stairs to the second floor.

There was moonlight moving across the floor of my bedroom. I didn't even know there was a full moon!

I stood looking at the silver light that seemed to arrive in streams. I followed the light up and out the window to the tops of the giant Sequoias beyond my garden. The moon was so silver it seemed to burn through the dark night sky.

I could see navy blue clouds passing in the distance like ghosts of a time. I watched with intent as though I was having a dream.

Then I saw Dreygon. He appeared out of the silver streams of moonlight and his figure was dark and alien inside its glow.

His wings were spread and his unworldly yellow eyes glowed without the presence of a face. He was motionless inside the moonlight as if held up by some unseen force.

I heard his voice inside my head. He said, "Human, you are doing well. You have grown accustomed to what you cannot know."
If this was a lead into our next journey, I'm sure it would be the unexpected. So I answered, "pray tell me of your existence?" For this was our greeting.

My heart pounded in my chest. I didn't move. I stood staring at this unbelievable vision in the night sky.

I don't know how I am able to do this. Maybe it is my will, scientific mind, and blatant curiosity that drive me. It is from the windows on the second floor of my bedroom, that I have these experiences.
This is unusual.
There could very well be a dimensional portal above the giant Sequoia trees beyond my garden. This was pure speculation. So I readied myself as a scientist and observer. I was still watching Dreygon from inside my bedroom.

He disappeared into the silver moonlight. I went over to the windows and opened them. I could see his enormous shoulder just outside.
Dreygon was waiting. I climbed out the window and on to his shoulder. I am always amazed by the size of his head and his iridescent color. Dreygon's bright green mane brushed the side of my face and I grabbed on. I closed my eyes and I began my inward descent. My breath quickened and I felt like I was falling down from the inside.

My head began to spin and once again I thought I would go insane from the pressure. I heard myself yell from deep inside. I could feel my body begin to peel, layer after layer. I screamed. It felt as though it would never end and this was for all eternity. I saw a very bright light. I heard a loud clap!

I opened my eyes and I was once again suspended above the planet with Dreygon. We were motionless.

I was breathing heavy, but I knew I was ok. Once again Dreygon and I were looking at this incredible view. The blue green planet sits in absolute blackness, yet there is light everywhere. The dark light is a place and everything is inside. The infinite possibilities of the universe become very evident from this view of the Big Ground.

One can easily imagine the utter vastness as yet unseen.

Dreygon turned his enormous body and we picked up speed. We were headed into the dark light behind us. It was beautiful and foreboding and it consumed us like nothing I could have known. The Big Ground could no longer be seen and from here I could not imagine it even existed. Dreygon's voice was in my heard. He said, "I know the Relms of the Agnamani. You cannot know what will happen until your arrival."

My mind raced. I wanted to see Elbah, and I had thought about it several times. She was the only other Human I knew that traveled the Relms.

I was seeking validation for this extension of my reality. Meeting Elbah was key for me. Dreygon knows the Human psyche. This was another revelation for me.

We were flying fast through the dark light. The distance between the stars is more than a Human mind can imagine. But in the Relms everything changes.

These stars appeared like small lights and closer together. They seemed to be in a field and were giving off an energy that radiated like a mist.

If we are of the stars, I was being bathed. Everything seemed to slow down as we move through this field of stars. It was as if we were riding on a stream.

We arrived at a point outside the star field.

Dreygon stopped moving and waited.

The blackness of deep space was in front of us. I held on tight to Dreygon's mane. I looked behind me and there was the star field. It looked like a photograph. It was hard dealing with the feelings this vision evoked. I resigned myself to letting go of all that I thought I knew about reality, so that I could fully experience this.

A small bright light deep in space appeared in front of us. It grew to a horizon that was deep red in color.

This had been the color of the Big Ground in the Rainbow Relms.

I wondered was there some kind of connection. The deep red horizon was also the Relms of the Agnamani. Dreygon made his move and I felt like we dove.

We flew in an arc and we did not arrive immediately. This deep red horizon was distant and we were moving fast. Dreygon and I both looked intently at the Relms to calculate which horizon. Several other lights appeared now.

The red horizon was our destination. It appeared as a giant red crack cross the blackness of the cosmic.

We finally arrived and Dreygon and I entered this red horizontal crack in deep space. We just slipped through, moving slowly.

It was vast, red, and empty inside. I looked in disbelief. It looked like another world.

The Relms shifted to the left and we went down and through deep red atmosphere. I wondered if this was the Relms we saw on our last journey. I thought of this non-possibility giving the nature of the Relms, which is forever in a state of the shifting. This is the color of the Relms. I saw the Humans and the remnants of their possessions and passions.
I had heard the echoes of their dark desires.
Once again Dreygon could hear my thoughts. In my head I heard him say; "Human, we are in the Relms of the Agnamani".

We stopped moving and remained motionless. Dreygon suddenly lowered his huge shoulder for me to climb down. I hesitated because I could see no surface below me. There was only the deep red atmosphere. I descended Dreygon's shoulder, but I stood very close to him.

I looked at the environment in front of me. It was intense in the color of deep red. I wondered how Elbah could be in a place like this.

The red atmosphere became unstable and began to change. It swirled and the red became lighter in color. I could see someone approaching from far inside the red atmosphere. It was eerie for they were arriving without moving. I stared for a moment. It was Elbah!

She was standing inside an oval opening in front of a golden red sunset. The Relms she was in moved her right in front of me. I was unnerved! Dreygon disappeared behind the veil of mist.
She immediately began to speak.

"Vishnu, somehow I knew I would see you out here again. How did you find me?"

I thought to myself; was it that obvious? I mean we were in the Relms. I could just be here by accident. I heard a rustling behind the mist. It was Dreygon. I knew he heard what I was thinking. I wanted to laugh, but Elbah would surely take that as admission of my search for her. She continued to speak and her face grew more lucid and even more beautiful. I watched, as I am accustomed to do with all my attention.

Elbah said, "I have been here a long time this time. It seems harder to leave because there are so many young in the Relms. I want to show you something."

At that moment I took notice of what she wore. The garment was of an unusual dark violet color. It had a high collar and the shoulders were pronounced. It was held closed by a silver chord. It seemed large for her frame and she wore it with great confidence.
But she was opening her attire and there was a shift inside the Relms she stood. Before I could comment, I saw of what she spoke.

Suddenly I could see what looked like an eternity of young faces. I've never seen that many faces at once. Too many to count, but I could see them all! They were standing in front of the golden red sunset and they could all see me.

I don't know if I've ever had that many eyes on me at once. It was bone chilling!

Then I heard a rustling behind the mist, Dreygon. I said nothing and I stared for what seemed like forever. I could feel the energy of their eyes.

Elbah sensed my response and said, "It's okay; you will grow accustomed to these realities of the Relms. You must remember I am Agnamani. I'm here a little more often than I am on the Big Ground. I am the guide for all whom you see. Remember what I told you. The experience of one is the experience of many. As I guide one, I guide all others."

I understood, and I stared at their faces. There seemed to be no duress.

They were waiting.

Elbah adjusted her garment. There was another shift inside the Relms she stood, and all the faces moved to become the face of one!

I was startled and Elbah closed her jacket. I watched her tie the silver chord that held it closed. Now only the golden red sunset could be seen behind her.

She was looking at me and then she said, "I know you wonder how I am able to be here and on the Big Ground. It all seems unreal to me until I arrive in the Relms. It is from here that I have a better understanding of existence on the Big Ground. It is the piece that is missing as to whom we really are as Humans. I'm speaking of the ability to know and become aware of the *inner map*."

Once gain I was hearing about this inner map. I decided not to ask her anything about it.

I smiled and told her I was glad to meet someone who was having a similar experience. I made no mention of Dreygon.

Funny, Elbah never asked me how I was traveling, but I think she knew. I wanted to tell her I thought I saw her in a street on the Big Ground. Somehow it seemed out of place. She was Agnamani.

"You are probably wondering how I became Agnamani," she continued. This is a state of awareness. I cannot tell you how, because this is what I am, Agnamani. Most nights when I close my eyes to sleep, I almost immediately experience a physical transformation." Elbah did not describe her changes. I knew this was impossible to do.

She continued to say, "In a flash of light I am transported into the Relms. The young ones from the Big Ground are waiting just as you have seen. If they arrive here, they are lost and are not aware of the *inner map*. I don't show them where to go; I just help them become aware of the Relms of possibility. Some may choose to travel the Relms. Some will return to the Big Ground, and others will not."

Now I thought of the Navigator and the blue Being.

"It's more than most can imagine, she said. There are others traveling the Relms. This is only the beginning of that which has no end."

She began to smile as though all the wonder of life was consciousness. Maybe we really are immortal. Maybe the knowing of the Relms is a preparation for the return, and the *inner map* was needed. It had all the coordinates.

Once again I heard a rustling behind the mist; it was Dreygon reminding me of his presence.

The golden red sunset of the Relms in which Elbah stood began to bleed through the garment she wore. She was being consumed by the golden red color. "Time to go", she suddenly said.
Her face eventually became the sunset. The oval opening of the Relms retreated, shrank, and just disappeared.
I was amazed. I had come here to see her, she arrived, and now Elbah was gone!

The mist lifted with a rustling and there was Dreygon looking at me with his intense yellow eyes. He immediately lowered his shoulder and I climbed on without a word.

Dreygon spread his enormous wings and we began an upward assent. The Relms became colorless and then we passed out the crack we entered. I turned to look behind me at where we had been. The red crack flashed as it closed and was gone!
We were back in deep space traveling through the dark light.
I could hear Dreygon speaking to me, so I listened. "We are on our way to Arahnubia," he said.

"Do you mean we're going to where angels live?" I asked but I wasn't serious. I could see the light of a smile arrive from where I sat on his shoulder. This light shaped his face and was the smile of Dreygon. "No, we are in the Relms and angelic is what you understand. Angels is a concept from the Big Ground. This is an idea that describes a possibility, but has no meaning in the Relms, Human". This is what Dreygon said.

ARAHNUBIA

Dreygon and I were still moving, and this time I tried to understand our location. We had arrived back at the edge of the star field. It seemed to end at a specific location and we were flying along the field where it ended. I looked up and we were at the bottom of a wall of stars!

Once again I had to prepare myself for the reality of the Relms.
As we continued moving pass the star field, I turned my head to look in the direction of the vastness of the dark light of deep space. It was opposite the star field. The light coming from the star field extends pass us in a soft glow.
It seemed to lie across the blackness. It was both beautiful and foreboding. The visuals are always overwhelming in the Relms.

I have to constantly remind myself to remain the observer. Dreygon turned his enormous body and now we headed directly into the dark light.

The star field was behind us but the light stretched out in front of us like a silver causeway and then it just disappeared.

Dreygon picked up speed. The blackness of the dark light engulfed us like a womb. I held on tight to Dreygon's bright green mane.

He suddenly banked to my left and I could see an intense yellow light in the distance. I saw a small flash as it opened to a thin yellow crack across the darkness. It seemed far from where we were and I wondered how could we go there?

Our speed increased and I felt as though we were moving on an unseen crest.

As we neared, Dreygon slowed down. He began to tell me of our destination. I heard him say, "We are going to the place of my origin. You will not see others like me. They never go to the Big Ground. We are going to the Relms of Arahnubia. In Arahnubia, the Twelve arrive to become one. It is a vibrant place where there is no sorrow. It is a place of higher knowledge, and many come to travel the Relms."

I was excited! Again I thought of the Navigator and the Blue Being.

"Why do they travel to the Relms?" I asked.

"It is not the Relms as a place but what it represents in infinite possibilities, Dreygon continued.

The most evolved cannot know the Relms, for it cannot be known. It can only be experienced. Each experience is a continuum of the last. In the Relms, one's experiences are always the beginning of the next. This is the great beauty of unknowing knowing."

We finally arrive. The crack was larger than I had imagined. The atmosphere seemed to be moving inside. We flew right through it. We entered a pale yellow mist and continued to travel into the interior as it swirled around us. Dreygon headed deep into the atmosphere of a place I could not see.

The mist cleared and there was Arahnubia, golden in color!

The city was transparent and suspended inside of something too large for me to comprehend. The structures were made of a substance that was similar to membranes and I saw no doors. This was fantastic!

Dreygon stopped moving and we were motionless above the city. He began to rise and now a horizon became visible beyond the city. Arahnubia was suspended in one of the Relms.

If you have not been here before, you would never find this place. Arahnubia was indeed beautiful, and to behold this place was to be my most profound experience.

This was truly a city of golden light. We began our approach and descended into the glow. The golden light streamed my face and the body of Dreygon.

Dreygon's incredible wings and body turned an iridescent golden color. His eyes burned a bright yellow that withstood the gold color of the environment. His bright green mane turned vibrant, and he seemed to be guided in. We were landing in a field of very strange plant life. The plants were enormous, colorful, and semitransparent. The plants swayed very slowly as Dreygon floated down. When we touched the surface of Arahnubia, the plants loomed tall above my head. The city was no longer in view even though it seemed near. There was no sun here, but Arahnubia was as bright with light as any sunny day on the Big Ground. I looked up to a golden sky, knowing this was not the color of the sky I knew.

The golden sky extended forever like sky on the Big Ground.

Dreygon lowered his enormous head for me to climb down. I floated down. I was now standing next to Dreygon. I watched the eyes of the Twelve turned golden, move across his flanks.

Dreygon turned his head and looked directly at me. His unworldly yellow eyes were softened by the incredible colors of the ethereal plant life behind him. The golden sky above his head complimented his size. Dreygon's bright green mane moved as though there was wind and he flicked his intimidating golden tail of great thickness. I heard his voice in my head.

He said, "Vishnu, this is Arahnubia. It is the place of my origin. A place you will forever know and the knowing of which will forever change your reality."

I was sure I understood.

We began to move now through the vegetation toward the city that was a very short distance away. The plant life parted as we moved.

I had no tread and Dreygon seemed to glide through the colorful swaying plants. I have never seen this type of vegetation. Some leaves were long and thin, and some grew in a spiral. The plants were close together and continued to sway. There was no wind on Arahnubia. I saw nothing that looked like a tree.

This was an environment of every shape of leaf possible. I looked closely as we passed through the leafy vegetation, which seemed to grow from deep within the surface. I didn't understand how the plants could be semitransparent and in such an array of colors, some of which I have never seen.

All the leaves were huge!

They loomed above my head, but not Dreygon. They barely reached his huge shoulders. I didn't try to touch them because they kept moving out of my way as I walked. I looked down at my feet. I saw very small-multicolored leaves that did not move as I stepped on them but folded backwards as if to lay flat. I saw no insects, only the plants. We soon reached the entrance to Arahnubia that appeared suddenly in the plant life in front of us. There was no door. I looked up to see a very large entrance that was made visible because of a gold colored membrane that appeared inside the plant life. It bore no visible shape. Dreygon glanced at me, and his large yellow eyes penetrated my very soul.

Then we began to pass through the membrane-light entrance. Dreygon suddenly disappeared!

I was shocked to find standing next to me on the other side of the entrance, a Being of a different nature. He was much smaller in stature and he glowed! This Being was similar to a Human except for the top of his head, which seemed to extend into the glow that surrounded him.

162

"You look surprised, said the Being. It is easier this way. We cannot show you how we become Dreygon. I'm sure you have tried to imagine this. I am one of The Twelve. My name is Sunimul. I carried the light of one. I will be your guide in Arahnubia."

Sunimul glowed, and I looked at him in amazement. His true features were hidden by his brightness, and he seemed to enjoy my curiosity. This was feeling like a dream. I tried to remain an observer having this experience. I heard Sunimul say", Shall we"? And we began to move into what was Arahnubia. We were on a very wide walking road. I saw no vehicles.

Arahnubia was amazing. It glowed golden and all was translucent. The city seemed to be made of thin gold colored membranes.

Sunimul and I took the way filled with very tall and very colorful Arahnubians. Their appearance was almost human. I stared at them as if they were in a dream. They began to fill the golden walking road we were on. I was trying to understand them physically. It was as though I could only register part of their appearance, but I felt all of their presence.

They took no notice of me. I had to look up to see them.

Sunimul and I walked through the crowd of Arahnubians toward what looked like a market place. Here the Arahnubians seemed to be trading something. I kept looking to see if it really was something I recognized.

I saw small cubed cubes and cubed balls just like the ones the Navigator used! This was amazing. I stared making sure of my observation. One very tall and colorful Arahnubian seemed to be holding a small transparent box filled with these objects. Others were gathered around him as he held up one of the cubed cubes in what appeared to be his hand. Sunimul did not stop to offer an explanation. We passed the group unnoticed.

I wanted to ask if I could be seen, but decided not to because I couldn't see the Arahnubians clearly. I was only here to observe.

Arahnubia was a city made of huge structures. I saw no windows. Perhaps this was because there were no doors and the city itself was transparent. Arahnubia consisted of large round buildings, and square buildings that were made of several archways stacked on top of each other. Everything here seemed to be without the matter I knew on the Big Ground. The whole city glowed golden.

We continue walking and now we were entering another part of the city. I could see something shimmering on a horizon as we approached. The golden sky of Arahnubia hid them from view momentarily. Slowly the structures became visible. I was awed!

Pyramids were on both sides of the walking road, and they were white in color! They gave off some kind of energy. I could feel it, as we got closer. There were Arahnubians everywhere. But I still found it hard to see them clearly. They looked mystical and almost like Gods. It was here that I saw the Arahnubians consuming something as they passed. It had an egg shape and it glowed. I watched as they put it into their mouths and swallowed it whole.

It was something that I have never seen. It seemed to glow in their mouths and light up their throats just as it disappeared from view. I stared and did not ask Sunimul any questions. I tried again to see their faces.

I was still trying to see what they really looked like. I couldn't understand their physical bodies, no matter how focused I became.

The Arahnubians still did not seem to notice my presence. What was I doing here?

Sunimul began to speak as though he heard my thoughts.

"Vishnu, you have many questions to ask. I will tell you some of the answers," he said. I turned to look at him. He glowed so bright it was hard to see his features. I stared, wanting to see whom I was with. I could see a change of expression. Again he seemed to find my curiosity humorous.

Then Sunimul said, "This Relms is matter three times removed. It is like moving back in time to experience the origins of matter. Meaning this Relms is the beginning and the return of light energy, ethereal from matter. The Arahnubians are light beings. They come here to experience the Relms as infinite possibility. They are forever in quest of unknowing what can be known."

Then he smiled and I thought I saw the face of Dreygon! I was silent and once again unnerved.

Sunimul continued, "We know no pain or sorrow and there are no transitions of old age and what Humans call death. We do not have the experiences of being Human. This Relms is Nirvana, but not the one that Humans speak of. I have used

165

this term so that you can understand this with the emotional part of yourself."

I could understand this. I was stardust and I still carried memory of the Big Ground. Again, I wondered how I could be here.

Sunimul was smiling through his glow and said, "Ahh Stardust, this is a good thing. This stardust is everywhere and it moves on the Stellar Winds that sometimes blow through the Relms. It is how you are here. Only you can know why you are here. I am your guide."

We continued moving through this part of Arahnubia. We were in a section of the city with enormous Pyramids. They lined both sides of the walking road and were so large I could barely see their tops. I counted twelve in number, six on each side of the walkway. They were made of something unlike the other structures in Arahnubia. The strange leaf plants grew in between the white pyramids in single rows. These plants were similar to the ones outside the city.
They were all transparent colors and they swayed as though a breeze was passing. I wondered how they got here and how this was something that could be real. I stared and I began to breathe deeply. I wasn't sure why my breathing changed. I couldn't control what was happening to me, so I just relaxed. I began to feel energy coming from the Pyramids. It was powerful and it seemed to penetrate far into Arahnubia. Sunimul didn't tell me about the energy of the Pyramids. We passed through this entire section of Arahnubia and ahead of us; I could see a very lush garden. We walked in.

I stared. The plants were moving and there was no wind.

These plants were similar to the ones on the Big Ground, but there was something very strange about their appearance.

Sunimul began to tell me something about cosmic memory and that what I knew began here.

I listened and watched the plants move as we passed. I noticed they varied in size and color as if here was the blue print for every plant on the Big Ground.

But their shapes were odd and they looked as though they were not meant to attract bees or any other insect. There was no smell. The flowers seemed to exist as an expression of beauty. This is what I felt. I looked up and the sky was still golden. I looked down at my feet and I could still see the small-multicolored leaf plants lay flat as I stepped upon them. I could not see a horizon or to where the garden might end. But suddenly Sunimul and I were in front of a very large set of stairs.

I glanced up to see where they might lead. I could not see above the first step. They looked like pink marble so I reached out to touch them without thinking. My hand lit up and I felt my stardust start to leave. It was happening so fast, I couldn't pull my hand away. I was being sucked into the wall of the stairs!

I felt my whole body hit the stairs. I was inside before I knew it. It was as though I was inside a giant pink crystal.

My arms flailed to no avail. I could hear Sunimul's muffled voice from outside as I continued to move

forward. A small set of stairs appeared deep inside the crystal. My feet came to rest on the bottom step. The steps were small and narrow and I knew I had to climb them to get out. I reached out to touch whatever might steady my climb, but quickly withdrew my hands fearing another surprise.
I steady myself and began my climb to the top. I arrived without incident at the top of the stairs and stopped. It took a moment for my eyes to adjust and then I saw the unexpected.

There was an immense open space before me. This space was of unimaginable proportions!

I could feel its immensity and I became very unsure of myself. I didn't know what I should do next. I looked behind me. There was nothing there! Then I look down to see if the small set of stairs were still present. They were gone!
I was standing in an open clear space. So I looked into the Relms in front of me without moving, for here in the Relms some things can be seen.
I saw a thin white mist approaching from deep within this space. As it continued moving, it became dense and had the appearance of an approaching white storm. The thick mist continued to roll forward in my direction and then it stopped.
I waited and watched.

Suddenly, I could see them.
Arahnubians were appearing out of the mist: very tall, luminous, and colorful. Vibrating rotating discs could be seen on all of them. The discs were each a different color and pulsed by opening and closing. The discs were evenly placed beginning at the top of

their heads, and continuing down the front of each Arahnubian. I counted seven discs.

It took a moment to register.

In their hands they carried a cubed cube and a cubed ball, one in each hand.

My mind was trying to understand the possibility of this experience. The Arahnubians soon filled the entire space in front of me. I didn't remember seeing the discs on the Arahnubians in the city. In fact, I had been unable to really see them. Now I could!

The Arahnubians didn't seem to notice my presence at first. They moved toward me and I stood still. In their incredible luminous hands I could see the cubed ball and the cubed cube. These were the same ones I saw them looking at in the market place. I remember seeing these cubes with the Navigator.

I knew I was standing in the midst of infinite possibility. How it would all play out would be the great unfolding.

I was still a scientist, and this was beyond anything I could imagine.

The Arahnubians occupied a space so large it was impossible to see it all from where I stood. They were many and too tall to count. I stood silent and I dared not move as their luminous bodies brushed passed me setting my stardust a glow. This was cool. I watched my dust turn luminous. I felt deliverance and I still couldn't explain why.

It was now when they had all passed me in this great open space, that they turned to notice my presence. All energy was directed at me. I say energy for I felt a pulse from them. They stared at me for a very long time. I had to look up to see their faces. They were extremely tall, luminous, and beautiful. And like Humans, each one had a different face. These were faces that took a moment to understand. Perhaps it was the shape of their luminous heads that made their appearance difficult to see.

The Arahnubian head was long and flat at the top. The top of their heads revealed a disc that pointed up. There was a disc in the middle of their foreheads.

They had large expressive eyes. I saw a color, but I didn't understand it. I could only see dark pools with shimmering light that floated across them.

I stared at their long slender forms, and the line of all seven vibrating discs that extended from the top of their heads down the length of their bodies.

I looked for expressions, but their faces revealed nothing. Then I noticed their eyes. It was here expression was revealed. Everything shown on a Human face was only in the eyes of the Arahnubians.

I was overwhelmed with my own emotions.

One by one the Arahnubians looked away from me and up at what was above where we stood. It was at this moment that I realized there was open space above us and I could see the blackness of the dark light.

Above my head I was in deep space. Small lights blinked in the distance. This was fantastic! Somehow I knew what they were looking for. The Arahnubians held the means of travel in their hands. The cubed cube and cubed ball gave unimaginable capabilities to the holder. I remember the experience I had with the Navigator, which I also knew as the man with the crystal eyes.

I suddenly realized this was their means of traveling the Relms.

The Arahnubians were looking for the lights that would become the horizons to the Relms. This was incredible.

I could not tell how long I waited in this space with the Arahnubians. Eventually, small bright colored lights began to appear. The lights sparkled like diamonds. They were many and distant. Then it began.

I watched as each Arahnubian began to manipulate the cubed cube and the cubed ball. Their hands became one with their objects.

The Arahnubians luminous hands pressed the cube into the ball and the new-formed object became the same colors as the opening Relms above us.

The seven discs on the bodies of the Arahnubians began to open then close and turn like a kaleidoscope. I watched. The intricate detail of the discs on their bodies became evident. The colors inside the discs had a liquid quality, but were not liquid.

It was impossible to comprehend them all, at the same time.

I decided to watch one Arahnubian. He was closest to me and I saw him staring at something in the deep space above us. It was emerald green. The light became very intense and after a while it flashed open like a long horizon. It was a beautiful emerald crack across the dark light of deep space.

Somehow I could see that far, but could not imagine traveling that distance.

The Arahnubian began to manipulate the cubed object in his hands. The cubed object began to glow and then turned emerald green. He did nothing more with the object and looked toward the opening Relms.

The Arahnubian's eyes were large and very dark. I watched the pool of light move across eyes showing his expression. His eyes began to change as he gazed at the emerald green horizon of the opening Relms. He was peering through the crack. The story was unfolding in his eyes and some of his expressions were unknown to me.

The Arahnubian could see through the crack of the emerald green Relms. He was looking at what I could only imagine. At first I thought I saw fear. But I realized I was using menial interpretations that were Human to understand this story unfolding in the eyes of the Arahnubian.

I continued to watch him. The Arahnubian's eyes continued to change. And now they looked surprised. His eyes changed again and I saw all the emotions that were Human move through his eyes like ripples in a tide. I felt myself shudder on the inside.

The Arahnubian's eyes changed again and I saw every emotion that I knew as Human evolve and become one emotion. It was almost like seeing emotions move as energy. I looked in disbelief. Everything became one thing as I watched his eyes.

I saw his oneness, with what seemed to be inside the emerald green crack in the Relms above us. Did his eyes say love?

I have never seen this love in anyone's eyes on the Big Ground.

The Arahnubian gazed into the emerald horizon with eyes of one expression that contained all expressions. I thought it must be incredible to see what he sees. Somehow I knew that oneness of expression had to be the tool for me to understand what he gazed upon.

I read all these expressions without the awareness of time. The eyes continued not to search, but in observation.

His eyes said he understood the nature of occurrences in the Relms and the conditions that are always present. Sometimes I could not read his eyes.

I only watched him observe what was in the crack of the emerald green horizon above us.

There was no struggle in the Arahnubian's eyes. I'm not sure if what I understood was true for me, for fear did exist in my consciousness. But this was the Relms, and they knew this existence.

I looked again at all the other Arahnubians here. I wanted to remember this visual with all its impossibility. The Arahnubians were Relms travelers. I was staring at them, and they began to leave one by one.

It was as though hundreds of stars that were not stars had become visible and each opened into a colored crack in the dark light of deep space above us. I gazed at thin threads of color that were at a distance I could not travel. These were the horizons of the Relms. As soon as the horizon became visible, the disc on the top of the head of the Arahnubians pulsed a beam of violet color. They began to leave, headfirst!

I felt as though I was watching moving rainbows, from the place of origin. The Arahnubians carried in their incredible luminous hands the new cubed object. The cubes were now combined and opened like a beacon that was the same color as the Relms they would travel to.

The Arahnubians were using the cubes as navigational devices.

They followed the beacons through the dark light into the cracks of the Relms that appeared above where we stood.

I heard a rumbling so deep; I felt it on the inside of myself. The sound was coming from the direction of the opening Relms. I was afraid.

This was more than I could handle. I had to remember to stay the observer. There were Hundreds of Arahnubians leaving for the opening Relms above me. I could see their seven vibrating discs opening and closing; then rotating and changing colors. Their eyes were gazing upward toward the colors of the opening horizons of the Relms. Thin pools of light crossed their very dark colored eyes.

Their tall luminous bodies glowed like living stars. I watched their bodies become streaks of light moving in the dark space above where I stood. I could hear the rumble as each reached their destination and the crack to the Relms closed and disappeared.

It seemed to take a very long time. I'm sure it was only my perception, for suddenly the space was empty. All of the Arahnubians were gone except one.

In their absence, the space regained its immensity, and I once again became overwhelmed by the size of this place. Above me I could still see the blackness of deep space.

The one Arahnubian remaining moved toward me quickly as if to prevent my sensory overload. His size increased as he came closer, and I almost felt trepidation. I stared at his long luminous head and into the pools of light moving across his dark eyes. I felt a touch.

I looked at the seven vibrating discs on his long luminous body and I felt really strange. The stairway appeared in front of me. The Arahnubian's eyes told me to climb down. So I did.

I felt my feet touch the bottom step. I looked up to see the opening for the stairs almost closed. I saw a flash above my head and I heard a distant deep rumbling. I'm sure it was the departure of the last Arahnubian.

I could now hear the voice of Sunimul. I turned around as I tried to get a sense of direction. I was back inside the pink crystal stair. I could see the fractures of light. Somehow, I just moved forward with my arms outstretched. I was being drawn by the voice I heard. I slipped through, but it was backwards! I could see my hand still on the giant crystal stairs again!

Sunimul quickly moved my hand away from the stairs and said, "This is not the moment".

The moment for what I wondered? I had just reemerged from the stairs I had disappeared into. Was Sunimul laughing?

He said, "This is the home of Dreygon. On this journey you are at the stairs. As you can see they are much too large for you to climb for a reason. This is not the moment."

He said this to me as though I had never been absorbed by these giant crystal stairs. For me it was a replay! Sunimul was smiling and pointing in a direction for us to go. I offered no resistance and asked no questions.

We went back through the garden. I could not tell how long we had been gone. I could not remember anything I saw on the way, and on the return all was new.

Sunimul said, "As soon as you stop looking, it changes". The Stellar Wind brushed passed us through the garden. It made the garden appear like a garden on the Big Ground. For a moment the plants did not glow, but took on the same quality as the plant life I knew. This was brief and a moment of infinite possibility.

Sunimul began to speak, "You are probably wondering if there is any danger here for you. The *inner map* tells you how to move through the Relms, but you must always do this with Dreygon. He is your guide. You can become lost and be here for a long time before you find your way out."

I wondered what would be happening to my body made of matter on the Big Ground.

Knock! Knock! Nobody home? The whole idea was a little scary. Somehow there has to be an automatic homing device used while in the Relms.

"Ah, you are beginning to understand the Relms", said Sunimul. He heard my thoughts. He then seemed to draw something in from the Stellar Wind that was passing. Now he became more visible. I could see his face. His eyes were deeply translucent and revealed another world of light. I could still see the same smile. His face looked so human. This vision of Sunimul was brief as the wind ceased and everything returned to its original state. I turned to see where we were and a group of Arahnubians was approaching quickly through the garden. I was surprised to see them.

They moved passed us as though we were invisible. After they passed all heads looked back and seemed to be staring at me.

The Arahnubian faces showed no expression. Their eyes told the story to my soul. I suddenly felt as though I knew them. They did something with their luminous hands. I could not see clearly. The Stellar Wind moved through the garden again, and now I saw part of their form. I could see the Arahnubians circular discs, seven in number. The discs pulsed different colors and then became transparent.

The Arahnubians turned and moved away and were gone before I could respond. Sunimul was watching me and only smiled and nodded for us to continue through the garden.

We were at the entrance to the city, and I was amazed at how quickly we had arrived.

I was passing through the golden membrane before I knew it. I could see Sunimul next to me, but Dreygon greeted me just as I arrived on the other side. He was in a resting position amongst the huge leaf plants in front of the entrance.

I smiled at my old friend. I was so happy to see him. The sky was still golden, and I looked back to see the entrance to Arahnubia for the last time and it was not there!

"You're looking in the wrong direction". It was Dreygon's voice.

I turned again to find the huge membrane entrance to Arahnubia to the right of me. It was as though everything shifted and we were not exactly in the same place as when we arrived. I looked at Dreygon and the eyes of the Twelve now golden moved across his flanks. I wondered which eyes belonged to Sunimul.

I'm sure Dreygon heard my thoughts for he suddenly looked at me. His yellow eyes searched my soul. He lowered his enormous head and I knew it was time to go. I climbed onto Dreygon's shoulder. His bright green mane brushed my face and I grabbed on. I have nothing to compare the feel of Dreygon mane. It's more like I become a part of him. I am with him when I hold on.

Dreygon stood up and spread his enormous iridescent golden wings. We began to rise above the colorful leaf plants of Arahnubia. He turned his enormous body all the way around and flew upward through the pale yellow mist. The mist began to clear and we went out the golden crack into the blackness of the dark light of deep space.

Dreygon was flying at an incredible speed. The blinking lights of deep space were passing like one long flash. I closed my eyes. I could sense the passing of time. Thousands of years moved through me, and then time stopped! Light filled my head.

I heard a loud clap! And I was back!

This time I was standing up on my arrival. Imagine waking up and you're standing in the middle of the floor of your bedroom. I was freaked!

I found it strange that my right palm was on my chest and my left hand was at my side. My head was bowed. I stood there. I really felt peaceful.

I looked up and I could see the wind blowing through the Sequoias outside my windows. I heard the birds, but saw none. I headed for my bed and fell in. Sleep was deep.

THE RIDE

It was Saturday and I could sleep in, but I was up and dressed before ten.

"Know where I fly
The center of the eye
The knowing of a sky."

Dreygon's words floated into my consciousness. My reality on the Big Ground would never be the same again. Consistency is the desire of most.

My mind was searching for a constant. Some things are, like the sun's arrival this morning. I was rambling to myself. There was a lot to think about, like my encounter with the Arahnubians.

This last awakening journey was more than I could have ever imagined. So many things happened. Another incredible event was the meeting of Sunimul the Luminous. I'm still not sure who he really was. I just slipped back through the membrane of Arahnubia and found Dreygon and not Sunimul. It was more than I could digest at once.

I began thinking about Elbah. She seemed easier to think about than the Arahnubians.

My phone buzzed.

I got a text from some friends. Everyone was meeting at the park for a bike ride, just what I needed. I grabbed my bike and I was out the door.

The bike ride to the park is nice. It's a twenty-minute ride from my house. When I arrived, the park was alive with people.

The sun felt good and brought smiles to everyone's face. I could hear music blasting in the distance. It was the perfect day. All my friends came to the park, ready to ride. There is a group of us, about eight people who seriously bike.

There are no cars in the park and a lot of people have the same idea. We ride with the wind.

Somebody yelled, "Wind ride!"

And we took off on our bikes.

The ride through the park is amazing. This park has old growth and a lot of indigenous vegetation. In some places, the park looks like a jungle with thick over growth both sides and lots of wild life. The bike path rolls through for more than 20 miles. You can smell the ocean and hear the calls of several species of sea birds. We were riding hard and I was silent.

"So dude, what's that growing out of your back?" It was the voice of my friend, Jones Harper. I call him Harper. He was riding behind me when he commented. I almost fell off my bike when he said

181

that. I had to really get a grip here. Harper fell out laughing. "Man, what's up with you?" It was funny, and I just put out my arms and pretended to fly. How else to play this off?

I felt no sensations on my back, but I could sense something going on in my head, maybe on my head. They all started to laugh. This was good for me. I needed a reality check. Harper was now passing me on his bike.

He said, "Dude, I really did see some wings on your back. Ok, I could be hallucinating in the sun. Maybe my head is still tight from last night. But there's something different about you. It's not bad! Just different."

I was laughing now. Might as well play up the mystique. We were now passing through a very large grove of redwood trees. The wind started to blow and for a while it was hard to pedal. We rounded a bend and the wind stopped. In the distance, I could see a group of bikers approaching us. They were on the bike path a little further into the park moving at a good pace, like how we like to ride.

The air became very still as they got closer.

Harper was the first to say, "Oh man, do you feel that?"

"Yeah!" everyone answered in unison. And then it happened. We could see them passing us through the trees. They moved passed us as in a dream. Everything seemed to slow down. I was looking really hard at the faces of the people on their bikes. Then as in very slow motion, I saw someone I knew. It was the face of Elbah!

Without hesitation I yelled, "Elbah!"

She was looking right at me, and I heard her yell back, "Vishnu!"

But the group kept riding and we rounded a bend and they were no longer in sight. We stopped.

All eyes were on me.

"Did you see that? Did you see that?" They were all saying the same thing.

I sat down on the ground next to my bike. Everyone was still talking at the same time.

I started to smile. I saw her and she saw me! This was so cool and very surreal.

"Did you know those people, man?" Harper asked.

"No! I mean I saw someone I knew," I said. How would I explain Elbah?

"Everything seemed to slow down!" one of my friends said.

"This is unbelievable!" said someone else.

Harper did not take his eyes off me. "Okay man, did you set this up?"

"Dude! How could I set this up?" I said in a loud voice.

Harper looked worried, and then relieved.

Whatever caused this to happen, it was very possible that I might have an idea, but dare I go there?

I played dumbfounded, like everyone else.

I was surprised!

It was obvious something unusual was happening.

I wanted to meet Elbah on the Big Ground, but this was weird. There she was, and then she was gone! Not only that, but what was up with the stopgap in time?

Slow motion?

I wasn't worried about it at all. This was mild compared to what I have experienced. I wondered what would happen next.

We finally gathered ourselves together and finished the bike ride. It was loud on the way back.

Everyone had an opinion. Finally somebody said it really didn't happen. That statement didn't go over too well. We all had experienced the same thing. So it happened!

The ride was long on the return. I was glad to be off my bike and walking up the hill to my house. I told my friends I'd check in later. I went inside to sit down and think about the day.

I told myself the Relms were not merging into the Big Ground simply because I saw Elbah and she'd seen me. This was just how it was happening. I knew from my journey with Dreygon, all cannot be known. I started to laugh. Yes! This was really becoming a part of my reality. I can handle this. I was doing it. That slow motion thing that happened today with my friends was gothic.

I was glad I hadn't had this experience alone. Maybe the law of association was at work here. Harper really looked at me hard, like he knew that I knew. I really didn't.

I was just like him and everyone else.

This was not the Relms. This was Big Ground magic.

I was tired. I took a shower, put on some sweats, and took a nap.

I woke up hungry. It was time to roll out of my flat.

I got dressed for the ladies.

We were all hooking up at our hang, the Daygone. We love this place.
It has an international atmosphere and the music rocks. The music is always a mix of different genres from all over the world. I was ready for some nice sounds, good food, and a nice drink. We all say there was not a "day gone by" that we are not at the Daygone.

I called a taxi. I was still a little tired from the bike ride and the Relms. My thoughts alone were endless.
I wanted to ask myself, "Dude, who are you?"
Of course, no one could answer that except me. This was not the serious answer. This was the answer that had no answer in the Relms of infinite possibility.

The taxi came and I got in feeling really good. The ride through the city was nice. The sun was setting and the sky was blazing with the color of sunset. I arrived at the Daygone just as the crowd was arriving. We always have a table by the windows. I made my way pass the tree and the red bench in the middle of the restaurant. A table full of friends was all waving hello. It was so cool; I must say I felt the love.

I sat down. There were different kinds of wine already on the table and some really nice glasses. The chefs' board of: fresh bread, grapes, European cheeses with Turkish olives and raw honey was put in front of me. I didn't hesitate to indulge myself. The music was on full throttle. This time it was ragas played by India's best musicians.

We were about to order when I caught a glimpse of someone out of the corner of my eye.

No, couldn't be—I didn't want to entertain the thought of seeing Elbah. I took a sip of my wine and continued to laugh and talk with my friends.

We order dinner. I had fresh blackened salmon with jasmine rice and baked sesame seed vegetables. Everyone at the table orders something different so we have the opportunity to taste everything. The food is always beautiful to look at and delicious.

Dinner was great and at the end of the meal, there was nothing left on any plate.

The music in the Daygone changed and now it was on groove!

I thought I heard somebody singing along with a song that was playing. The last note came, but the person sang something different. It was the note I heard on the street a while back!

My face froze, and everyone looked at me. I laughed and played it off, but I kept my ear pealed to the sound of that last note. Yeah, that was it!

I didn't turn to see. One can hope that things just happen. This was passive on my part. I think I just wanted to experience something else. There was a round of applause and lots of laughter. No one at my table heard the note. Everyone continued to laugh and talk and listen to the music.

My curiosity got the best of me. I excused myself and decided to walk pass the table on my way to the WC. Sure enough our eyes met as I was passing a table full of people. Elbah stood up and came around the table to greet me.

"Vishnu!" She gave me a very big hug.

She said nothing more, but looked in my eyes as she had always done in the Relms. Her eyes were green.

I was smiling and for some reason very comfortable with our meeting.

"Nice to see you on the Big Ground", I said jokingly.

Elbah laughed and said, "I know, this is amazing!" She held my hand like I was a good friend. I was really jazzed. "What should we do now?" she asked.

I knew she was joking. I looked at the table she was sitting and everyone's eyes were watching us. We both looked at the table I came from.

For some reason I cannot imagine, everyone there had stopped talking and was staring in our direction.

We both laughed.

"See you later," I said as I walked away.

"Yeah, in the Relms!" Elbah replied.

Someone at Elbah's table asked, "What are the Relms?" I didn't hear her reply, but my face was in a full smile when I walked away.

"Who was that?" one of my friends asked when I finally returned to our table. I was honest when I answered.

"Oh someone I met in the Relms." I knew none of them would believe me so it was okay to tell the truth. They say I'm a great storyteller. I didn't tell them anything really.

The Relms could be my neighborhood as far as they knew. I also understood, for the moment this was all they could understand. They would all have to find the *inner map* without me. We were all evolving at a different speed.

I wondered if they were ready for the realization of remembering their night journeys.

The gift was that we get to arrive at our own chosen time. No rush, just intention. I didn't say this either.

I thought a lot of things I never said. Timing was always an issue. What's the point if no one understands?

It was time to go. We all left the Daygone at the same time. I could see Elbah waving through the crowd of her friends. I waved back through the crowd.

I know I anticipate situations sometimes. Not always the best. Especially if things turn out nothing like anticipated. This is really a reality check on control. We are not in control. I say this, but I do the opposite.

I said good night to my friends and took a walk before calling a cab. The evening had been a lot of fun. It was incredible to run into Elbah at the Daygone. But then, I always said the most incredible people I have ever met, I met at the Daygone. Elbah was hanging with a real happy group of folks. This speaks to who she is on the Big Ground. Being Agnamani is who she is in the Relms. Incredible!

I called a cab. The ride is always cool. I was glad to turn the key and go into my house.

Time to get ready to hit the 'hay", I'm sleep.

It had been a full day, and there was always tomorrow.

JOURNEY TO RAMUDAH

My bed was a welcomed sight. I stood in the
mirror brushing my teeth and looking at my head.
I looked in my eyes to see if there were any obvious
changes. I looked to see if there was anything
glowing on my back. I was serious and somehow this
was not funny.
The fact that I was actually doing all this was funny.
So I laughed, and then I thought I saw some kind of
colored smoke coming out of the top of my head!
My head seemed to be changing its shape.
Was my forehead always this large? I saw a strange
light in my eyes. I blinked in shock! Whoa!
I had to get a grip on myself. Yes, this was hilarious!
Okay, I was done with the teeth. Sleep was
calling me. I was so tired and my two realities seem
to be crashing into each other. I had another day
before I was back at work. I was so glad.
This was non-stop!
I could also find myself on the way to the Relms.

189

I got in bed. I drifted and was fast asleep for a long time.

A breeze came through the windows of my bedroom and ruffled my covers.

I felt the breeze on my face as I slept and I woke up. I knew it was Dreygon.

I was no longer tired. I suddenly felt energized, but I didn't move. I waited because I couldn't see him.

The breeze blew again and ruffled the leaves on a plant sitting in the corner of the room. I sat up.

I glanced over and was startled to see a set of eyes. The eyes sparkled in the darkness of the corner and moved up toward the ceiling.

What were two became too many to count.

I watched in awe and unfamiliarity. Together they began to take on the shape of a tiny comet as they moved toward the dark ceiling in the corner of my bedroom. The eyes looked as though they were smiling.

I had a sudden flash of a childhood memory of seeing them a long time ago as a child.

Now at this moment the memory of the eyes returned and they were still a mystery to me.

Without warning they changed direction and moved towards me.

They stopped and swirled over my bed. They made an opening and I could see a section of a cloud filled universe.

I looked pass the large white clouds, but saw nothing.

I sat there looking up and waiting for something to happen.

The view began to change its perspective.
What seemed distant was now becoming near.
I watched the edge of this universe move toward me
from deep within itself.
I saw deep inside was Dreygon.

His huge iridescent wings were spread and he
was suspended in a turquoise sky. The white clouds
passed in front of his unworldly yellow eyes.
His bright green mane waved and he looked larger
than I remembered.
I tried hard not to show my astonishment.
I wondered how he could arrive in so many
dimensions.
The edges of the opening began to close.
The opening to a view of this universe was rapidly
shrinking in size!
The opening above my head grew smaller and
smaller until it was the size of a dime. Then it just
disappeared in the darkness above my bed.
I was astonished!
The night air ruffled the leaves of the plant in
the cornered of my bedroom.
I thought I heard some kind of laughter.
No, I'm sure it was just my imagination.
Then I head Dreygon's voice.
He said, "Human, tell me of your origins."
This was his greeting. It made me feel like I was all
of humanity. That was not Dreygon's reasoning, of
this I was sure.
I am a human dweller of the Big Ground and my
name is Vishnu.
My life was becoming extraordinary.

No one knows about the Relms but me, and now I had met Elbah. I really needed to be able to relate to someone Human. I'm sure this was part of Dreygon's plan.

He was guide to the Relms and now my trusted friend. I was ready to see him and travel the unimaginable. I got out of bed and went over to my windows. I opened them and gazed up at the night sky beyond the giant Sequoias. There was no full moon. The moon was crescent and stars could be seen in a very dark sky.

Dreygon seem to appear from inside the crest of the moon, and was headed in my direction. His silhouette cast the form of an alien being, that I knew. I am still amazed by his relationship with me. His burning yellow eyes could suddenly be seen in the night sky. He was close. I readied myself both mentally and now spiritually for our journey.

He soon arrived into tops of the giant Sequoias. Dreygon's iridescent body was barely visible. He left the trees and was headed for my windows.

I watched his huge iridescent shoulder move under my window and stop.

I climbed out and onto Dreygon's shoulder.

I closed my eyes.

I was sure I had to get off the Big Ground the same way I always did.

My head felt like it was shrinking from the inside. I started to breath heavy and I had that old feeling of falling down from the inside. The peeling of my layers was unbearable and the pressure intense. I heard myself yell. I saw a very bright light, and heard a loud clap! I opened my eyes and we were above the planet! I was breathing heavy. The view of the Big Ground was surreal.

I needed a minute. The journey in, to get out, was always intense and Dreygon's unusual arrival was still in my head. I have to always remember my whole self is present. I knew my whole body went from matter to stardust. It felt like a great inner pull: greater than anything imaginable. Even my mind felt pressurized.

Dreygon's voice entered my head. He said, "Human, you are doing well. We will go to the Relms of Ramudah".

Dreygon turned his enormous body around with his incredible wings spread. We flew in the direction behind us into the dark light. This time we were moving in a glide. The dark light is all consuming. I always felt as though I was in one incredible dream, but this was no dream.

The journeys were becoming even more intense for me as I always came back to be Vishnu: the scientist and Human dweller on the Big Ground. I admit it was exciting to spend my evenings in Relms travel.

The reality of the two worlds would someday merge and I would know the reason for my new perceptions.

We were in deep space now and small silver lights blinked in the distance. Dreygon stopped and we waited. I knew he was looking for the lights of the Relms. The very bright colored lights began to appear and without a word Dreygon began to move toward an opening Relms. I could see its turquoise crack glowing in the blackness of deep space.

Dreygon picked up speed and moved in an arc. It's always a rush for me.

We arrived at this turquoise crack just under light speed.

We slipped through this enormous opening into an amazing world that had appeared in the middle of the blackness of deep space.

Evergreen shadows were floating in a turquoise space as we entered this Relms. I could not determine what they were shadows of, and I marveled at the contrast of color.

I could feel a wind and I watched my clothes move as though I was in the wind on the Big Ground.

I was a little unnerved. I held on to Dreygon's mane even tighter.

Dreygon began to move down in a spiral. Down and down we went through the turquoise atmosphere.

The evergreen shadows passed us like ghosts, long forgotten. I felt the strange sensations of the spiral down. We finally stopped. The cloud cover cleared. We were moving above a world very similar to the Big Ground. It was as though we were looking at Earth as an idea. This world was round and it was moving, but inside of something vast. It was smaller than the Big Ground, but with the same intensity.

There was stardust everywhere. It seemed to be floating eons from the planet and it glowed. Dreygon was explaining as we approached.

He said, "This is the Relms of Ramudah.

This Ramudah holds one possibility of a beginning.

We know this because when we leave here it will not be seen again. It can be seen here because we have asked to know the map to Ramudah."

I was confused and I asked, "Do you mean no one else has seen this place?"

"Others may find Ramudah, but it will not be here in this place, Dreygon answered. This is where Ramudah is for you."

I knew I had to absorb Dreygon concepts. I did not use logic to understand. There wasn't enough room. I accepted it as being something not known on the Big Ground. I had to find a place for this in my understanding.

Dreygon and I glided down through the stardust and came even closer to Ramudah. There seemed to be a turquoise cloud cover.

We moved through the clouds and there was Ramudah, a site to behold!

Ramudah was green and lush. Plant life that never existed on prehistoric earth was in full bloom here. I've never seen so many strange flowers.

The flowers were huge! Some were the size of trees. Very small plants that looked like green ivy clung to the surface of Ramudah.

What I saw next was so shocking it was beyond belief. Thousands maybe millions of very strange beige colored life forms of all shapes and sizes were in a full run across the surface of Ramudah.

As they ran across the green ivy, I could see the most primitive looking were at the rear of the hoard.

They ran on any number of legs! The most advanced forms were running in the front. They ran on two long slender legs!

Dreygon began to descend closer. Now I could see them more clearly. They had every head shape imaginable. I saw no ears. But their eyes faced sideways like prey on the Big Ground. Their eyes appeared vacant and their heads were pointed forward and never moved. We came close.

They were running at top speed as if pursued by something. Then, they would all slow down to a halt. I watched as they began to eat the huge flowers. Some nibbled at the bottom of the flowers and others ate the tops of the flowers when they fell. The flowers seemed to glow and I could smell fragrance and something else that was so familiar. This was an old smell, an ancient smell of earth and sweetness. I did not see trees and I wondered about this strange ecosystem.

Dreygon kept moving and soon we arrived on the other side of Ramudah. I saw seas covered in an aqua mist. The aqua mist seas rippled on the surface. In some places it extended completely around Ramudah. It was beautiful and frightening at the same time. I realized real beauty is almost scary.

Dreygon suddenly stopped and we were motionless above the aqua sea. I looked down and I saw something strange.

The rippling stop and very peculiar looking dark green life forms began to crawl out and onto the surface of Ramudah.

Once on the surface their dark green colors began to fade to beige. They crawled slowly at first and then into a full run.

It was here the strange life forms we saw on our arrival to Ramudah, had their beginnings.

I was witnessing an evolutionary process in a matter of moments! There were millions of them.

Dreygon changed direction and we began to follow the hoard onto the green ivy surface. At first the aqua mist hid the creatures from complete view.

As we continued to follow them the mist began to clear.

I was shaken to see what was waiting on the green ivy surface of Ramudah below us. Thousands, maybe millions of light Beings were waiting amongst the enormous flowers. Their posture told me they were ready for a chase.

The light Beings had a soft glow.

Their bodies were eerie pink and blue colors that seem to mix together and move around on their forms. A thin yellow line formed an outline making their forms visible. I could see no obvious facial features, but I could see their eyes, small and intense. They seem to burn with a very strange glow. As the creatures neared, the chase began.

The light Beings ran from inside the flowers and onto the green ivy cover. They pursued the creatures as if it was their only purpose, and indeed it was. Some ran upright.

They took long aggressive strides. Some looked
Human and I became a little nervous at seeing what
I could not imagine.

Others ran low along the surface, and none
took notice of Dreygon or I. We remained aloft and I
witnessed the incredible. The light Beings faces
became visible just as they neared those whom they
pursued.

The light Beings eyes burned like fire as they soon
overtook the beige colored life forms. They were all
sizes and they leapt into the air and entered through
the heads merging into the bodies of the life forms
on Ramudah.

The heads of the life forms snapped to one side and
their eyes rolled back in their heads.

The newly formed entity rolled upon the surface of
Ramudah and stopped.

It seemed they became aware of themselves because
their eyes opened as if to see for the first time.

I watched as this continued.

Thousands became millions. I could not believe my
eyes. All this took place on the green ivy and among
the huge flowers that covered Ramudah.

As the transformation continued, some stood
upright and gazed upward toward the tops of the
giant flowers. I've never seen such facial
expressions. I could not understand: perhaps
because emotion was not present, but awareness
was. What was the meaning of this—the two that
became one?

It seemed both violent and beautiful at the same
time. I knew this was a Human perception.

The air above Ramudah flashed and glowed as some took flight with transparent wings. I could see their faces and their eyes looking as though they could see for the first time.
They flew in erratic swoops and dips. Some landed on the tops of the giant flowers. Even the smallest of the new creatures seemed to admire their new forms.

It was almost eerie and I became overwhelmed. I had to really relax to be okay with what I just witnessed. Dreygon and I saw the secrets of Ramudah. I wondered what my purpose here was. It was a terrifying experience.

The facial expressions of those that stood upright were etched in my mind. Their eyes burned with life fire. Their faces contorted to express this new form awareness.

Millions of creatures succumbed to the light beings on the green ivy of Ramudah, and then it ceased. The union was finally complete.
The new life forms seemed to occupy three levels of Ramudah, which were: terrain, upright and airborne. These light Beings that became a part of the life forms here had done this as if on a hunt.

I could hear a voice come into my head. It was Dreygon. He said, "Human,
The life forms of Ramudah did not have what is known as awareness.
It is with awareness that one can experience memory. Awareness and memory make possible the experience of time. Now with the integration of the light Beings they have awareness of memory inside of time".

Dreygon turned his enormous head to the side and looked directly at me. His unworldly yellow eyes watched my expression as I sat on his shoulder perplexed.

I knew I could not understand everything that was happening beneath the giant flowers. Some things were still hidden from me.

I gazed down and saw all eyes looking aloft as if they could see us. Perhaps the new life forms were remembering their flash into Ramudahian existence. Awareness not had until they merged with the light Beings.

Dreygon shifted his gaze at something that seemed to appear out of nowhere. The Relms were shifting and a temporal rim of a giant circle appeared above Ramudah. Dreygon and I began moving across the planet toward the temporal ring. He began to spiral into the temporal ring. The visual and the sensations were incredible.

We entered the ring and suddenly we were in aqua skies. Dreygon flew up through the aqua skies of the Relms of Ramudah and out through the enormous crack. I turned to look back and I witnessed a turquoise flash as the Relms of Ramudah disappeared from site.

I held on tight to Dreygon's mane. I was overcome by the experience. I wanted to ask Dreygon about Ramudah and how this was possible. I was in the Relms and I knew possibilities were infinite.

Dreygon was headed into the dark light of deep space.

Sometimes colorful cosmic cracks of the Relms would open as horizons, close and another would appear, but not in the same place. They would appear as random destinations that had been hidden for what we would call eons. Their distance was impossible to understand by any human.

I finally understood the Relms could not be known without the *inner map*. It is the use of the *inner map* that enables the understanding of an unknown destination that is waiting. This was hard to fathom. I could not use just my mind, but my whole existence to understand the infinite possibility of me.

This was my journey and it was a good idea to own it. I felt relief for the first time since arriving in the Relms.

My friendship with Dreygon had changed what I knew as reality. Now I could see the depths of my existence beyond the Big Ground. But for now, the Big Ground would always be home. I was ready to be home.

And like some incredible dream had just ended, I woke in my bed!

The room was very quiet, not even the birds were singing. My head felt heavy. I looked at my arms, and there was no luminous residue. Everything was normal. Where was Dreygon?

I closed my eyes and there he was like a fading vision in front of a small light.

Then Dreygon was gone!

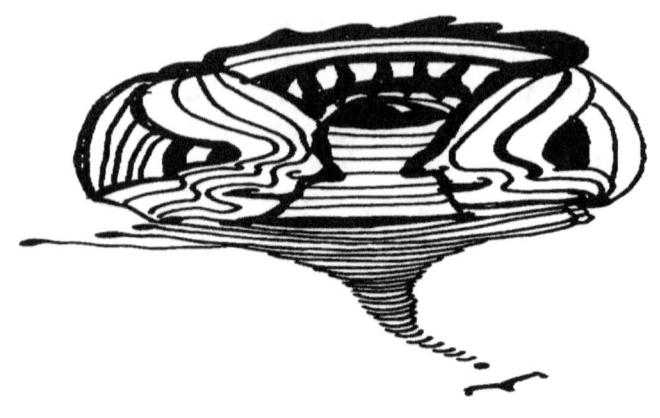

MEETING ELBAH

Life seemed to return to its usual after Ramudah. It had been weeks since I had traveled the Relms with Dreygon. I admit I had a hard time not just kissing it off to a really bad dream.

I say bad dream, because when I thought about it, it was terrifying. I laughed at the end of those kinds of thoughts. Had to. I was determined to stay abreast of this. Keep my sanity. Live in both worlds. I knew about the map. I had a guide. What more could a person want?
I knew how to answer my own questions.

Somewhere in the back of my mind, I was hoping I would run into Elbah again. Like kind, seeking like kind.

We met in the Relms and now we had met again, here on the Big Ground at the Daygone. This was very exciting to me. And then there was the bike ride! This was an amazing occurrence witnessed by my friends who really had no idea of the underlying story.

What would happen or when we would meet again was up to chance. I wasn't even in control of my journeys to the Relms, so who was?

There I was again thinking someone must be in control, as opposed to going with the flow.

OK, flow it is.

It was Thursday, and I left the office early. It had been a very intense couple of weeks with deadlines for our project. The Hieroglyphic chip was coming along nicely. We finally figured out the sound frequency for a lot of people.

Recording a note from almost every human on the planet was still an undertaking. My colleagues and I agree it is a beautiful idea and concept.

We also agree it communicates the complete information of what each Human is by means of their sound. We also knew that in the future we would be able to detect a healthy human from a sick one by means of this same technology. I also think certain notes or sound frequencies have the ability to heal at the cellular and energy level.

I thought it might be time to take a little head break. But my mind gave me no rest. So I left my office for the day.

I was so glad to be outside in the Sun. People love the sun, especially in the city. Sunny days in the city can make one forget how deep life really is.

Man has his ultimate structures and engineering feats to baffle the imagination. None compare to the great pyramids. Again, the sun was of great importance, and maybe the Sahara wasn't all deserts back then.

The Nile River ran directly in front of the great Pyramids back then. The Big Ground is always evolving along with its inhabitants: the big coming and going of life forms and their relationships to earth.

The Humans look upon extinction as unnatural, a catastrophe. They are the only inhabitants of the Big Ground aware of its history and their discoveries made it so. If the Humans had never discovered the dinosaur bones, who would have known of their existence?

So I was the witness, as Dreygon said. I say and there for it is, for this is the part I play in this divinely Intelligent universe that wants to see itself. My own awareness was key in this.

I turned the corner and headed for the "hang". It had been a while since I checked in with the Daygone. I was ready to do the late lunch.

The Daygone was quiet for a Thursday. I knew this would not last. I was in the lull and I was happy with this. I sat at a table by the windows and ordered a café latte. I checked the menu and ordered my favorite breakfast; eggs benedict baked purple Peruvian potatoes and a bowl of fruit. I was having breakfast and lunch.
It finally arrived, and I ate with good appetite.

The Daygone started to fill up and the music was great as always.
I was really enjoying myself when I saw a familiar face in the emerging crowd.
It was Elbah!
She was headed my way!

I couldn't believe it. I was so glad to see her. I stood up to greet her and gave her a full body hug.

Elbah the Agnamani was here!

How did she know I would be here?

I knew I would have to wait to see how she explained it.

The moment had finally arrived and we were together again. She sat down across from me and I looked to see if the lights were still in her eyes.

I could see eyes so green that her brown face would just disappear. Her hair was deep auburn and very curly. I was amazed and really attracted to her. Elbah started talking to me right away.

"Vishnu, how are you? I knew you'd be here. This is so serendipitous."

I was just watching her, and did not hear her question. The Relms seeped into my mind, and I flashed on the last time I saw her there. I had not even begun to deal with what had been happening to me since then, or if I wanted to tell her. So I just smiled and waited for her to bring it up, and she did.

"How did you get to the Relms? Who are you, really?"

I started to laugh. I think I was flattered that she had asked who I really was.

She smiled and began to laugh with me. It was funny, and we both were just bathing in this world only we knew.

"Would you like something to eat?" I asked her. I was ready for something stronger than coffee. Elbah said, "Yes! And you can have a drink and talk to me while I eat."

Sounded like a plan to me. Now this was a woman who seemed to be handling herself. She was in the flow. I was really enjoying her company.

We had a lot to talk about, probably enough to last a lifetime. Now that was a thought!

We ordered and Elbah began to tell me openly of how she became the Agnamani.

"I think I knew something about the Relms when I was a kid," she said. I don't think I ever went anywhere, but I remember seeing things at night when everyone was asleep.

I have some unusual memories: being born. I know that sounds impossible, but I do. I remember being in a place and there was nothing there.

I was sitting in a circle with some people wearing long robes. There was an opening in the middle of the circle. We all looked down into it. Where it went was hidden. They said to me it was time to go.

I didn't want to enter the hole. Too late, down I tumbled headfirst. I heard my own voice cry out as I fell through, and seeing the green walls of a room. There was a dark space and I heard something beating. It was so loud. Then I saw a blinding light. There I was, a new baby!

I was upside down.

I remember the first time I saw my mother's face.

I cried.

It was her smell, which finally soothed me. I would never tell my mother that I cried when I saw her face."

At this point in the conversation we both began to laugh.

It was obvious Elbah had a great sense of humor, even though she was speaking of something in her life that was important.
Elbah continued, "Some people still think a newborn baby can't see, but I could.
I remember my mother's hands massaging me. I always felt better.
One day I realized I had hands. I remember moving my hands and thinking to myself that I was inside of something. I remember it being a strange sensation.
At this point Elbah stopped talking and she had a faraway look in her eyes. Then she was back, smiling her wonderful smile and waiting for me to tell some secret.
I had none to tell.
The world had always been my playground.
But I began to tell Elbah something about me.
I said, "When I was two, I thought everyone knew me. Here I was this little kid walking with my mom looking at everyone with a smile on my face. My mom would just watch me amazed. She told me that when I was around six years old, I had a way of calming the other kids.
I was a welcomed sight at any party where the parents brought their children. As soon as I walked in, all the kids would just calm down. I was a kid, never even noticed."
Elbah was smiling as I continued to tell her of my childhood.
"The best story was the story about the bees. My mom told me that she took me to the park every day when I was still a toddler. We always sat on the grass. I remember how soft and green it was.

The honeybees would be foraging on the small flowers that grew in the grass. I was a baby, sitting in the middle of them. Never got stung.

When I was around four years old, I use to suck them up at the end of a straw. Their little legs would be kicking. I thought it was pretty funny. Then I would let them go and they would just fly away. Bees like me", I said.

Now Elbah was laughing.

It was funny. Then she asked me, "Was your mom worried about stings?"

I said, "No, my mother recognized the fact that I had no fear in me. I think she believes children are in tune with nature, and that parents sometimes instill fear instead of wisdom. She thought she had an amazing kid."

Now Elbah and I both started laughing.

This was really good. Elbah was as weird as me. I would never tell her this. I was smiling. My drink came along with her lunch. Everything looked really good and arrived at the perfect moment.

"Saluda," I said as I raised my glass and took a sip. She held up her fork and dug into a smoked salmon and black bean salad. I sat back and relaxed. The music came to the forefront.

My favorite tune was playing, an oldie by the Rolling Stones called "Give Me Shelter". Couldn't get any better.

We spoke about our friends, the weather, and the economy while she ate. I was glad. I needed time to gather my thoughts.

I wasn't sure how much I could tell Elbah.

I knew I could not mention Dreygon. I was sure of one thing, and that was meeting Elbah was no accident. We were meant to be friends, and a lot of this relationship had to do with the Relms.

The waiter came and removed her plate. She ordered a glass of a really good rosé. I admit I was very surprised by her taste in wine. I think I was just surprised she drank wine. For Elbah, it was chilled and strong enough to relax and converse.

The Daygone was now full. Everyone seemed to be enjoying him or herself. Sounds of laughter filled the air and once and a while someone sang along with the tune.

Finally, Elbah asked, "How do you know about the Relms?
It's okay to take your time and answer. I know you can't tell me everything. Some things we can talk about. I would be really happy to share what we can of what we are both experiencing in the Relms.
I'm sure that's part of the reason we have met. Besides, I really need to talk to someone about it. I'm sure you find yourself having to also balance the reality of the Big Ground."

Big Ground? How did she know that term?
I didn't ask, I would ask her later.

She continued, "I know you are wondering how we both can do this. I have no answer. It wasn't anything I planned. It was birthed in the intent of my spiritual self."

Then Elbah began to smile, and the smiled turned into laughter. She was surprised by her own words and the absurdity of having to explain something so deep. It was beautiful, and I realized she was an eloquent speaker.

She was looking more like the woman of my dreams!

Ha, the woman of my dreams?

Now this was even literal, because we had met in the Relms. I was smiling big.

Then I said, "I've had some very unusual conversations recently".

Now she began to howl with laughter. I was shocked. I had been trying to be serious. No, we were not having that conversation, is what she was trying to convey.

Elbah took another road and a sip of her wine. So I sat back and enjoyed the view.

Then she leaned over the table and began to whisper. "Can you imagine the conversations we could have about all you have seen with me?"

"Do you know why you are here to have these conversations?" I asked her.

"Yes, I do", she replied. "I am Agnamani and I have this ability."

I sat back in my seat. I was silent, and I looked at Elbah. I could see she had become a whole being. Her green eyes were intense.

"Do you have a guide?" I asked.

"I do, but I cannot see who or what it is.

It remains hidden."

It became obvious to me that we were having very different experiences as to how we go to the Relms. I had Dreygon, and she was with an unseen guide.

"I have been going to the Relms for a few years now, she continued. You are probably wondering how this all began. I was a student living in Istanbul. I was working on the study of lost languages and ancient scriptures.

The University had given me an apartment in Arnavotkoy, a town along the Bosporus Sea.

The building was at the top of a hill with a view of the Bosporus. This was a beautiful neighborhood with all the houses built on a slope. This area is part of the famous seven hills of Istanbul on which the city was built.

My dwelling was an apartment building with what I would call: unusual architecture. It had a Turkish shield over the marble entrance.

Once inside, a winding marble stairway led up to my flat on the third floor. My apartment was nice, but even when I walked inside; it had a certain vibe about it. It was painted stark white and nicely furnished white furniture. There were glass doors that opened to a deck that was the length of the top floor. I use to watch the huge cargo ships travel up and down the Bosporus. They say it's very deep in the middle.

The living room and dining room had hardwood floors, open and spacious. Marble floors in the kitchen, can you imagine?

The bedroom was off a small hallway. It had a door that opened to a small deck that had a pitched tiled roof. There was another room that had the slope of the roofline at the end of the hallway. This room was a little strange. There was some kind of residue on the far wall when I moved in. I had the repairman paint over it. The bathroom was fairly large and tiled with the pictures of a goddess bathing. There was lots of energy there, not negative, but noticeable."

This was getting interesting so I leaned across the table to listen. Elbah continued her story:

"Someone had written something about a portal on the molding at the entrance to the bedroom. The details of which elude me. I just know that my first night there was really strange. I got ready for bed, climbed in and turned off the light. It felt really weird in there, and I couldn't sleep. I sat up in bed and looked around; at first I thought I was seeing dust or some kind of play on my night vision. Not so.
There in the darkness I saw some odd things floating in mid air. I'm not even going to tell you what I saw. You would surely think me insane.
I thought I might be dreaming. No! It was no dream. I'm brave, but I almost ran out!"

At this point we were both laughing. Elbah had a great sense of humor.

She continued, "It was the same in this room every night, and every night I slept on the couch. I was really scared. The Dean of my school lived across the hall. I certainly could not tell him that my flat was haunted. One night I decided to just deal with it. I got ready for bed and I went into the bedroom. I lay down waiting for whatever might occur.

It was not long before I had my first visitor. I was laying there in the darkness gazing up at the ceiling. I started to fall asleep and then I felt something change in the room. Out of nowhere above my bed, a man with shoulder length black hair stepped through from some place I couldn't see.

He was only half way through to where I was. I could see his dark hair blowing. Half of his face was present and the other half looked ethereal. He looked as though he might be Egyptian descent.

He wore no shirt, but some kind of ancient looking skirt around his waist. He wore a stone bracelet on his left wrist. He glanced down at me, extended his hand and said, 'Come with me, I want to show you something." I wasn't sure if I should but I wasn't afraid of him. I did ask his name. He said he was Cireon. I didn't ask where he was from because I was so taken by his arrival. So began my journey to becoming Agnamani".

Elbah stopped speaking and smiled. Then she said, "There is so much to tell—small doses and it does not include what you already know about me".

I knew she was done talking about herself. She would have seemed insane to me had I not met the Dreygon. It all made sense. How could I tell Elbah that I met my guide resting in the giant Sequoias in the grove of trees behind my garden? It couldn't be any stranger than what she told me.

"Elbah, that's an amazing story." I said. "It's okay. We have plenty of time. It's impossible to tell someone your life the first time we meet. There isn't enough time. I have a guide and I can see him. We have been traveling the Relms for a few years now. The meeting of my guide was definitely the most amazing thing that has ever happened to me in my life, other than meeting you in the Relms. I am still trying to wrap my head around it. It makes me wonder who we really are. I mean this in the most profound sense—our purpose. In the Relms this is not a conversation. This conversation would be considered pointless in a universe of infinite possibility. There is no time to ponder purpose. It is in the being that we become closer to the mind of divine intelligence".

213

Whoa, I couldn't believe I had said that. I now sat watching Elbah's face, her green eyes. The music flowed in. We both paused to check it out. It was amazing how chilled out Elbah is.

Then Harper appeared out of nowhere. "Vishnu, Sky Man, what it be!" He was coming toward our table with a big smile on his face.

We all laughed. Harper is one funny dude. Harper has New York humor. He grew up doing the "dozens". The dozens is a kind of quick wit humor, not always flattering, but really funny.

"This must be the Sky Lady!" Harper was on a roll. Elbah smiled and introduced herself. Harper grinned and bowed as he took Elbah's hand and kissed it. It was really cool. She loved it.

Harper said, "Vishnu, Sky Man! This is the best day in many a day, Dude! "The Daygone is 'jamming' with women and all the ladies are from other planets!"

We started to laugh again. Harper had all the facial gestures to go with what he said. Harper was having fun. He continued his New York humor and said, "They are all smiling and wearing scents that blind the third eye!"

At this point even the people at the next table were laughing. I wondered where he got his sense of humor.

"Sky Man, I just met the woman! I was sitting over there under the tree on the famous red bench waiting for a drink. This tall beautiful woman wearing some outrageous scent sat down next to me. My head snapped around to look at her. It was hilarious. I asked her name. She said, "One Who Remembers". So I asked her if this was long for instant recall. And she said, "No, it's short for Tanudahsatnahani". And then she started to laugh. She tried to beat me at my own game!"

"Harper, she got you, Dude!" I said. We were all rolling with laughter.

Harper said, "I know that's not her name. Can't be! She was trying to read me like a cheap novel and I loved it". Harper was still laughing. "Got to go, got to go!"

Harper had exiting music. He kissed Elbah's hand and backed into the crowd and was gone.

We were still in Harpers aftermath.

"I like him, Elbah said. He knows more than he lets anyone know. He's a good friend to you."

"Yeah, Harper's a childhood friend", was my reply. "We go way back. It's kind of cool, having a friend who has known you for a long time. Harper's special. It wouldn't surprise me if he knew about the Relms."

Elbah just looked at me.

Then I said, "Elbah, I think we are traveling the Relms for very different reasons. I think there are many experiences you can have in infinite possibility. You are Agnamani and I am visiting Relms that boggle the imagination. Yet our Relms crossed and we met there before we met here."

"How else should we have met?" Elbah said with a smile.

Good answer, I thought. The waiter came and I ordered another round of drinks. The conversation was moving at just the right pace and I felt comfortable. We approached each subject with patience and openness. There was so much to understand.

215

"Vishnu, I know it's hard to understand the Relms if you look at it from here. When you go there everything just makes sense. It's like being someone you're just meeting for the first time. I think it's better if we don't try to explain what we do. Can you explain it?"

"No, I can't, I said. I didn't think I was looking for an explanation as much as wanting to discuss the scientific aspects of it. The guide has nothing to do with science. We change molecular structure to travel the Relms. By traveling in to get out, we become something different."

As I was saying this I had a flash of Ramudah. I could see the Light Beings overcoming the other life forms and entering them through their heads. There must be a connection. Maybe we were now doing what we remember. Perhaps we were experiencing the very old knowledge buried eons ago and Ramudah was the Relms of its beginning. I didn't tell Elbah what I was thinking. It would have taken all night to explain what I was doing on Ramudah.

"I wondered about that also, Vishnu, Elbah said. I leave in exactly the same way as you do. I travel in to get out. It is in this state that the change occurs and we are able to travel the Relms. Perhaps we have discovered something that will not have scientific proof. Maybe here is where the *inner map* has its greatest meaning. Maybe we really are Relms Travelers."

I just sat listening and thinking. What Elbah was saying was so true. Besides, who could we tell? I never imagined telling anyone before now. No need. I wasn't even sure how or why this became part of my life and reality. It just did, and I am eternally grateful. Yes, maybe we are Relms Travelers and are the first to know about each other.

This was interesting and seemed to have a natural timing to it.

Our time together at the Daygone went by quickly. We hadn't even begun to tell each other what we did for a living on the Big Ground. I wanted to ask Elbah about all the young that I saw her carry under her cloak. I thought better of it and decided to keep that conversation for another time.

I'm sure Elbah saw the flash across my face. She eyed me with a smile.

It was nearing time to go.

This had been a big surprise.

We exchanged numbers and info. Now we were friends. This was going to be good. Elbah agreed. She was up and hugging me goodbye. I must have looked really happy, because she gave me a kiss on my cheek and told me, "Soon".

We both walked out of the Daygone and stood there for a minute just checking out the end of a really great day, the sunsets here are beautiful. I waved as Elbah headed down the street. She turned and waved and laughed. She did this several times. I thought, Wow! She's really lost it. Then I remembered who she was and realized this was what I liked about her—her openness.

The wind came up. I turned and walked quickly in the other direction. I turned the corner and walked down the block. It had already been a long week and I was ready for the big chill. I flagged a cab and I was glad to arrive home. I thought about Dreygon as I entered my house.

It's amazing how quickly I'm back thinking about the Relms. I answered some emails and texted a few friends. Hollered at Harper. He texted back saying he was still with Tanudahsatnahani, and that was her real name! I was rolling with laughter. This was incredible. Harper's text said he was having a great time. I realized it had been that kind of day for both of us. Today was a day I would never forget.

I still had some laundry to do and some bills to take care of first, so I sat down and finished the mundane part of life.

It was late evening before I knew it. The day seemed really long. I had done a lot in one day. The most amazing was running into Elbah at the Daygone.

I was hungry again, so I called out for delivery. I was in chill mode. Dinner arrived in good time and I was ready. I had ordered Indian food and it smelled really good. I ate dinner on the deck overlooking the garden. The night air was warm and the moonless sky beautiful. It was definitely a starry night. I finished dinner, washed the dishes, and headed for my bedroom on the second floor.

I brushed my teeth and thought about having seen Elbah at the Daygone. This was really cool. I got undressed and headed for the bed. I was in and asleep before I knew it.

Morning came slowly. I had to go into my office. The clock seemed to crawl. What was happening? The norm would be for the morning to be on speed. Not this morning! It was moving at a crawl. I felt so relaxed! I could get use to this really quickly. I wondered if anyone else was having a morning like mine. I even got to the office early.

218

Everything was in the flow, even though I was really busy. The day went by slowly, but before I knew it, it was time to go! I was home again. How long could this last? Not the thought to have, just enjoy the moments.

I changed my clothes and headed for my garden. Everything was in bloom.
My thoughts went to Dreygon. I was talking to myself. Getting my mind ready. I was trying to decide if I should tell Dreygon that I saw Elbah on the Big Ground. That thought did not fit the situation. He helped me find her the second time in the Relms. I bet he already knows. I think Dreygon wanted me to know Elbah.
Perhaps he thinks it's important to have a close friend, especially if you travel the Relms.
Ah yes, some thoughts on Elbah. She's really beautiful: her very green eyes and her brown skin and that insane auburn hair! She was amazing. I think if I had met Elbah without knowing about the Relms, I would still sense something really special about her. Our meeting was the most unusual meeting two people could ever have. It bordered on bizarre. I didn't want to over-think this. Flow, just stay in the flow.

I decided to eat the leftovers from the previous night. It was Indian food and better than I thought it would be. I finished some home projects and listened to some great music. I stood on my deck at one point just staring at the giant Sequoias beyond my garden. It's still hard to believe all that has happened since I first saw Dreygon resting in the tops of the trees. I was resolute.

It had been a while since I had seen him, and I just knew I would again really soon.

It got late and I was ready to go to bed. Sleep was slow to come, but finally it did.

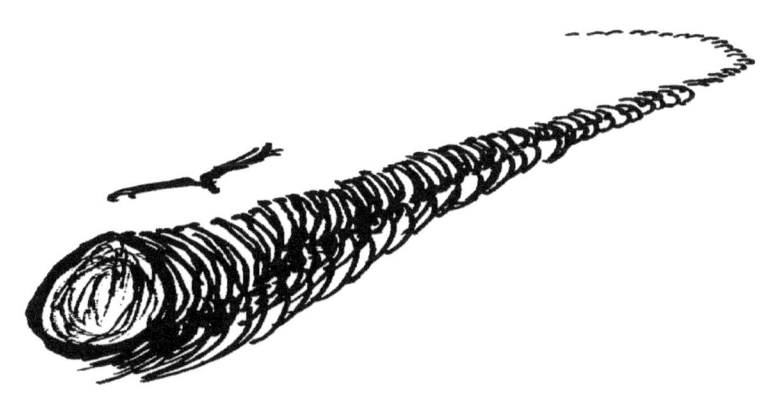

FLIGHT IN THE STELLER WINDS

I never know how Dreygon will arrive. Maybe it's the shifting of the Relms on his way to the Big Ground. But the Big Ground wasn't on the map. I still found this hard to believe and humorous, but I learned to accept the fact that I had become aware of different physical physics. I was part of this new knowledge and so was Elbah. She was my validation of this truth and I was hers. Knowing this put me at peace.

I had been asleep for a few hours before Dreygon arrived. At times, he arrives in a dream. He is always something to behold. This time I saw myself reaching out to touch him and I woke up. I looked around the room. It was so dark that I thought I was somewhere else. I wasn't, it was just dark. Then it became unusually quiet. I waited. I felt a breeze. I could not tell its origin for it did not come from the open window. My blanket moved up and I closed my eyes. I wasn't sure I wanted to see, what

221

might be present. I felt pressure in the back of my head.

When I opened my eyes I was sitting on top my blanket.

I heard Dreygon's voice. "Ahh Human, you are doing well."

I looked toward the windows. I could see the shadow of giant wings and two intense yellow eyes piercing the darkness of the night.

There was no moon and the stars were so bright I didn't recognize this sky. I watched as an outline of light become Dreygon's smile. His huge head became visible just outside my windows. I'm always unnerved.

I said, "Pray tell me of your origins?" for this was our greeting.

I took a moment to gather my thoughts. Then I got out of my bed and walked over to the windows, which were already open. Without hesitation, I climbed out of my windows and onto Dreygon's shoulder. I could see the giant Sequoias. They looked like dark giant sentinels standing watch beyond my garden. Now I looked to see where I was. I was looking at my windows from outside. Very strange perception and I thought I saw someone sleeping in my bed. I did not ask myself how. Dreygon was here and I was used to seeing the unusual. I was ready to travel the Relms. I closed my eyes.

I began to feel the sensations in my head. I was moving inward very fast. I felt the big fall and the pressure so great I yelled. Then came the tearing of layers of flesh, which felt like every molecule of me. I thought I would go insane. I saw a very bright light and heard a loud clap. I opened my eyes and we were above the planet. It wasn't getting easier to go through these physical changes. There was no other way to travel the Relms.

We stayed motionless looking at this incredible view. Gaia was really green now, and I marveled at how different the planet appears from time to time. Then Dreygon turned and we headed out into the dark light of the deep space behind us.

We were flying through the blackness swift and smooth. I always have the sensation that I am inside of something and I will never know what it is. There were millions of blinking lights, and I had no sense of direction. Dreygon was master here. We began to pick up speed and I could hear Dreygon's voice in my head. He said, "There is something to know about how I travel in the Relms. We are here to catch the Stellar Winds."

This was going to be an experience. I had often wondered how he was able to travel across the vast blackness of the dark light. Dreygon stopped moving. I saw his incredible yellow eyes searching the deep space in front of us. A small very bright blue light appeared in the distance. I think this was a marker. As soon as it opened to a horizon, Dreygon move in an arc just under light speed. I was holding on to his mane as tight as I could. The sensation is like none I have ever known. I think maybe I turn to light, and that I make a sound. I'm guessing because it's impossible for me to tell the speed of which we travel. In other words, it's so fast I can't remember.

Suddenly there was a dimensional change and I was unnerved because I could feel it.

It was like a wave, a ripple in space that I could feel physically. It passed over us unseen.

Dreygon stopped moving. We were in deep space. I could feel the intensity of the dark light here. It felt heavy and consuming. Maybe this is just a perception caused by the blackness of deep space. A small golden light could now be seen in the distance.

It seemed to be moving toward us at an incredible speed. It was moving fast and it was growing in size and intensity.

I could hear Dreygon's voice in my head. He said, "Human, you will ride inside your first Stellar Wind. This wind is like no wind known on the Big Ground."

What I had perceived as light was actually the approaching Stellar Wind.

It seemed to slow down, as it got closer. Dreygon moved above it! It reminded me of stardust. It was light tan in color and filled with particles that sparkled like dust. It was moving below us, very slowly. Dreygon floated down and began to fly inside the Stellar Wind. His huge iridescent wings were open, and his unworldly yellow eyes pierced the atmosphere of stardust. This was atmosphere that could not be felt physically. I wasn't very physical, so I must have been sensing all of this with something else. This was my first journey inside the Stellar Winds.

Dreygon continued to fly into the wind and it increased in speed and in density. The atmosphere of the wind became filled with stardust particles. The further we flew into the wind the more intense the stardust became.

I looked at Dreygon's face from where I sat on his shoulder. He glowed and the stardust particles clung to his body and he seemed to increase in size. I saw the eyes of the Twelve move across his flanks. They became visible through the dust of the Stellar Wind.

I was having an unexpected reaction. I am stardust, so it had the unanticipated effect on me.

How does the wind see? I asked this question as I observed myself disappearing in the Stellar Wind. The wind blew harder, but what does this mean when there is no flesh to detect movement? But I could see everything.

Something was happening and I could not distinguish myself from the stardust of the Stellar Wind. I looked at my arms and I could not see them. They had merged with the dust of the wind. I felt my face leave, but my eyes became even more focused. The speed was terrifying. I blew where the Stellar Wind blows. I began to see what the wind sees. Here the Stellar Wind blew far into the Relms and was a constant even as the Relms shifted.

It blew through distant Relms but not everywhere. I saw the far reaches of the galaxy. Here only a few particles of stardust looked to see what was beyond where stardust finally came to an end. The vastness was incredible.

I turned to look at Dreygon because this reality was overwhelming. My stardust began to move toward me immediately.

I watched as my arms returned from the dust of the Stellar Wind. I could almost feel the return of my face. It was an incredible rush and I felt my hand hold on tighter to Dreygon's mane.

Dreygon knew this wind. The whiskers on his face were back and he was flying through the Stellar Wind without resistance. He was engulfed and inside. I looked ahead to see where we were, but nothing could be seen.

Dreygon began to move up and out of the stellar dust cloud. It continued moving below us as though it had a life of its own and knew where to go. The Stellar Wind had the appearance of a golden snake moving through utter blackness. I was shaken.

The eyes of the Twelve moved across Dreygon's flanks and peered out. He was gazing into the dark light in front of us. We were motionless. I could hear Dreygon's voice in my head. He said, "I am waiting for the next Stellar Wind, this time you will ride. I will take you to Zenzibanouke.

The Relms of Zenzibanouke can only be reached by way of the Stellar Winds."

We were wind hopping. How cool was this! I sat eagerly on Dreygon's shoulder. We waited for the golden glow to appear that would be the Stellar Wind to Zenzibanouke.

"What is Zenzibanouke?" I asked Dreygon.

"Zenzibanouke is the Relms in which its inhabitants live in duality. You will be surprised by what you see," replied Dreygon.

This was the first time Dreygon had ever prefaced where we were going. Perhaps this was going to be a real challenge to my reality and Dreygon wanted me to be aware.

The golden glow we were waiting for appeared now in the distance. It was moving towards us fast. This was the Stellar Wind. As it approached I realized how wide it was. It looked like a dust storm on the Big Ground. It was incredible to see. It was coming from another part of the Relms. It was moving like a golden serpent. This time it looked as though it was full of other Travelers!

The Stellar Wind seemed to slow down, as it got closer. There were no Travelers in the front.

The wind's approach reminded me of a gathering storm on the Big Ground, slow to arrive and hell later. The tail of the Stellar Wind extended deep into space, for this is where we were.

The color of the wind was changing to a dark-tan. Dreygon positioned himself above the approaching wind. On the Big Ground you feel the wind, no skin, no wind. Here in the Relms you can only see it coming. Now Dreygon and I were going to catch a ride, and with some other Travelers!

Riding the Stellar Winds was a mode of travel in the Relms. This was new, and in the Relms of possibility things infinitely occur. The Stellar Wind increased its speed, and was moving below us fast. Now it was time for Dreygon and me to merge into the wind. It was amazing. Down he went and this time we were flying with the wind. Dreygon entered in a glide. We were immediately in the speed of the Stellar Wind.

At first I couldn't see anything. I think I must have closed my eyes.

When my vision cleared, we were inside and moving fast. Dreygon was in his element. His face changed. Everything on his face moved back. It was a face meant for the Stellar Wind.

His unworldly yellow eyes burned through the golden stardust of the wind. Dreygon's gigantic wings look as though they were on fire. I held on tight. I was having a cosmic rush, but my mind was clear. I had become accustomed to the unusual. I was ready for this.

I peered deep into the Stellar Wind as we flew. It was hard to see anything. The golden stardust clouded my vision and I couldn't see The Travelers. I felt the Stellar Wind shift, and then they came into view. They seemed larger than usual and bore no resemblance of any Humans I have ever seen. I saw no outline that could be Human. They were riding on neon discs!

I held on tighter to Dreygon. I looked again and this time I saw faces, all manner of faces that seem to blend into the wind. I felt the Stellar Wind shift and all the faces disappeared, only to reappear. This time one of the Travelers turned his face in our direction. Dreygon took no notice.
I had the feeling that he knew them.

The Traveler was not of stardust, nor did the Traveler resemble the Arahnubians. He had no discernable features. His essence was gaseous, his form slightly human and he bore a triangle in the middle of his brow. His eyes were white and seemed to wrap around the side of his face. Through the wind I could see that he road on an elongated disc that looked like neon. Then I noticed his gaseous essence was blue.

The Traveler was incredible to behold. His size alone was awe-inspiring. The Stellar Wind blew through the blue gaseous form of the Traveler. He seemed to extend into the Stellar Wind. He suddenly turned his head and stared at me. I felt his white eyes reach into my very soul.

The Traveler smiled through his blue gaseous form and the wind shifted. He seemed to move further into the wind, and could no longer be seen by me.

The Stellar Wind shifted again, and this time the Traveler came closer.

I looked at his face, which wasn't really there. His eyes glowed in a strip around his head and his blue color was like nothing I could have imagined.

The triangle on his brow was a metallic color. I looked inside the triangle and it shimmered. I looked at him with an expression of amazement. I think he knew for the wind shifted again and he was close enough to touch. The Traveler took one more penetrating look at me. I stared and said nothing. Then I smiled and the Traveler began to move away and disappeared into the Stellar Wind.

There were others, but none were near. The size of the Stellar Wind across was phenomenal. I could barely see the Travelers riding inside. Again I peered through the dust of the Stellar Wind. Another face appeared but it was far into the moving wind.

Then the Stellar Wind shifted and a Traveler came near and into view. The Traveler was riding on a neon disc! This Traveler also bore the triangle in the middle of the brow and was of the same blue gaseous essence.
The outline of the triangle in the Traveler's head glowed. I stared and I could barely see eyes that seemed to be closed on a gaseous face.
The blue gaseous form floated back into the golden stardust of the Stellar Wind.

Only the light from the triangle in the brow could be seen. Then I noticed something very strange.

There was something inside the triangle on the Travelers forehead. It seemed to be looking at me from inside the triangle. The blue gaseous face became more visible and I realized it looked female. The features looked almost human.

The triangle glowed brighter and the Traveler came closer to me. Again, Dreygon took no notice. I felt the triangle light up the brow on my forehead and burn its way in.

Then I heard the Traveler say, "Welcome to the Relms. I am the Blue Being you saw with the Navigator. I am called by no name. I am what you would call 'Symbol." You will know me by this symbol in the Relms".

I felt the triangle glowing on my brow, but I didn't try to touch it. I wanted to see her face, so I looked with greater intent. I could see a copper colored face in the triangle. It was close to Human. The face within the triangle bore a triangle on the forehead with a copper face inside. This face bore a triangle on the forehead with a face inside; and so on until nothing more could be seen. The Stellar Wind shifted.

The blue Traveler that was Symbol moved away and was gone!

I could still feel the triangle on my brow and Dreygon had begun to rise above the Stellar Wind. We merged out into the blackness that still held starlight. We had arrived at our destination in the Relms. We became motionless. I could see the Stellar Wind below us moving fast. It now had the appearance of a golden serpent moving through the dark light of deep space.

The last of the Travelers could still be seen. Their blue gaseous forms blended with the stardust of the Stellar Wind. I could just make out the neon discs they rode, and then the gold light at the end of the wind as it disappeared from sight. I could no longer feel the triangle on my brow. I was now with Dreygon motionless in the blackness of the dark light. Dreygon no longer had his face for the wind and I relaxed my grip on his mane. I heard his voice in my head.

Dreygon said, "Ahh, you have had your first journeys with the Stellar Winds, Human. You have also been given a Symbol for traveling the Relms so that you will remember this journey and its *inner map*."

It takes time for me to comprehend the events that occur while traveling the Relms with Dreygon. Nothing slows down for me to contemplate. Every experience is in the moment and of the present.

My reality expands because I am a participant. I am not in control of this. I'm still not sure I understand the *inner map*. But maybe I'm being shown how to use it. Perhaps I already know, but have somehow forgotten, and now I am on a journey to remember.

ZENZIBANOUKE

Dreygon and I waited in the dark light for the appearance of the Relms to Zenzibanouke.

My thoughts were on the Stellar Winds. We were far from the Big Ground now. It was impossible to calculate the distance we had traveled by means of these winds.

I felt like I was on the other side of the Universe. Where is here?

An incredible violet light appeared in the distant blackness of deep space. It glowed with almost violent intensity.

I watched Dreygon's unworldly yellow eyes focus on the violet light.

The light flashed open to a thin horizon. Against the blackness of the dark light it seemed unapproachable. Dreygon began to fly toward its direction.

I could hear his voice in my head. He told me, "Human, the violet light is the Relms of Zenzibanouke.

It is here you will see another possibility of the duality in your existence."

Again, I'm never sure the meaning of Dreygon's parables.

The darkness of deep space with its blinking stars felt unnatural to me. I had only imagined this view from the safety of the Big Ground. The violet horizon increased in size as we neared. It appeared to be a violet crack that was larger than anything I could know. It extended into the darkness in both directions, to my left and to my right. This is my only means of calculating direction in the dark light.

We entered the violet crack.

Zenzibanouke appeared out of nowhere.

My head reeled, and I held on tightly to Dreygon.

There it was, directly in front of us! This was not a world.

Zenzibanouke was strange. It was a place. It was floating as if on a plate in the middle of twilight. It appeared to be a place of outlines.

I could see violet light that seemed to be burning everything into existence. Dreygon's huge iridescent wings were spread and we glided toward Zenzibanouke.

This time Dreygon called me by my name.

He said, "Vishnu, you have seen many things. What has begun will not end, for how can you understand end if you are not present? Zenzibanouke has a meaning. The meaning is; I am two becoming one."

Was this another of Dreygon's riddles, or was he preparing me for what I was about to see?

We were close enough now for me to see Zenzibanouke, but I saw no inhabitants.

I saw a place that brought confusion to my visual understanding of things. It was true.

Everything on Zenzibanouke became visible because of a burning violet outline. I stared in disbelief.

We were moving across Zenzibanouke and I could see no end.

It was larger than I could imagine and beyond the possibility of existence.

I was entering a place that was in a state of twilight.

I alluded to this because it appeared to be a place where the light was in a perpetual state of beginning.

The dark sky above Zenzibanouke was streaked with a white hue. Below me was nothing but the burning violet outline of plant life.

There seemed to be two of everything! The plants continuously burned their way into visibility by means of this violet light.
All of them were at different stages of two becoming one.

Violet was not the only color. I could see green outlines deep inside the foliage.

I watched, as the green outlines became a color that bled into the plants making them completely visible.

Then it bled out and the plants became just the violet outline of themselves.

Some plants bled the green color into each other, and then would bleed out to the violet outline.

Then I noticed the plants were different sizes of the very same plant! They appeared to be just the tops of long slender foliage.

I could hear Dreygon's voice in my head.

He said, "We are in the Twilight Relms of Zenzibenouke". Dreygon then glided down and into the foliage. He flew through foliage that was just above our heads. The foliage brushed against us and fluttered like plants on the Big Ground.

The plants began to bleed in green from their violet outline. I was astonished.

We stopped suddenly and were motionless inside the now green plant life.

Dreygon continued to speak saying, "You can climb down now but will not be able to touch the surface. This is better for you since you are not of this existence, but a visitor.

Your journey to become one is hidden in Zenzibanouke."

Dreygon lowered his head and I climbed down but remained suspended inside the plant life. Below me the tall plants were so close together, no surface could be seen.

I stood close to him and I was tempted to touch the unusual plants. I knew no other way of experiencing their texture.

I decided not to touch. We waited and soon the inhabitants of Zenzibanouke came.

The green foliage began to move as though there was wind.

At first I was not sure what I was seeing. Once again I find my Human mind unable to comprehend the visual.

Inside the green foliage I could see the beginning of a violet outline. Something was burning its way into visibility.

It glowed the outline of an inhabitant who resembled a human and male. There seemed to be two.

They seem to share most of their body.

He wore no attire, but was not naked in the human sense. I was visually shaken. Dreygon was silent as this first inhabitant approached us.

The inhabitant was coming through the bleeding plant life, which continued to move as though there was a wind.

There is no wind on Zenzibanouke. Somehow those concepts from the Big Ground did not apply here.

I saw no separation in his form. The violet glow outlined the two making them one.

The only obvious separation was the head. Both heads were visible having rounded features at the top and a slightly longish shape to the heads. I saw no ears, only faint outlines of what might be faces.

I wondered if the violet color would change. It did not change. Both heads were visible, one behind the other. The inhabitant was looking in my direction and began his approach through the green plant life. He seemed to move in utter harmony with his form. Two walked as one. This was unnerving.

"Zenzibanouke!" the inhabitant said. I bowed my head and said Zenzibanouke; I am Vishnu, for I assumed this was their greeting.

I could see his faces now. The violet outline glowed bright.

Both heads had faint outlines of what would be facial features. A very faint outline made both sets of eyes and both mouths visible.

There seem to be on both heads a curvature where a nose could be, but on neither head was it evident.

He was colorless.

Both heads spoke. "I am Casuke," the inhabitant said. "I have almost completed my understanding of two becoming one.

We are all at different stages here. You may see some things of which you are not accustomed.

Here on Zenzibanouke we have no memory of being one.

It is as though it is has always been as you see."

Casuke made no mention of Dreygon. When I turned my head to look for him, no outline could be seen. Dreygon was hidden inside the now green foliage. I was spooked when I saw that his intense yellow eyes were closed. Maybe Casuke did not notice because Dreygon is twelve being one.

Casuke continued to tell me about Zenzibanouke.

"I think it's better if you do not try to move around too much on Zenzibanouke."

I could see the outline line of a smile on Casuke colorless faces.

He spoke to me as though he had been expecting me.

Perhaps anyone who arrives on Zenzibanouke is expected. This is not a place you just visit.

Casuke explained, "If you are not an Inhabitant, a trip across the Zenzibanouke country side could be dangerous. The color of the plant life always bleeds in and out of existence. Duality is at home here.

What is here will stay with you, so you must experience only that which you can understand."

The visual in the twilight Relms of Zenzibanouke is like seeing a world burn its way into existence.

It was very possible that I could just get lost here because it seemed dark to me and the plant life was so unnatural. This was my first experience in a world of such obvious duality.

The bleeding of the plant life was difficult to comprehend. How do plants bleed in and out of existence?

I decided to stay objective.

Casuke was still telling me about Zenzibanouke when the plant life began to bleed out of its green color.

I watched as the whole environment changed to nothing but a violet outline.

I was silent and looked with no understanding of this experience. Twilight seemed to increase its hold on Zenzibanouke and there was an eerie stillness in this semi-lit environment. Then the plant life began to bleed in the color green once again.

The plants began to move as though there was wind.

I watched and waited. Inside the now green foliage I could see the beginning of a violet outline.

I saw the violet outline burn the inhabitant into visibility.

His heads were long and round at the top, the same as Casuke. But he was different in appearance.

The inhabitant was two in duplicate moving in complete unison as one as he began to move through the foliage. They wore no attire and were both colorless. The facial features could barely be seen. But only the feet were joined. The inhabitant began to move quickly through the foliage and approached us with the same greeting: "Zenzibanouke!" I was staring because I was trying to register this experience.

I was out of my reality.

"Zenzibanouke!" I replied.

Casuke greeted the newcomer in the same manner, "Zenzibanouke!"

The two joined at the foot spoke together. This inhabitant immediately introduced himself.

He said, "I am Suke and I am at the beginning of understanding two becoming one. Only my feet are in agreement of where I will go. Where I was before I began, I realize only now that I am at the beginning."

I did not understand.

Suke was looking at me and I could see the two. His facial features were almost nonexistent on both parts of him. But I could feel the eyes of both watching me.

It was so strange and my sense of things was being challenged.

239

The two that was Suke said nothing more. He turned and moved past us and entered the green foliage behind me.

I turned to look at Casuke. He was looking at me with both heads.

He said, "Vishnu my friend, there are many parts to any possibility before it becomes what you know as reality".

I saw his colorless faces smile inside the violet outline of both heads. I had to get use to his appearance.

The plant life in front of us began to bleed out of the green color. I stood with Casuke and watched as this same process took place again. I felt unsure of myself but I remained attentive, as the plant life became the violet outlines of itself. The intensity of twilight returned along with the eerie stillness. Then without warning the plant life began to move as though there was wind on Zenzibanouke. The plant life began to bleed in green. The next inhabitant was burning his way into visibility by means of the violet glow.

The eerie color of twilight lent an atmosphere to make one's blood run cold. I could see two and they were joined from the feet to the knees.

The inhabitant looked male and his colorless features were more obvious. He wore an expression of recognition on both faces. I could not imagine why. He walked in complete unison with himself towards us through the green foliage. His violet outline became prominent in this twilight.

As he neared us he was visually both eerie and beautiful. I shuddered.

He was greeting us while he approached, but he stood directly in front of me. I stared at him for a moment.

Both parts of him looked exactly the same. I stared at where they were joined together, the place where you could see only one.

He said, "My name is Eusuke. He did not wait for me to introduce myself.

"My feet agree where to go and my knees now follow the direction of my soul. I am not aware of my beginning only of my new destination, which is always the present."

I was surprised by his words. I could see both of his faces watching my expression.

I stood staring at him not sure of what to say. He leaned forward and looked at me with both his heads.

I could see the outline of the two and I felt the intensity of one. I was shaken! He turned and moved quickly away and entered the plant life behind where Casuke and I stood.

I watched the two that was Eusuke joined only to the knee disappear into the bleeding plant life.

The plants covered any trace of him and were now bleeding out of the color of green to the burning violet outline. They move ever so slightly.

I turned now to see what might be approaching from the plant life in front of us.

The twilight atmosphere seemed to increase its intensity as part of the process for the return of the green color to the foliage. I waited.

Now the plants began to move as though there was wind. They bled in the green color, in the dimly lit twilight of Zenzibanouke. I watched.

I could see just the beginning of the intense violet outline as another inhabitant burned into visibility inside the foliage.

This time the inhabitant in the plant life looked female. She wore no attire but was not naked and the shape of her form was different than the male inhabitants.

I could see the violet outline joining the two perfectly. She was joined only to the hips. She parted the plant life and walked towards us. She said nothing at first. Casuke greeted her, "Zenzibanouke!"

Her attention was on me. Her long heads were round on the top and both faces were colorless. I could see vague outlines of her features, but the outlines of her eyes were prominent.

I could see her staring at me from two heads, but I could not see her facial expression. Then she said, "My feet agree where to go. I am following the direction of my soul and I understand the possibility of two that make one. I have no memory of my beginning, only my destination."

She did not take her eyes off me and at times both faces were hard to see. She made no mention of her name like the others.

I felt this was intentional. Then she said, "You are the one becoming two. I am the two that become one."

I was shocked by her words, and I said nothing.

I could see the two looking at me. She did not leave immediately, but stood in front of me as though she was waiting for my reply.

242

I had none. I was adjusting to the fact that she was female. I was still having a problem with the reality of her physical form.

I looked for expressions on her two faces, but there were none. I could see her eyes on both heads staring at me.

Suddenly she said, "Zenzibanouke" and moved past me into the foliage behind us. The plant life bled out the green color to the violet outline as she disappeared from view.

What was happening was a lot to digest.

I looked up into the semi darkness of a twilight sky. I felt uneasy. I gathered myself together and looked for Dreygon in the foliage. I could see him hidden in a resting position and his unworldly yellow eyes were closed. I was still spooked but reassured. I saw no sign of the Twelve on his flanks.

Casuke and I waited inside the plant life for a while before the next inhabitant arrived. He said nothing as he kept watch on the foliage in front of us. I had no questions that would be pertinent.

The plant life in front of us began to wave as if a gust of wind had arrived, and then bled in the green color.

Deep inside the foliage I could see the intense violet outline as it burned another inhabitant into existence.

He was male, colorless and without attire. Only the intense violet outline that gave him form was present. I could not imagine where he was coming from or where he had been.

I wanted to ask him, but I knew I was not ready for an answer that was only relevant in the Relms.

243

He parted the foliage as he approached us.

He looked almost human in his state of two becoming one. His physical form was similar to Casuke.

Both his heads were round but were separated, one behind the other. His facial features were very visible on both heads. He bore no obvious expression. He moved through the foliage in my direction and stood in front of me on his arrival. I could see both faces, one behind the other. Who might he be?

The faces spoke together as one face. "Zenzibanouke! I am Tasu. He then began to tell me something incredible. He said, "My feet have finally agreed where to go. My soul knows the way I should travel. Now I understand the two who make one. My heart knows my will and compassion. My hands and my arms have the power of truth. I speak of love and now I wait to understand."

Tazu did not leave immediately, but stood watching for my expression. I showed one of revelation. I could feel his presence at my core. Tazu turned now to Casuke. I stared at them both.

I tried not to become over whelmed by their appearances. It would have been easy to experience trepidation. I think they both felt my fear for suddenly all four heads looked in my direction.

There was a long moment of silence. Tasu suddenly turned to look at the plant life behind me. Then without another word he walked around me, and into the foliage. I turned to watch him disappear and leave no trace.

My head filled was filled with confusion.

The inhabitants of Zenzibanouke did not seem to be aware of the strangeness of their forms.

They were all at different stages of the same reality. They all shared the same journey of two becoming one, but each were having a completely different experience based on their awareness. Perhaps by saying "Zenzibanouke" the inhabitants embraced the potential of his or her physical oneness.

Maybe they were all saying: I am like this because I am on my way to greater understanding through the wholeness of myself.

I know at times I have felt my own feet wanting to go where my heart did not. Perhaps this is "Zenzibanouke".

Maybe the inhabitants were the physical manifestation of what it is to be human.

I could feel the Relms suddenly shift. It was like feeling the rotation of a cosmic plate. My uneasiness returned with a vengeance.

Now deep inside the bleeding plant life, I could see the appearance of the violet outlines of thousands of inhabitants as they began to burn their way into visibility.

There were so many violet outlines burning through the twilight of Zenzibenouke into existence, that twilight became another color.

It looked as though they all were arriving from a place I would never see. The inhabitants in the plant life of Zenzibanouke were all at different stages of two becoming one.

They all began moving through the plant life and at first they took no notice of Casuke or me. I saw no children. I did not ask why, but I wondered where were these inhabitants of Zenzibanouke going?

They all just disappeared into the foliage behind me, but not before looking directly at me. I tried to read expressions, but couldn't. The physical appearance of so many was almost frightening. The plant life became very green and rustled as each vanished. I watched with disbelief.

Casuke turned to look at me with both heads. He said, "Vishnu, you have been seeing with the absence of understanding".

Just then, the plant life stopped moving. I saw no more inhabitants burning their way into existence inside the foliage in front of where we stood.

I turned to look at the foliage behind us where the inhabitants of Zenzibanouke had disappeared.

Everyone was gone and the plant life bled out its green color to the intense violet outline.

Twilight returned with all its intensity and everything seemed to fall silent. It seemed dark here again and the intense violet outline of the plants made Zenzibanouke a frightening place. Casuke continued looking into the foliage in front of us.

He said nothing more and we waited.

Soon the plants began to bleed in the green color and they fluttered as though a breeze was passing through them. I felt nothing and my apprehension returned.

I waited and watched with Casuke. Then, deep within the now green foliage I could see an intense violet outline appearing and it burned one solo human looking inhabitant into existence. The features looked female and I saw no separation in her form. Her entire body was colorless and she wore no attire.

Casuke seemed to be surprised. She parted the plant life and approached us. Before he could say "Zenzibanouke", she introduced herself.

She said, "I am Enuvah, Zenzi".

I saw no other violet outline burning into existence in the plant life behind her. I stared without saying anything. It was Casuke who spoke first.

"Zenzi, Enuvah!" he said.

Her head was round and perfectly formed. She was colorless but she had eyes that were very pronounced.

I could see their outline, and some of her features. She had a face that was like film.

The glow of her violet outline was intense.

Enuvah looked directly at me and she bore no signs of separation.

Space existed behind the features of her face.

I stared. I have never seen a face like hers. The spaces behind her features seem to extend to some kind of spatial eternity that extended beyond what I could understand.

I saw her face smile. I was overwhelmed and I felt my heart beating.

She emitted something that made me become aware of myself here, and that I slept on the Big Ground.

"Would you like to come with me?"

She asked with a mouth that had only an outline.

I stared. She came closer so I could feel her energy.

"Yes", I answered.

She continued, "As I have said, I am Enuvah, Zenzi. I will show you Zenzibanouke for you cannot possible see what it truly is from where you are."

I turned to look into the foliage on the side of me. I could see Dreygon.

His eyes were still closed and he remained hidden inside. The bleeding plant life was moving again as though there was wind. It still had its green color. I could finally understand its beauty.

"Vishnu my friend", it was Casuke speaking. He was looking at me now with both faces.

He said, "Go with Enuvah. She will show you Zenzibenouke. There are many possibilities that can arrive, to make what is infinitely possible".

He looked at me with both heads for what seemed like an eternity. I saw his faces smile as he turned and began to walk into the green foliage.

I watched his intense violet outline and both heads disappear into the bleeding plant life behind me.

Enuvah's hand that glowed violet reached for mine. Before I could respond in fear, I felt the pressure of a hand and we began to move down through the foliage.

We had been at the top of the plant life all this time!

I could see the violet outline of Enuvah's other hand as she parted the bleeding plants as we continued our descent.

Down and down we went.

The bleeding plants were gigantic. There was suddenly a lot of space in between them. It was almost scary.

The plants began to bleed to their violet out lines. Sometimes they almost seemed to disappear. Then they would bleed back into green.

We finally stopped our descent. I remembered what Dreygon told me.

So I knew could not touch Zenzibanouke with my feet.

One touch and I would become as aware of my duality as the inhabitants. For me it would be like coming apart at the seams.

Enuvah let go of my hand. We were deep inside the bleeding plant life of Zenzibanouke.

She moved out in front and turned to face me. I could see her film like features that were over shadowed by her large eyes. She pointed up. I looked and I gasped in shock.

The bleeding plants grew for miles up into the atmosphere of Zenzibenouke. Some were so large their tops could not be seen from where we were.

I realized up there is where Dreygon and I had arrived in Zenzibanouke.

The dark twilight sky could still be seen even from these depths. The twilight made its way down to where we were.

It seemed to be woven inside the plant life. I could feel its eeriness and now I saw twilight from here.

"Tell me your name?" Enuvah asked. "I am called Vishnu" I replied.

She said nothing more and pointed to the interior. She took my hand again and we began to move through the foliage. I looked down and I couldn't see any surface between the plants. I didn't understand how the bleeding plants were growing.

There wasn't anyone here and I wondered why all the inhabitants were aloft.

Then I noticed something on the leaves of the bleeding plants down here. At first it was hard to see its shape clearly.

We were moving through the plant life slowly enough for me to finally catch a glimpse.

There were small violet pods clinging to the bleeding plants above our heads. Something else was living on Zenzibanouke.

Their numbers increased on the bleeding plants as we moved further into the interior of the foliage.

They gave off a soft glow that extended up through the foliage above our heads. We came near enough for me to take a closer look.

The pods were clear.

I saw the violet outline of small creatures curled up inside. They glowed and pulsed inside the pods. They did not look Human. Then I remembered Humans don't look very human in their embryonic state.

I knew they were connected to the inhabitants of Zenzibanouke. But I could not imagine how.

Enuvah said nothing but I know she saw me staring at the pods.

I understood we were not down here for that reason. I felt increased pressure on my hand and we continued moving through the plant life. Down here the bleeding plants had the width of trees. I had the sensation Enuvah and I were riding on something. I most definitely couldn't see it. I looked down and I could see my feet, but no surface. There was nothing

but colorless emptiness below the plant life. I
thought maybe I'm dreaming. I wasn't dreaming.
     We continued moving through the bleeding
plants, and then Enuvah stopped.
     There was an open space directly in front of
us. But in truth, it looked like everything just ended.
I saw nothingness! It ended and I was at the edge.
Enuvah pointed again for me to look up. I turned
and looked back to look up.
I saw the edge of this violet world.
The huge plants extended into the atmosphere above
us further than I could see. This world ended here,
and I was at the edge—the edge of duality.
The huge plants began to bleed into view.
Enuvah grabbed my hand and we went up along the
edge of this world. Zenzibanouke was just coming
into being.
The bleeding plants could be seen now in full view.
I looked down the edge. I could see nothing below
Zenzibanouke. It was beyond frightening.
     Enuvah touched the sides of the plants. "Can
you see? Here I touch the beginning, before this,
there was nothing? You say how can this be? Out of
nothing, something. I ask you how would you know
nothing if there were not something?
     More importantly, why do you need this
experience? Duality is the essence of you on the Big
Ground.
Yet you find yourself neither at the beginning of
reality nor the end, but in the present. This present
is the third of what you call trinity.
In Zenzibanouke you can experience divine
intelligence in all three realities: Nothing, something,
present.

I use these terms so that you can understand. It is an actuality and not a concept. All three exist at the same moment. This is the beauty of Zenzibanouke. The becoming one with oneself is to be the present. This is the third of the three."

We were close to the tops of the plants now. Enuvah continued to hold my hand as we began to move across Zenzibanouke inside the foliage. It bled in and out of existence. It was the most incredible sight I have ever seen and felt. The burning violet glow was unnerving.

The plant life bled into the green color as we passed through it and then it would bleed out again to the violet outline. It was more than I could fathom.

It would have been impossible for me to find my way back to Dreygon.

I could finally see us approaching him through the bleeding foliage. He was still hidden as the plant life bled into green.

We stopped near Dreygon and Enuvah let go of my hand.

She said, "Vishnu, you walk with all parts of yourself. Inside the three is the view. Use your inner map. Here you will discover the true nature of yourself in all its infinite possibilities."

She took a long look at me. I could feel her eyes searching my very soul. I saw a smile on a face that looked like eternity.

Enuvah turned now and entered the foliage from the direction she came.

I saw her violet outline burn out of existence!

The twilight of Zenzibanouke was all encompassing now.

The plants began to bleed out to their violet outline.

It was a very strange place to be in and I admit I was a little scared. I immediately thought of Dreygon and looked for him inside the plant life.

I was glad to see him still there. His unworldly yellow eyes were open and he looked directly at me.

His iridescent body shimmered in the twilight and he spread his enormous wings. The eyes of the Twelve moved across his flanks and peered out at the bleeding plants.

I heard him say, "Ahh Human, you have met Enuvah, guardian of those unborn into duality.

You have had the experience of Zenzibanouke and seen a possibility of your true self. It's time to leave."

The Twilight Relms of Zenzibanouke began to shift.

I could feel a change and the semi dark sky above appeared to be moving. Its dim glow of light became unstable. Dreygon lowered his huge head so that I could climb upon his shoulder.

The Relms was shifting fast and with his huge wings spread, we ascended high above the bleeding plant life.

A violet horizon appeared in front of us like an enormous crack. Zenzibanouke began to move toward the horizon as though it was being compressed into one beam of light.
The Relms was closing.
Dreygon flew at what felt like just under light speed. We passed Zenzibanouke and slipped through the violet crack just as it closed.

There was a violet flash across the dark light of deep space. Zenzibanouke vanished!

Dreygon and I were flying fast.

The dark light engulfed us as he flew faster than I can ever remember traveling with him.

I closed my eyes. Everything in my head looked like black and white specks. I forgot where I was. I think it was so intense that I fell asleep, because when I was conscious again, I was lying in my bed. Eyes wide open! I sat up wondering what had just happened and what did I see?

Then I remembered Dreygon, but not Zenzibanouke. Sometimes my re-entry from the Relms is so intense that I forget where I am or what has happened. I closed my eyes and there was just the peaceful darkness.

Thank you my friend, I whispered to him and I fell asleep.

THE DAYGONE

My cell phone was ringing, but I couldn't tell where the sound was coming from.
I opened my eyes slowly and decided not to answer. There was a sensation on my forehead. I touched it, only to feel a real pulse.
Then I remembered the Traveler named Symbol. I closed my eyes. I knew it was time to get up.
I was moving slowly as I climbed out of bed and went into the bathroom. I almost dreaded the mirror, but took a look to check my head.
I saw an inverted triangle on my forehead and it was lit and pulsing! I yelled, "Oh no!"
Then I woke up!
Did I just dream of a pulsing triangle on my forehead?
My head felt strange so I touched my forehead. I thought I had better check to make sure. So I got up.

This time I went into the bathroom for real. I took my time before I looked into the mirror.

I think I was waiting for it to subside before I looked, because I could still feel the sensation.

The inverted triangle was not there. I touched the area between my eyes where I had felt it pulse.

I started to remember everything and everywhere I had gone with Dreygon last night.

I stared at my face. Dude! Who are you?

Then I began to remember Zenzibanouke. I felt strange. I could still feel the energy of Enuvah. I looked deep into my own eyes to see if there was a change; I wasn't sure what I would do if there was. There wasn't anything noticeable and I began to think Zenzibanouke was just a vivid dream I had.

I knew I was lying to myself. This was avoidance of the mind.

I'm a scientist and through this medium I had already discovered that the Universe was more bizarre than any science fiction imagined.

The Relms was off the charts.

There was no logical explanation or mathematical formula to address where I had been. I took a deep breath. I decided to sit down, close my eyes, and meditate to clear my mind. I felt better after this.

Okay, time for some java. I took a shower, brushed my teeth, got dressed, and went down stairs.

I went into the kitchen and made the java while I balanced my thoughts about my life.

Once again the Relms was having an incredible effect on me.

I knew I had to take my time and be back on the Big Ground. I drank the java. It was better already.

I felt grounded like the grinds. The sun was shining through the glass doors to the deck outside. I opened them and took a step outside.

The morning was bright and I could see the ancient Sequoias beyond my garden.

I took another sip of the java. I had to find resolution. Everything that I had experienced in the Relms was moving around inside of me.

I was looking for a place to put it. I took a deep breath. I had experienced what I could never have imagined. My reality was expanding and I was living it! I'm a scientist and my Human self was screaming for recognition.

I thought about Elbah. Was she in the Relms last night? My head began to playback all the visuals.

All the Beings I encountered, and all I experienced rushed to my head. I needed time to contemplate all this.

I took another sip of the java and it was time for a refill.

The Big Ground was looking really different to me as I stared into my garden. It definitely seemed more amazing. Everything was so alive and full of color.

I really needed to see Elbah. I had to tell someone about all this. I'm sure that's why we met. I had her number. After work I would give her a call.

We could hook up at the Daygone. Sounded like a plan to me. I was feeling better already.

My inner confusion subsided and left me with a feeling of well-being. It was time to head for my office.

I finished the java, grabbed my briefcase, and was out the door and into another reality, the reality of the Big Ground.

The sun was shining and the streets were busy. Everything looked really bright.

I checked out the faces of people as they passed me on the street.

They seemed to be checking me out too. We held gazes, which was most unusual. Most of the time people are in their own world.

Now that was an interesting thought. I was definitely in my own world.

I arrived on time. The office was full of people. We had some visitors from another division.

I said, "Good morning!"

"Good morning," they replied in unison!

It was truly remarkable. I could tell what kind of day it was going to be. This was really cool.

The phone was ringing as soon as I entered my office.

A client from Rome called to tell me to please check my email. I always do, so this must have been important.

I went online and there was his email, with an attachment.

I opened the attachment to find some very unusual pictures.

These were pictures of a series of nebula taken by NASA. I looked closely. I could see the gaseous colors and stars behind them.

These were pictures beyond the rim. It had taken years for the probe to reach beyond what scientist call our galactic skin that was thousands of light years away.

I looked again and suddenly realized I had seen this before! Everything stopped as I took the realization to heart.

I sat back in my chair amazed. I assumed nothing. I just sat staring and smiling to myself. This revelation was a shock to my system.

I would never tell anyone what I was thinking. No one would believe a word anyway. I was definitely the "Sky Man" as Harper liked to call me. Still, it was strange that I would receive these pictures now. I decided not to dwell on it too much. My friend in Rome couldn't possibly know about the Relms. But the timing here was uncanny.

The day went by quickly at work.

My colleagues and I had begun to sequence all the notes. We had recorded them from each Human in both Hemispheres of the planet. Now we were programing them onto the Hieroglyphic chip. I'm excited about this process, and the progress we have been making on our project. It had been a very full day when 6pm finally arrived.

It was time to leave work and I was out the door and on my way to the Daygone.

Time to check in with Harper and see Elbah for dinner.

The evening was warm and the sun was almost setting. I took my time.

I found myself looking at everything as I walked. I'm sure people thought I was a tourist. I have walked this way dozens of times.

Today everything looked clear and vibrant and I marveled at a beautiful sky. Women love a setting sun. So you can imagine how many conversations I had on the way to the Daygone. My face was in full smile.

I had no thoughts of the twilight Relms of Zenzibanouke. I walked for a while before I finally hailed a cab.

The ride to the Daygone was short and sweet.

People were starting to arrive as I was getting out of the cab. There is always a nice crowd of people at the Daygone. Everyone wants to sit on the famous red bench under the tree and order drinks. The blue trapezes with the colorful trapeze artists hanging in the ceiling lend to a dream fun atmosphere.

The huge plants added to the positive vibe of this place. I passed the red bench and I could see Harper waving from a table by the windows. You can see the ocean from this part of the restaurant.

"Sky Man! What it is?" This was Harper's greeting for me every time I had been in the Relms. It's like he could smell stardust.

Maybe I looked crazy after a trip out. I didn't ask, because then I would have to tell him.

Harper was my best friend.

"Whasa? Whasa?" I answered.

I was really glad to see Harper.

I sat down. The waitress came right away. I order a pot of the Dragon's Well tea and two cups.

"Deep day?" the waitress said.

We both said, "Yes!"

Harper was smiling when he said, "So dude, I told you about this woman I met named one who remembers. Hey, Sky Man! Tanudahsatnahani, remember?"

"Yes, I do! I said. So what happened?" I was still smiling, big time.

Harper was looking serious.

He said, "I'm not sure. It was like this woman was from someplace else.

At first I thought she must be an actress because she's beautiful, or a writer working on a script because she was so articulate.

The more we spoke the more I realized this was her personality, who she was.

We had conversations I don't normally have with a woman. She spoke about traveling off the planet and the law of physics.

Then she said something else about the law of physics in other places in the Universe. Tanudah said something in an ancient language: *Auhna ma suk kah ni.*

I can't even tell you what those words mean. She said it was ancient Rishi.

How many people do we know that can speak a forgotten language?
I think I was pleasantly surprised.

Dude! When was the last time Dudes drank tea?"

I was laughing now and so was Harper. I needed a clear head.

Harper continued, "She tells me she's a Night Traveler. She would not say how or where she was traveling to, or even why. I saw her watching my eyes to see if I believed her or thought her insane. Funny thing, Sky Man, I believed every word of it.

It was fascinating. It felt familiar in concept, but that was all.

She told me she had a PhD. in physics. This was her field. She said she studied ancient languages, concepts, and mythology.

It was one of the most interesting conversations I have ever had in my life. Perhaps all the things I think I understand about me have a beginning somewhere and no ending."

I was surprised by Harper's last words. He was looking at me as though he was hoping I understood. I did. Infinite possibilities were the way of the Relms.

Harper was right on it. I sat smiling and continued to listen as he filled me in on some more details.

I found myself laughing out loud.

I have never seen Harper so excited about a woman. Harper is extremely intelligent. He has more than one degree, so for him this was the "sweet meet" of the century.

We drank three pots of the Dragon's Well tea during our conversation. This was a first.

It was getting close to dinner and Harper had an appointment.

"So Sky Man! How's the Sky Lady?"

We both laughed. "Elbah is cool, I said. I'll tell her you asked about her."

"Copasetic!" Harper said, as he got up to leave.

This had really been an amazing day. I knew it from the start and it wasn't over yet.

Elbah would be arriving soon, and I had to decide how much of last night I was willing to talk about.

Symbol, who is Symbol? She said I would know her by just that, a symbol.

Not only that, I saw an inverted triangle on my third eye this morning in a dream. Now I'm talking about a third eye? Must be the Dragon Well tea. I was smiling to myself.

The view at the Daygone was great—the golden red sunset over the blue ocean.

I relaxed and took it all in.

Symbol riding a neon disc was back in my head. She was one of the most amazing Beings I had ever met, and she welcomed me to the Relms.

Symbol said she was the Blue Being with the Navigator. Now there was even more to think about.

Until now I had not thought about my journey to Zenzibanouke. Maybe it seemed personal, so it stayed hidden in my memory until this moment of reflection.

It floated in like some alien thought. Perhaps I needed more time to think how anything could burn its way into existence.

The experience was fresh in me and I had not allowed it to rise into thought. I needed more time before contemplation of what to me seemed to be almost a dream.

I turned my gaze toward the entrance of the Daygone. At that moment I could see Elbah making her way through the crowd.

I stood up to greet her. She was as beautiful as I remembered with her face so brown and her eyes so green.

Her curly dark red hair was up in a bun. She wore a fitted white shirt and light blue pinstriped pants. She had on a beautiful pair of sandals.

Elbah arrived full of great energy. I hugged her warmly.

"Vishnu, how nice to see you again!" she said, and sat down across from me.

She immediately began to tell me about all the things that had happened on the Big Ground since the last time we met.

It was a really different kind of conversation. She always refers to the Big Ground as the location for what happened.

I really wanted to smile, but then I would have laughed. Not because it was funny, but because here I was living two realities and there was someone with me. The Universe must have a sense a humor, big time! How else could we all know laughter?

The waiter came and we both ordered a glass of wine while we looked at the menu. The food at the Daygone is great. As we ordered dinner, I could hear a tabula at the beginning of some raga music. The drumming of the tabula floated across the Daygone. There's always a different "flavor" of music here. Tonight it was music from India. This music is meant to take you someplace else. The Daygone was suddenly rocking in Bangalore.

It seems the right song always plays at the right moment.

I asked Elbah: "How do we talk about the Relms? How can I tell you about these places I go and have it be understood?

Last night I was in the Relms. I traveled on the Stellar Winds and visited worlds that baffle the imagination. How do I speak of this?"

Elbah spoke softly, "You aren't meant to really tell me everything you have seen.

I've had so many journeys of my own. I think it's really special that we met there. Somehow you will always be able to just find me. As Agnamani, I am always changing Relms. I have never been in the same one twice. Remember infinite possibility, the continuum."

I knew this word.

Now I remembered. I heard this in one of the Relms at the Wall of Souls.

I didn't say this out loud. I was just thinking about these things as Elbah spoke to me.

"You probably wonder how this can continue." She said with a smile. "How could it not?

Each time I become the Agnamani, I am in the Relms to guide the young ones who leave the Big Ground in duress. This is how I am Agnamani.

The Relms are constantly changing. We are all experiencing infinite possibility while traveling there.

Imagination and awareness are intertwined with the condition of the Humans as they leave the Big Ground.

I am talking about the physical dying of Humans". Elbah continued, "No one arrives in the same Relms, but similar Relms. Remember, they move in and out of each other. Yes, you are there for a different reason. Your reason is experience and knowledge of the *inner map.* We share the ability to travel the Relms. Perhaps as individuals we have both evolved enough to have the experience of the Relms. And this is how you and I were able to meet.

We have experienced its existence and now we hold the Relms in our reality.

It becomes accessible and your knowing of the Relms has changed it.

Each time we visit we add something to what is there and leave a trace of our existence behind. Pretty cool, huh?"

I was listening and analyzing at the same time. I realized I had never told Elbah I was a scientist.

I have never asked her how she survives on the Big Ground. Maybe this was a conversation irrelevant to why we had met. It really didn't matter what we did on the Big Ground for a living.

We go off planet. This was the relevant conversation to have with each other for now. The waiter came bringing our dinner.

I was glad for a pause in the conversation. I took a moment to digest what Elbah was telling me. It was interesting.

I realized I might never know everything she sees on those journeys to the Relms. I also understood it was impossible to tell her everything about mine.

Maybe when we are old and no longer Relms Travelers we can share stories. We will have a lot to tell each other.

"Do you have a companion when you travel?" she asked. I could not tell her about Dreygon. He was my spirit guide and I never spoke his name to any Human.

"Yes, I do. I have a spirit guide."

"Then you cannot tell me his name nor of his origin," she said.

I was surprised by Elbah's response, but not really.

We understood each other even though we were new friends.

"You're right, I can't, I said. I'm so glad you understand. I can tell you that I ride the Stellar Winds."

She just looked at me with a twinkle in her eyes. I told Elbah about the winds. It felt good recounting some of last night's journey.

I didn't tell her everything. Some things just wouldn't come out. These are the words not necessary according to Elbah.

I was experiencing something unusual. There was harmony with Elbah, some kind of music.

I only hear it when I'm with her. Maybe it has something to do with that *note* I heard on one of my journeys to the Relms. This was okay with me and kind of special.

The dinner was great! Elbah had Canard Comfit and I had Grilled Jumbo Shrimp. We shared an organic salad and some baked blue potatoes.

My favorite dessert is the chocolate bread pudding. I shared it with Elbah. She loved it.
The music was now on full load.
The Daygone is still notorious for the music. It was a full house!
People were singing with their favorite song. Peels of laughter could be heard and the clinking of glasses filled the background. Elbah and I had a lot of fun. The time went by quickly.

It was getting late. I paid the check and it was time for us to go.

It's always hard to leave the Daygone. We made our way through the restaurant.

"Vishnu, thank you so much for dinner. This was so much fun," said Elbah.

"Yes, I had a great time", I replied.

We were on the street.

The evening was warm, and I walked with Elbah under a navy blue sky. We both marveled at its intensity and stars that could be seen even here in a city. We stopped and she said,

"Well here's my car, so good to see you, Vishnu. I hope I see you again and definitely in the Relms."

We both laughed, gave each other a hug and she got into her car.

I waved as she drove away.

I continued to walk. The city was really beautiful. It was only Monday and the week had just begun. I had the feeling this was going to be the longest week of my life, or I would go to bed and wake up and it would be Monday...again!

I flagged a taxi. I was really tired.

I just wanted to sleep. As soon as I got home I went up to my bedroom. I did my routine and got into bed.

I slept until morning and woke up refreshed.

It was Tuesday and I was ready to work on the Hieroglyphic chip. I was excited about the chip containing notes from most of the Humans on the planet.

I showered and got dress as fast as I could. I decided to stop at Zenobia's Cafe and get a java to go. I hailed a cab and drank it on the way to my office. It was really good.

It had been really nice seeing Elbah last night. I decide she was my Relms companion.

My life was full. I was also in constant contemplation of my reality of the Relms.

I thought about Symbol, the Blue Being. I could still see her riding a neon disc inside the Stellar Wind.

I saw a copper colored face inside a triangle on the forehead of her blue gaseous form! This was like something out of science fiction!

The inverted triangle she placed on my forehead told me we were destined to meet again.

I suddenly realized that I have never asked Dreygon about any of the Entities we encountered. It seems I am destined to have the experiences of the Relms and it can only happen with Dreygon. Somehow, infinite possibility and my existence had finally lined up.

I was becoming aware of the *inner map* through my rumination of the Relms with him.

The taxi stopped and I hopped out. I went directly to a meeting in the *wheel room* with my colleagues. We had already begun sequencing the data the day before.

We sat listening to the notes sung by Humans from the Northern Hemisphere of the planet.

It was incredible to hear all those people singing just one note that told the story of their existence.

We realized there were too many to hear. This brought smiles to everyone's face that we were attempting such a feat.

No one moved and we actually continued to listen until it was time to leave at the end of the day.

The notes sung from the people of the Southern Hemisphere would be next. I was sure we would hear a difference base on environment and location. I made a joke that it was also because their heads were pointed down. We all got a laugh.

This was fantastic for us.

There were still a lot of small details to be worked out. I was glad to go home at the end of the day.

My head was full of Human voices singing one note.

I decided to make dinner when I got home. I put everything in the oven: potatoes and chicken. I made a salad.

I poured a glass of wine and sat on the deck while everything cooked. Beyond my garden the giant Sequoias still stood with reverence.

There was something comforting about home and being so close to the ancient trees. For me these trees were the Big Ground in all her living glory.

I heard the bell from the oven.

The food was ready and I was hungry. I ate under the evening sky on my deck. I wanted to take a siesta from all the things that traveled through my mind during the day.

A warm breeze came up and I could hear the leaves moving through the tops of the Sequoias. Dinner was good. I put the dishes in the dishwasher and headed for my bedroom on the second floor. The wind was blowing outside my windows. I turned on the lights of my nightstand and just sat there. I was still in siesta.

It was late now and I headed for my nightly routine. I read for a while and tried not to think about Zenzibanouke or the Relms. I was glad when my head finally hit the pillow.

Rest was what I needed. Sleep was deep and long.

SYMBOL

It had been awhile since Dreygon's last visit. Fall was fast approaching. I have become accustomed to these interludes of no travel to the Relms.

I reestablish my sanity for the Big Ground.
I am always certain of Dreygon's return on the nights when the sky seems to be unusual with starlight or a raging full moon.
This was neither or I just didn't take any notice. I had been working long hours with my colleagues on our project, and I was really tired.
We order Chinese food at the office and ate dinner together. I was glad to finally get home. I did my routine. Got into bed and fell right to sleep.

I was dreaming. Someone was asking me a question. I could barely hear the words. Then the words became clear.

"Human, tell me of your existence?" It was Dreygon. I felt myself laugh in my sleep. It seemed as though he had been gone for eons.

Perhaps I had finally synthesized my experiences. Now I was ready to travel with him. Relms travel causes a time shift in consciousness. It's almost like everything happens at once, and then there is no one thing.

I have no other way of explaining how to conceptualize this sudden awareness of time, no time, no place.

I was still dreaming when two unworldly yellow eyes suddenly appeared and they looked directly at me. I was use to this from Dreygon. Sometimes I wonder if he found my fear humorous.

"I beseech thee tell me of your origins," I said. This was our greeting.

Then I woke up and sat up in my bed. I immediately looked toward my bedroom windows.

The wind was blowing and white clouds could be seen moving quickly across the night sky.

I was filled with anticipation. The giant Sequoias beyond my garden looked like dark guardians.

I sat watching the night sky waiting for Dreygon to appear. I saw him move from behind a passing white cloud in the distance.

Dreygon's huge wings were open and his iridescent body would appear and disappear as he approached.

I could see his unworldly yellow eyes piercing the night sky.

The passing white clouds sometimes hid him from my view.

I got out of bed and went over to the windows to wait for him.

I was excited because I knew my travel to the Relms with Dreygon would be incredible.

He arrived and I saw his huge iridescent shoulder pass just outside my windows. I opened them and looked out.

Dreygon was just below the windows and the eyes of the Twelve suddenly moved across his flanks. I will forever be unnerved.

I say to myself each time I climb out of the windows that I must be insane to do this. But I'm scientist.

Why would I not explore? I climb out the windows and onto Dreygon's shoulder. His bright green mane bushed the side of my face. I grabbed on to it and held on. I closed my eyes.

The sensations within returned with intensity. I could feel myself moving inward very fast. My breathing became heavy and I felt like I was falling down from the inside. My head started to reel and the pressure was so intense I yelled.

The peeling of the layers of my body began and continued for what felt like an eternity. I could feel layer after layer peeling.

I thought I would go insane before the physical change was over.

I saw a very bright light and heard a loud clap.

I opened my eyes. Dreygon and I were above the planet!

I will never get use to the physical changes.

It took me a moment to gather myself together. I know this is how it has to happen. Dreygon was motionless as he always is before we begin our journeys to the Relms

I looked at Earth, the Big Ground. It's always amazing to see it from here. It's beautiful and intimidating. I felt small even as I sat on the shoulder of the Dreygon.

Then without warning, he turned his enormous body around and we flew into the dark light of deep space behind us.

Dreygon was flying smooth and swift. The blackness engulfed us and the blinking lights of millions of stars could be seen.

The further we traveled the brighter the stars became. I looked around at an incredible view. I could not understand how Dreygon knew where we were. There is no up and down here, no east, and west. I sensed we had traveled a great distance when I felt a sensation on my brow.

I could feel it pulsing. I touched my forehead. The inverted triangle was there and it was lit!

The triangle pulsed and I saw a glow coming from my forehead.

I began to panic because I didn't understand what was happening to me. Then I remembered my last journey riding the Stellar Winds, and Symbol. This was incredible!

I was ready for the unimaginable. Symbol and I would be meeting again.

The further we traveled into the dark light the more intense the pulsing of the triangle on my brow. I felt a shift as though we passed through some kind of flux I couldn't see. We were in deep space now.

The light of Dreygon's unworldly yellow eyes extending in front of us like a beacon cutting through the intense blackness. I heard his voice in my head.

He said, "The Stellar Wind is approaching with the Travelers",

I could see a very bright golden light that appeared out of nowhere.

The light was approaching us with unusual speed. Dreygon became motionless and waited for its approach.

The color of the Stellar Wind changed to a golden tan as it neared us. It was huge! It still had the appearance of a giant golden serpent speeding through the blackness of deep space.

The wind drifts in at first and has the appearance of slowing down. This is an illusion.

Dreygon moved above the Stellar Wind's approach.

I felt the inverted triangle on my brow continue to pulse, and it remained lit. I knew I was going to see Symbol again. I wasn't sure why.

I did know it had something to do with her welcoming me to the Relms on our first encounter.

I remember Symbol telling me she was the Blue Being with the Navigator. Somehow destiny was at work.

We waited, and now we could see the Travelers approaching inside the Stellar Wind. I looked in awe.

They were all riding on something incredible. I saw the neon discs.

Dreygon made his move and I held on tightly. The descent into the Stellar Wind was flawless. Dreygon was in his element. Everything moved back on his face. This face was meant for the wind.

We were inside and moving fast.

I was riding The Stellar Wind.

This time I could see through the golden stardust of the wind.

The inverted triangle on my head was lit.

The Stellar Wind shifted and we seemed to change direction. I held on even tighter to Dreygon's mane.

The golden stardust of the Stellar Wind was beautiful, but it moves like a storm cloud.

I tried to see the Travelers inside the wind. The stardust cleared briefly and I saw many! They were riding the neon discs.

The Stellar Wind shifted again and all the Travelers on the neon discs disappeared inside the golden stardust.

The inverted triangle on my brow was still lit and continued to pulse, as I continued looking deep into the wind.

Symbol was inside and I could see her moving in my direction.

Her blue gaseous form looked almost human riding a neon disc.

I was astonished!

It seems to take a long time for her to arrive. There is a trick to moving laterally in the Stellar Wind.

The rider has to pass the other Traveler and allow them to catch up as you move over close. It was so cool.

I could see Dreygon's unworldly yellow eyes burn through the stardust in front of us.

He never looked to see the approach of Symbol. I'm sure he knew.

The Blue Being that was Symbol was suddenly next to me. We were riding together.

Symbol's blue gaseous essence moved out behind her and mixed into the Stellar Wind.

Her features were not obvious and her blue gaseous essence molded a face that could be seen.

I look at the symbol of a triangle on her brow. It began to rotate.

I watched and held on tightly to Dreygon's bright green mane.

I could see a face inside the rotating triangle. This was not a face made of flesh. She was the color of copper. Her eyes were large slits with blue in the interior.

Her mouth was full but I saw no nose, only a line above her lips. Her head was covered by a metallic looking cloth. She had a neck and shoulders, but she did not look Human.

She spoke—if she had not, I might have been overwhelmed by her appearance.

"Welcome to the Relms", she said. "I am Symbol. We met the first time you road the Stellar Wind with the Travelers."

I heard her thoughts for nothing could ever be said in the Stellar Wind.

I did not respond. I wasn't sure what to say. I kept looking at her face inside the rotating triangle and her blue gaseous essence riding next to me on a neon disc in the Stellar Wind.

A smile came over my face. I heard Symbol's voice in my head.

She said, "Where I am from we are not called by any name. You will know me by this Symbol".

It was the pulse I felt on my forehead.

She continued, "I have been in the Relms for all of my existence. In the Relms, we evolve essence and infinite possibility becomes home.

I don't have what you call memory of some place before.

Perhaps for us everything occurring before was necessary for the arrival to now. There is only now.

For me it's traveling the Relms on the Stellar Winds. We are many.

These winds carry the Travelers to no specific destination. The Stellar Winds move through the Relms.

Only the Travelers themselves know to which Relms they journey.

This keeps true to infinite possibility. It is inside the Stellar Wind that we have the opportunity to greet other Travelers.

You are a Being of stardust from the Big Ground. You are riding with those of us who have left that essence behind long ago. And yes, we know Dreygon", she said.

I was surprised to hear Symbol tell me that the Travelers knew Dreygon.

I took this moment to ask Dreygon via my thoughts if he could see Symbol.

I heard a very loud, "Yes!"

The Stellar Wind began to shift.

This time I could see the front of the wind as it banked out into deep space.

I watched it move as though it had intelligence.

I held on tightly to Dreygon.

My brow was pulsing, and the speed I was traveling was faster than any human could imagine.

Telepathy was the means of communicating in the Relms. I was becoming accustomed to this. More importantly, it was how I had been communicating with Dreygon since our first meeting.

Symbol continued, "I know of this Big Ground where you dwell.

We say here in the Relms, it is the place of smell. You must breath to be in that reality."

I could see Symbol's face smiling inside the triangle. Then she said, "I don't remember smell. Perhaps I have never dwelled on the Big Ground. It must be interesting for you, Stardust."

She called me Stardust, and I wondered how she knew. I just left it at that.

"I don't know smell, Symbol continued. I only know of my existence, which is to experience the Relms.

It is almost like smell, but with infinity attached to it. The infinite smell, the smell of infinity."

Symbol seemed to have a sense of humor. She had jarred my reality.

"We don't know what you would call extinction here in the Relms", she said.

I think she was reading my stardust. She continued, "There are no transitions of death in the Relms.

My existence evolves.

We do not imagine not being. These are thoughts only known on the Big Ground".

I could see her very strange blue eyes that peered through slits on her copper colored face.

She stared at me and then she said,

"The existence of the Relms is an extension of the Human reality that can be known on the planet of smell, called the Big Ground. You will know the evolution of stardust".

The Stellar Wind shifted and Symbol moved away and disappeared inside the wind.

I waited for her return.

The wind shifted again and I could see Symbol moving fast in my direction on a neon disc.

She was back and riding next to me again.

I think she could read my thoughts because she said, "Stardust, you are in your journey. You will want to ask me if existence ends. You may ask this question desiring an answer, that will not be relevant in the Relms".

I thought about the *inner map* and me arriving at this moment with Symbol.

The triangle was no longer rotating on her gaseous brow. The being inside the triangle seemed to move toward the front of the triangle.

Her copper colored face suddenly filled the space.

I looked in disbelief. Symbol was looking at me. The blue color that filled the large slits of her eyes was penetrating.

She looked vaguely human.

The stardust particles sometimes hid her from view.

But I could see that she had the same symbol of the triangle on her brow, and inside another copper face like hers that peered out. And that there was another triangle on the brow of that face and another face like hers peered out and another triangle on that brow with a face like hers that peered out until I could see no more.

I was shocked and amazed. I stared, and I'm sure my facial expression revealed what I thought. I felt the triangle on my forehead brighten in its intensity.

I didn't know where I was for split second. Boom! I was back and still holding on to Dreygon riding inside the Stellar Wind.

"Stardust, we will meet again."

Symbol moved away on her neon disc and disappeared inside the Stellar Wind.

It seemed as if we had been in the Stellar Wind for an eternity.

Dreygon made the move.

He moved up and out of the wind with the smoothness of a master.

The Stellar Wind filled with Travelers continued to move below us at an incredible speed. Dreygon remained motionless and I watched as the Stellar Wind continued moving out into the dark light of deep space. I could still see Travelers riding neon discs inside as the wind slowly faded into the blackness. It looked like a single golden thread before it vanished into the darkness.

The blackness of the dark light seemed to rush in on us.

Dreygon turned his enormous body and we flew swift and silent toward some blinking stars.

His unworldly yellow eyes were like beacons in the dark light.

I could still feel the inverted triangle on my forehead, but it was no longer lit. I heard Dreygon's voice in my head. He said, "Human, you are now a rider of the Stellar Winds.

You have seen the Travelers. They ride the Stellar Winds on neon discs into deep space. They are headed for the Relms. You have met the Symbol".

Dreygon began to fly across a very dense nebula that was suddenly below us. We both gazed at this incredible sight. The nebula was endless. It seemed to be moving and very far away.

Dreygon increased his speed and I held on tightly to his bright green mane. We began to ascend and then I felt us slip through an unseen flux and he suddenly stopped. Dreygon remained motionless and his unworldly yellow eyes penetrated the darkness of our location.

A very bright blue light appeared in the distance amongst the blinking white lights that were stars. Dreygon arced his flight in this direction. This marker was far.

I could feel myself begin to fall asleep. Dreygon was speaking to me, but his voice began to fade.
I never heard a word. I knew I was on my way back to the Big Ground.
I was aware of the incredible speed by which we finally arrived. I felt me entering something. I suddenly felt as though all of my molecules were being compressed for the Big Ground.

It was happening so fast, I had no time to respond. I could hear a sound, almost like a hum. My eyes were still closed and I saw a flash of light.
I woke up and I was lying in a very dark room.

Tap, tap, and tap. There was a tapping at the windows. I lay there without responding. My mind needed a reprieve and I was waiting.

The tapping continued so I thought I should make a move to check it out.
I looked toward the windows and white clouds were passing in the night sky. I got up and walked over to the windows. I looked up at the tops of the giant Sequoias beyond my garden.

I could still see the clouds passing like white ghosts beyond the high branches of the trees.

The tapping was only a branch moved by the wind. I had experienced so much, and all of it was still fresh in my head.

I thought about sleep. Once again, sleep. I closed the windows and got into bed and fell into a deep sleep. I slept for a long time.

Eventually another tapping awakened me. What's up with this tapping thing?

This time it was at the glass doors off the kitchen. I heard a familiar voice from down stairs.

"Hey! Sky Man, dude! Are you in there?"

Tap, tap, and tap. It was Harper. Should have known.

I yelled, "Yeah, dude, I'm back!"

I thought it was funny, so did Harper.

I got out of bed and walked down stairs and into the kitchen to open the glass doors. The afternoon sun was shining on the deck outside.

I had been sleeping a long time!

No wonder Harper was at the glass doors at the back of the house.

I opened the glass doors and he immediately began to check me out.

"We had a hook up, and when you didn't show, I became concerned.

Where have you been? Have you seen yourself?"

At this point I became concerned.

I turned and headed back upstairs and straight for the bathroom. I checked myself in the mirror.

The tips of my hair had changed color and there was an inverted triangle on my forehead!

Even the color of my eyes had changed. I was shocked! I blinked, and it all disappeared.

I just stared.

I threw water on my face, got in the shower, and decided to keep my sense of humor. I wondered if there might be something different in my appearance now.

I had been riding the Stellar Winds all night in the Relms. There used to be an inverted triangle on my head, recently. Then I thought about the giant marble stairs in Arahnubia, and meeting Sunimul.

Sunimul the Luminous was one of the Twelve that was Dreygon. This was incredible.

I remember seeing some of my stardust leave, so I stared at my hand flexing my fingers. I felt a surge-- wow! Stronger than before!

This is really incredible. I decided to take a breather from all this recall right now. I finished dressing and went back downstairs.

"Harper! Dude, how about some java?"

Harper was smiling and relaxing on the couch as I re-entered the room.

Harper said, "Better man, much better. I'm not sure of what I saw before. Maybe I was hallucinating.

Sky Man! Your hair was different, and I saw a triangle on your forehead!

Ok, I'm wigging! Glad I am. No problem, my friend. I'm ready for the java!

It must have been from hanging out with Tanudahsatnahani. Boy, that's definitely a head full. Hard to believe, Sky Man!

There are some very strange things happening. Revelation! Dude! Revelation!

You and I have been friends for a long time. Dude, this could be our great evolutionary leap of consciousness. It has to be! Can't believe I just said that.

This woman, Tanudahsatnahani, appears out of nowhere in the Daygone.

And now here you are looking a little sky worthy.
Can you understand what I'm trying to say?"
    We both began to laugh!
I was in the kitchen making the java. This was going to be really interesting.
Harper and I understand each other. There is no pretense. Just a genuine love and respect for each other's vision. Couldn't be better.
    I considered myself fortunate to have such a good friend for life. I know we will be old one day with our women. Should be really interesting.
Right now, we were in the early stages, and that far ahead was only infinite possibility.
    The java was strong and tasty. Harper and I moved to the deck off the kitchen.
The wind was coming up and we sat facing the sunset. I couldn't believe I had slept the day away. I felt really good and guilt-free.
I would soon be doing everything from this deck. I was smiling big time!
I was thinking of working from home on part of the Hieroglyphic chip as it moves into its final stages.
    I would still have a few days at my office, but I was pretty much done with the daily grind of having to be there five days a week. I am a young man.
    Nothing comes easy. I knew I had earned this. Truly, I was surprised to have arrived already to my ideal.
I wondered if the arrival of Dreygon and all those journeys to the Relms had anything to do with it. Perhaps it was all a part of some higher plan.
    I was laughing to myself.

Harper had his eyes closed, and the sunset was golden on his face. It was deep. I just watched in wonder.

Stardust came to mind, and I had an epiphany that nothing was what it seemed.

I sipped the java and cast my eyes to the now golden glow. The planet was jamming!

This was a moment.

I could see Harper's face smiling as he opened his eyes. We watched everything turn red.

We were both looking at the horizon in amazement.

The horizon soon turned orange and then began to transform into pink. Harper and I were looking like we had never seen a sunset before. Harper said nothing.

"Dude! Do you see this?" I yelled. Harper began laughing.

"Sky Man, I'm checking it!" he said.

I took a deep breath. For the first time I realized, I was on the planet of smell I knew as the Big Ground.

These words played in my head as a revelation. My sense of things had definitely been challenged. Through my breath I was experiencing the whole planet. My skin felt and my eyes saw vibrations and made sense of them.

I would never be the same again.

I had added to my concept of reality.

I think the word that expresses where I am now is relativity—I'm beginning to understand how everything is relative to me.

I've had a glimpse of my possibility as pure energy and I have seen some of the secrets of light.

I have experienced my mass as stardust and I have become aware of space as my infinite location.

I am a Traveler of the Relms.

I have a guide. His name is Dreygon.

But tell no one!

TO BE CONTINUED.

www.ingramcontent.com/pod-product-compliance
Lightning Source LLC
Chambersburg PA
CBHW070443030726
47503CB00004B/872